Praise f...
Party-P...
How to ...

"The Killer Party series is ...

"Presley Parker is a prota...
She's been down on her luck but lands on her feet when she comes
up with the idea for an event planning business. For a mystery series, it's a near perfect occupation."   —MysteriesGalore.com

"This book combines humor with mystery and makes a wonderful
tale taking place at the de Young Museum in San Francisco. This
is a party that you don't want to miss."
—Once Upon A Romance Reviews

"Penny Warner has created a wonderful heroine in perilous Presley Parker. . . . With plenty of action on her investigation and several poignant moments, readers will enjoy the perils of Presley
Parker."   —Genre Go Round Reviews

"The second Party-Planner mystery is a delightful whodunit due to
a strong lead and the eccentric cast who bring a flavor of San Francisco to life."   —The Best Reviews

"Plenty of motives and suspects . . . a cast of lively characters."
—Gumshoe

How to Host a Killer Party

"Penny Warner's scintillating *How to Host a Killer Party* intro-
duces an appealing heroine whose event skills include utilizing
party favors in self-defense in a fun, fast-paced new series guaranteed to please."
—Carolyn Hart, Agatha, Anthony, and Macavity
award-winning author of *Laughed 'Til He Died*

"A party you don't want to miss."
—Denise Swanson, national bestselling author of
Murder of a Bookstore Babe

"Penny Warner dishes up a rare treat, sparkling with wicked and
witty San Francisco characters, plus some real tips on hosting a
killer party."
—Rhys Bowen, award-winning author of the Royal
Spyness and Molly Murphy mysteries

continued . . .

"There's a cozy little party going on between these covers."

—Elaine Viets, author of the Dead-End Job mysteries

"Fast, fun, and fizzy as a champagne cocktail! The winning and witty Presley Parker can plan a perfect party—but after her A-list event becomes an invitation to murder, her next plan must be to save her own life."

—Hank Phillippi Ryan, Agatha Award–winning author of *Drive Time*

"The book dishes up a banquet of mayhem."

—*Oakland Tribune* (CA)

"These days some of the hottest crime fiction revolves around caterers and chefs. The latest author to venture into culinary mystery territory is Danville's Penny Warner, whose Bay Area hero—party planner Presley Parker—runs into homicidal high jinks all over the Bay Area, starting with an Alcatraz wedding gone awry."

—*Contra Costa Times*

"With a promising progression of peculiar plots, and a plethora of party-planning pointers, *How to Host a Killer Party* looks to be a pleasant prospect for cozy mystery lovers." —Fresh Fiction

"Warner keeps the reader guessing." —Gumshoe

"Delightful, filled with suspense, mystery, and romance."

—Reader to Reader Reviews

"Grab this book. . . . It will leave you in stitches."

—The Romance Readers Connection

"Frantic pace, interesting characters." —*Publishers Weekly*

**Praise for Penny Warner's
Connor Westphal Mystery Series**

Dead Body Language

"Delicious, with a fun, irreverent protagonist."

—*Publishers Weekly*

"A sprightly, full-fledged heroine, small-town conniptions, frequent humor, and clever plotting." —*Library Journal*

"The novel is enlivened by some nice twists, an unexpected villain, a harrowing mortuary scene, its Gold Country locale, and fascinating perspective on a little-known subculture."

—*San Francisco Chronicle*

"What a great addition to the ranks of amateur sleuths."

—Diane Mott Davidson, *New York Times* bestselling author of *Fatally Flaky*

The Party-Planning Mystery Series

HOW TO SURVIVE A
Killer Séance

A Party-Planning Mystery

PENNY WARNER

AN OBSIDIAN MYSTERY

OBSIDIAN
Published by New American Library, a division of
Penguin Group (USA) Inc., 375 Hudson Street,
New York, New York 10014, USA
Penguin Group (Canada), 90 Eglinton Avenue East, Suite 700, Toronto,
Ontario M4P 2Y3, Canada (a division of Pearson Penguin Canada Inc.)
Penguin Books Ltd., 80 Strand, London WC2R 0RL, England
Penguin Ireland, 25 St. Stephen's Green, Dublin 2,
Ireland (a division of Penguin Books Ltd.)
Penguin Group (Australia), 250 Camberwell Road, Camberwell, Victoria 3124,
Australia (a division of Pearson Australia Group Pty. Ltd.)
Penguin Books India Pvt. Ltd., 11 Community Centre, Panchsheel Park,
New Delhi - 110 017, India
Penguin Group (NZ), 67 Apollo Drive, Rosedale, North Shore 0632,
New Zealand (a division of Pearson New Zealand Ltd.)
Penguin Books (South Africa) (Pty.) Ltd., 24 Sturdee Avenue,
Rosebank, Johannesburg 2196, South Africa

Penguin Books Ltd., Registered Offices:
80 Strand, London WC2R 0RL, England

First published by Obsidian, an imprint of New American Library,
a division of Penguin Group (USA) Inc.

First Printing, March 2011
10   9   8   7   6   5   4   3   2   1

Copyright © Penny Warner, 2011
All rights reserved

OBSIDIAN and logo are trademarks of Penguin Group (USA) Inc.

Printed in the United States of America

To Mom and Dad, Tom, Matthew, and Rebecca—I couldn't party without you.
To Bradley and Stephanie Warner, and Luke and Lyla Melvin—the party has just begun.

ACKNOWLEDGMENTS

Thanks to everyone who helped me, inspired me, supported me, informed me, and entertained me: Colleen Casey, Janet Finsilver, Staci McLaughlin, Mike Melvin, Ann Parker, Carole Price, Susan Warner, the mysterious "Lady Killers," the informative staff at the Winchester Mystery House, and my tireless Webmaster, Geoff Pike.

A special thanks to my wonderful agents, Andrea Hurst and Amberly Finarelli, and my outstanding editor, Sandy Harding.

"Nothing is more irritating than not being invited to a party you wouldn't be seen dead at."

—William E. (Bill) Vaughan

Chapter 1

PARTY PLANNING TIP #1

When hosting a Séance Party, be sure to contact an agreeable spirit who's willing to communicate with you. There's nothing more frustrating than a tight-lipped ghost who only mumbles, grunts, or rattles chains.

CONDEMNED!

I stared at the orange notice that had recently been posted on the front door of my office barracks on Treasure Island and skimmed the printed words.

"City of San Francisco . . . Barracks B . . . hereby condemned . . . dilapidated and unsafe, due to contamination with asbestos, plutonium, radium, and other substances . . . vacated by the end of the week . . ."

I glanced around, looking for the jokester who had graffitied my place of business. Spotting no one, I ripped the bright orange paper from its staples and got out my key.

That was when I noticed the padlock.

"You're freaking kidding me," I yelled into the early-morning breeze that swept across the man-made island—once home to the 1938–39 Golden Gate International Exposition, the Pan Am Flying Clipper Ships, and the U.S. Navy—anchored in the San Francisco Bay. Decades later, when the navy abandoned the island, they left behind crumbling barracks, empty hangars, and toxic soil. But a few of the fair's Art Deco buildings remained, along with breathtaking panoramic views of the city, and low-rent housing that suited my budget perfectly. Apparently my yell had frightened a low-flying seagull passing overhead; he dropped a load of chalky white poop at my feet, narrowly missing my red Mary Janes.

Where was a crime scene cleaner when you needed one? Or a breaking-and-entering expert, for that matter.

I heard the screech of tires and spun around. Speak of the devil. Brad Matthews had just pulled up in his SUV. Brad and I had officially met when he'd moved into an empty office in the barracks building. At the time, I'd thought he was a burglar, and he'd suspected me of being under the influence of alcohol. Since that auspicious beginning, we'd become . . . friends. He saw me standing on the porch and waved. I waved the orange placard at him.

He sauntered over, looking incredible in his black leather jacket and black T-shirt with the red embroidered Crime Scene Cleaners logo and catchphrase—"Our day begins when yours ends." His hands were stuffed into the pockets of his well-worn jeans and there were no bloodstains on his New Balance Zips. I wished I looked as good in the white "Easily Distracted by Shiny Objects" T-shirt and jeans I was wearing. Of course, he looked even better without anything on. Okay, so we'd become more than "just friends." But I wasn't ready to call him my "boyfriend" yet.

"Someone pop your balloon this morning?" he asked, obviously noticing my scowl.

I handed over the sign I'd snagged from the barracks door.

As he read it, his smile drooped.

"You're freaking kidding me," he said, only he didn't use the word "freaking."

"That's what I said. How are we supposed to get inside? All my stuff is in there."

Brad gave the notice back to me and sighed. "Well, I'm not too surprised. These barracks should have been condemned a long time ago. They're falling apart—that's why they're so cheap to rent. And they light up like a month-old Christmas tree when there's a match within a mile of the place. Remember that fire we had in the old building?"

How could I forget? I had almost been trapped in it. "But the low rent is the reason I took this place. Where am I going to go now? My Killer Party business isn't exactly turning a profit yet."

"I hear there are a few openings in Building One." Brad glanced in the direction of the Administration Building, also known as Building One. The curved Streamline Moderne–style Art Deco building, erected for the Golden Gate Exposition of 1939, was one of a handful of original structures remaining on the island. Intended as an airport terminal, the building now housed a number of eclectic small businesses, including the Treasure Island Museum, Treasure Island Wines, and the Treasure Island Development Authority.

"I can't afford the rent there! And besides, how is that

place any safer? One big earthquake, and the ground beneath it will liquefy like Jell-O. The whole island is built on landfill, and none of the old buildings was constructed to handle a major jolt."

"That might be a good negotiating point," Brad said. He was taking this condemnation awfully well. "Plus, I know one of the administrators—Marianne Mitchell. Considering the circumstances, she'll probably give us a deal."

I checked my watch. "Meanwhile, I can't get to my stuff, and I'm late to meet my mother for breakfast. She called this morning saying she had something 'urgent' to talk about."

"She all right?" Brad asked. He and my mother seemed to have hit it off immediately when they'd first met. I think they talked about me behind my back.

"I hope so. She wouldn't say more. But if she sees something she wants on the shopping network or doesn't like the dessert they're serving at the care center, she calls that 'urgent.'"

"Do you need anything from your office right now?"

"I guess not, but I will soon. And so will Delicia and Berk and Raj and Rocco . . ." I listed the other corenters, who ran their own small businesses and shared the barracks building with me. They often picked up extra cash by helping me out with some of my bigger events. Dee dressed up in theme-fitting costumes, Berk videotaped the parties, Raj provided extra security when I needed it, and Rocco served as my caterer.

"I'll get ahold of the housing inspector and see what I can do about getting our stuff. And I'll talk to Marianne. I'm sure she'll give us a deal you can afford. Besides, I thought you were doing well in your party planning business lately—"

"Event planning," I said, correcting him.

He grinned at my insistence on calling my new career "event planning." I thought it sounded a little less frivolous, especially with a name like Killer Parties.

"Whatever. You must have made some heavy change with that last event you hosted at the museum."

It was true. I'd recently had some high-paying jobs—the mayor's interrupted wedding, the de Young Museum mystery party. Unfortunately, both events had become victims of party fouls, which had not only been traumatic for everybody involved, but had nearly cost me my life in both cases. Still, in spite of the sensational headlines in the *San Francisco Chronicle*, people continued to call me for their parties. Apparently, guests like a little drama with their bubbly and balloons.

"I have to run," I said to Brad, who already had his cell phone out, ready to call the powers that condemn buildings. "If you get inside, will you let me know? I've got half a dozen requests for events that I have to answer. I'm going to need them to pay my ever-increasing bills."

Brad said, "Hold on," to the person on the other end of the phone, then covered the mouthpiece and nodded toward the paper in my hand. "That's a misdemeanor, you know," he whispered.

"What?" I asked.

"Removing the sign. See the fine print at the bottom?"

Penalty for removal:
$700.00 and/or 90 days in jail.

I wadded up the stiff paper and threw it at him, snowball-style. Missed by a mile.

"And that's littering," he called out as I headed for my car. "A hundred-dollar fine and a week of roadside cleanup!"

Ignoring him, I hopped into my red MINI Cooper. When I looked back, Brad was at the barracks door, holding the padlock in his hands. Knowing him, I was sure he wouldn't wait for any official to unlock the building. He'd MacGyver it open himself.

I drove along Avenue of the Palms, up Macalla to the Bay Bridge entrance. It was getting tougher to merge onto the bridge these days, thanks to generally increased traffic and bridge retrofitting. Finally I was able to squeeze in front of a slow-moving truck. I plugged earphones into my iPhone and listened to songs from my mother's day—Frankie Valli, Little Richard, Jerry Lee Lewis, and of course Elvis Presley. Thanks to her, I loved the music of the fifties. By the end of "The Great Pretender" by the Platters, I had arrived in front of the assisted-living facility off Van Ness where my mother currently resided. I parked the MINI in the loading zone and headed for the front door.

Using my passkey, I entered the building and found my mother waiting for me in an upright wing chair by the fireplace. She'd dressed more for a tea party than breakfast, in a coral sweater set and a floral skirt. Still somewhat old-school San Francisco, she never went anywhere without her hair and makeup done. At least she didn't insist on wearing gloves and a hat, like her mother had.

A handful of other residents sat around the "social room" at tables or in groups, many in wheelchairs, doing crafts and handiwork, playing cards and board games, or idly watching a morning newscast on TV. I glanced at the screen and saw a head shot of an older man, with a caption underneath that read: "Computer whiz found dead in his office." I couldn't hear the details, but the man looked slightly familiar to me.

"Presley!" Mother called, waving me over and distracting me from my distraction. She turned to a handsome silver-haired man in a suit who sat opposite her and spoke to him animatedly. She touched his hand every now and then as she made her point, and laughed flirtatiously after he spoke. Luckily I couldn't hear what they were discussing. Sex, no doubt, knowing my mother. Mother had been something of a party queen in her day, and early-stage Alzheimer's disease hadn't hindered her ability to charm men. She seemed to have a new beau every few weeks, even though sometimes she couldn't remember all of their names.

She spotted me and waved; the gentleman stood up and pulled at his suit jacket with one hand, the other falling to his side.

"Presley! You're here!" Mother reached out and pulled me down into a chair next to her. "I want you to meet Stephen Ellington! He's new here, and we're already great friends."

I'll bet, I wanted to say. Instead, I took the high road. "It's nice to meet you, Mr. Ellington." I clasped his cool, papery hand with mine and shook it. One of his blue eyes squinted as he gave a half smile.

"Stephen, this is my daughter, Presley. She's a party planner, just like her mother!"

"Event planner," I corrected her; then by way of explanation, I began rambling. "I used to teach at the university—abnormal psychology—until I was downsized—"

Mother cut me off. "Stephen is joining us for breakfast, dear. I hope you don't mind."

I eyed my mother. She was up to something.

"You said you had something urgent to talk about." I forced a cordial smile in her direction. "Wouldn't you rather just the two of us—"

She interrupted me again. "Oh no! Stephen is the reason I wanted to see you. We have a very important matter to discuss with you—something I mentioned a few weeks ago, after your party at the museum. Remember?"

Not really, I thought. But I remembered that that party had turned out to be a disaster. "Sure," I said as I headed for the desk in the lobby and signed us out. Stephen held the door as we made our way to the street. "That's my car there," I said, pointing to my illegally parked MINI. Sizing up Stephen's tall, lanky frame, I pressed my lips together, then said, "It's going to be tight."

"Dear, why don't you let Stephen drive? Then you can sit in the backseat. You're shorter than he is." I'm five ten, and there was no way I was going to scrunch myself into that tiny backseat. Besides, the old guy probably didn't have a license, and I wasn't about to let some stranger drive my car. Granted, in spite of his age—I guessed him to be in his seventies— and a slight droop on the left side of his mouth when he smiled, his cheeks were a robust color and his eyes twinkled devilishly. I wondered why he was living at the care home. If he had Alzheimer's like my mother, it wasn't something I could easily spot.

"I have an idea," I said. "Let's walk. Mel's Drive-in serves breakfast, and it's only a few blocks away."

Mother looked at Stephen, and he nodded.

"Let me move my car so it doesn't get towed," I said.

Mother and Stephen chatted in front of the building while I drove up the street in search of a legal parking place. I managed to squeeze in between a Smart Car and a VW bug. Then I locked the car and headed down the hill. Stephen was just closing his cell phone as I approached.

"Shall we?" I said, leading the way to the drive-in turned diner chain. The fifties decor, popular with tourists, featured wall-mounted push-button mini-jukeboxes that I'd loved as a kid. Mother came for the freshly squeezed orange juice, the silver-dollar pancakes, and crispy bacon. Why the woman didn't have high cholesterol, clogged arteries, and a weight problem was a mystery to me.

We nestled into a cozy padded booth, me on one side, Mother and her "date" on the other. I ordered a low-fat blueberry muffin, strawberries, and a double latte. Mother gave her usual order and Stephen had a three-egg omelet called Herb Caen's Favorite—ham and cheese—and black coffee.

Silence settled over the three of us for a brief moment after the waitress left. My mind flashed back to the man's face I'd seen on the newscast at the care center. I was sure I'd recognized him but couldn't come up with the details of where or when. But the silence didn't last long, not with my mother. "So, Presley," she said, placing a hand on Stephen's hand that rested on the table. "We have a job for you! Remember when I mentioned I'd met someone at the center and his son was interested in having a big party?"

Ever since I'd started Killer Parties, my mother had been booking me for parties at the care center. I'd already hosted a Red Hat Party and a Hot Flash Fiesta for her lady friends, but had put her off when she suggested a Mardi Gras Mixer.

Knowing Mother, I had a feeling there would be boob-flashing beads involved.

"Not really," I said truthfully. "Things were kind of a blur after that party."

"Well, Stephen's son, Jonathan, is president of his own computer company, and he's about to announce an amazing new product. Stephen wants to help Jon promote it by organizing a party for him. Apparently the product is something that could revolutionize the movie business, so the guests would include a bunch of special-effects bigwigs like George Lucas, Phil Tippett, and what's his name—that guy from CeeGee Studios."

The details sounded vaguely familiar. I looked at Stephen. "Does your son know about your plans?" A few months earlier, I'd hosted a "surprise" wedding event for the mayor, which had backfired because the bride wasn't in on the planning. I didn't relish doing any more surprise parties like that in the near future.

"Oh yes," Stephen said, glancing at my mother, his eyes sparkling. "In fact, he's looking forward to meeting you."

I blinked. This party sounded like it had started without me.

Mother's red-lipsticked smile went into overdrive. "Presley, don't you remember? He wants a Séance Party!"

"A Séance Party . . ." I repeated. Suddenly it was all coming back to me.

"Yes! And he wants to hold it at the Winchester Mystery House!"

I felt a chill run down my back. Oh God, I thought I'd dreamed that part. I'd visited the hundred-plus-roomed house on a scouting trip when I was in sixth grade. The mansion, built by Sarah Winchester to appease spirits she suspected of haunting her, was filled with secret passageways, winding hallways, stairs that went nowhere, and rampant ghost sightings. It had scared the crap out of me back then.

"I remember," I said, "but why there?"

Mother glanced at Stephen; they both looked like giddy teenagers. "Because Jonathan wants to bring Sarah Winchester back from the dead!"

Chapter 2

PARTY PLANNING TIP #2

Hold your séance in an atmospheric setting, such as a gloomy old mansion or creepy cemetery, where spirits are more likely to be found. Just make sure your guests aren't arrested for trespassing. Nothing ruins a party faster than jail time.

After hearing my mother's plan, I choked on the strawberry I'd been eating. Wiping my mouth as delicately as I could with a napkin, I took a catch-up breath and said, "Excuse me?"

"You're excused, dear," my mother responded.

"No, I mean, excuse me, as in, what did you just say?"

Mother flashed Stephen a beaming smile. "It's a brilliant idea, isn't it? You hold a party at an old haunted mansion like the Winchester Mystery House, give it a séance theme, and then contact the eccentric—and long-dead—former owner of the house, Sarah Winchester, to showcase the new product!"

Stephen turned his crooked grin on me. "Yes, you see, the

project my son is working on is the latest in 3-D technology. He calls it '4-D Projection.'" Stephen made finger quotes around the phrase. "I don't understand how it works exactly, but he says it has plenty of applications, especially for the movie industry. That's why I thought hosting a party that shows those Hollywood producers what this gizmo does would be perfect. And your mother said you're the go-to girl when it comes to parties."

Go-to girl? Up to this point I'd said little, listening in stunned silence to their preposterous idea. They wanted to rent the Winchester House—one of the biggest tourist attractions in the San Francisco Bay Area—for a Séance Party. To bring back the spirit of eccentric Sarah Winchester, dead for nearly a century.

Ludicrous. I wished I had a crystal ball so I could see where all of this was headed. But I needed the money, and according to Stephen Ellington, his son was willing to spend "a wad" to debut his latest creation. Now that my office was temporarily off-limits, I had to find another place quickly— and that meant a hike in rent, for sure. But the idea of raising the dead at my next party . . . ? I shuddered, recalling a recent party where a guest had actually died. What was it my mother had said at the time? Oh yes. "A corpse is not a party favor, Presley." Ya think?

"And your son . . ." I started to say.

"Jonathan," Stephen filled in.

"Jonathan, he's on board with this?"

"Oh yes. Jon said if I could find someone good to host the party, he'd love to do it." Stephen gave me a half grin. I could see why my mother was charmed by him. Gentle, friendly, and obviously proud of his son, he reminded me of one of those distinguished stars from the golden age of movies—William Powell? Laurence Olivier?

"I don't know . . ." I said, stalling. "The Winchester House may not be rentable. And if it is, it could be extremely expensive. Besides, I've never done a Séance Party . . ."

"Ah, but Veronica assures me you can handle this," Stephen said, glancing at Mother with affection. Or was that lust?

In spite of being in the early stages of Alzheimer's disease, Mother had kept up her appearance and was still an attractive and vivacious woman. No wonder she'd hooked up with another handsome, charismatic man.

The bell over the door to the diner chimed, announcing a new customer. Stephen turned to look at the young man who entered, then raised an arm and waved the man over. He was about my age—thirtysomething—a younger version of Stephen with blond instead of gray hair, smooth rather than lined skin, and jeans with a blue button-down shirt, instead of the tweed jacket and khaki slacks his father wore. Both had on brown Sperry Top-Siders—rich, stylish, and good-looking, like father and son.

Stephen started to rise.

"Don't get up, Dad," the man I'd guessed was Jonathan Ellington said. He leaned down to embrace his father, then straightened up, reached out a hand to my mother, and said, "You must be Veronica. My father has told me so much about you. I'm Jonathan." My mother blushed as she took his tanned hand.

There was no mistaking the resemblance between father and son. They had the same sparkling blue eyes, the same

perfectly sculpted thick hair, and the same tall, slim phy-
siques. The only real difference was the years between them.

Jonathan turned to me and grasped my outstretched hand.
He held it a little longer than was comfortable as he said,
"And you're Presley Parker, the 'party queen.' It's great to
meet you."

For a moment I thought he was going to kiss the back of
my hand. I pulled it away before he had the chance.

He flashed a white, toothy grin. "Mind if I join you?" He
slid into my side of the green vinyl booth.

O-kay.

I scrunched over, but Jonathan scooched up close enough
for me to smell his minty breath and heavy aftershave. I tried
to move over farther but was already up against the booth
wall. Literally and figuratively.

"How did you know we were here?" I asked, figuring his
arrival hadn't been a coincidence.

Stephen spoke up. "I called him, while you were parking
your car." I remembered Stephen being on the phone when
I'd returned from moving my MINI Cooper.

"You got here fast," I said to Jonathan.

"I live in the city," Jonathan replied. "Pacific Heights."

"Actually, it was my idea," Mother added, taking Stephen's right hand. "I thought the four of us should meet and
get this party started, as they say."

Jonathan started to touch my hand in a similar fashion
until he saw the knife I was holding. Instead, he picked up a
menu. "That's right. I jumped in my Benz and zipped on
over. So what's good here?"

While Mother praised the omelets, I quietly wondered

what I was getting into. Once Jonathan ordered his Mel-burger, it didn't take long to find out.

"So, as my dad probably told you, Presley, I'm founder and CEO of Hella-Graphics, the fastest-rising company in Northern California. . . ."

I tuned out as our food arrived. Jonathan continued to recite what sounded like a memorized speech, while I sipped my coffee and listened to "All Shook Up" that someone had selected on the jukebox. Could have been my ADHD (Attention Deficit Hyperactivity Disorder) or his NPD (Narcissistic Personality Disorder) but I checked out the fifties decor—old menus, posters of *American Graffiti*, pictures of carhops—until I felt a sharp-toed kick under the table. I glared at the smile pasted on my mother's face as I caught Jonathan's last words.

". . . exciting new product, an incredibly realistic four-dimensional holographic projector my research department developed, called 4-D Projection. Dad said you've had a few mishaps at some of your recent parties, so I'm thinking this event will not only be a great way to impress my future investors, but will also help you get your party business back in the spotlight."

Oh my God. What had Mother told them?

Now, after listening to the boring spiel in the pompous vocabulary he'd spewed—not to mention his condescension about my business—there was no way I could work with this egomaniacal player. And if my mother's new beau dumped her because I didn't take the job, then he wasn't much of a prospect, Top-Siders or no Top-Siders.

"Well, I'm not sure it's my kind of event—" I began explaining.

"Oh, I disagree," Jonathan said, interrupting me. "Any event planner would kill to get this gig, but after all I've heard about you, you're the one I want. Together I bet we could put on a great show. I'm sure your creative skills and my cutting-edge product will go hand in hand."

On cue, he laid his hand on mine. Kill me now, I thought.

"In fact, not only will 4-D Projection revolutionize the movie industry—think Princess Leia–slash-*Avatar* popping up at our table here, fully formed and as real as your sparking eyes—it also has potential for use in medicine, personal protection, even the military. And you can say you helped introduce it."

I removed my hand and reached for my latte. "But I really don't think—"

"Plus, it will make us both a hella-lot of money," Jonathan added, grinning widely.

I looked at Mother. She actually winked at me.

"Well, I'll check my calendar—I've got a pretty full lineup . . . a bat mitzvah, a *quinceañera*, two bachelorette parties. Oh, and a funeral—"

Jonathan's phone rang, interrupting my list of excuses. He pulled out his cell phone and answered with a loud "Yes?"

The three of us listened while he took the call.

"No way!" he said into the phone, his animated smile sobering. ". . . Screw him . . . Yeah, well if he tries, I'll wring his neck . . ." The irritation reflected in his reddening face morphed into anger. His voice grew louder, attracting the attention of the diners nearby. "Take care of it, Stephanie! That's what I pay you the big bucks for." He punched off with as much force as his thumb could muster and tucked the phone back into his pocket. Once again he flashed that superwhite smile, and said, "Sorry about that. Business. I'm sure my VP will handle it."

I shot a concerned glance at Mother. She raised her eyebrows. This guy was a chameleon, changing from charming to enraged in a matter of seconds. A red flag not only went up, but flew at full mast.

"Where were we?" Jonathan continued, oblivious to our reaction. "Oh yes. Just imagine—a séance at the rumored-to-be-haunted Winchester Mystery House. It's the perfect venue for debuting the product to possible investors. They'll all be blown away when our special guest suddenly appears— the ghost of Sarah Winchester!" He chuckled. "Wait until James Cameron hears about this. He'd kill for the secret to this new technology. But I'll be the one making a killing."

I'd had enough. I pushed away the plate in front of me and I pulled out my iPhone, pretending to check my messages. "Well, I hate to be rude, but I have to get back to the office. I'm meeting a client."

Jonathan made no attempt to move out of the way. "So, are we set?" he said, looking at me with confident anticipation.

I started to say, "In your dreams, buddy," but before I could get out a nicer version, I caught my mother staring at Stephen, her eyes wide with horror.

I looked at the older man. His eyes had rolled back and his lids were fluttering. He seemed to be trying to say something, but all that came out of his mouth were grunts and a string of drool.

Jonathan turned to see what I was staring at and jumped up. "Dad? Dad!"

Stephen's eyelids stop fluttering and his jaw grew slack.

"Stephen!" Mother said, grimacing and patting his hand.

Jonathan pulled out his cell phone. "Yes, this is an emergency," he said to the operator. "It's my father. I think he's having another stroke."

I witnessed a new side of Jonathan Ellington materialize as we waited for help to arrive at the diner. Leaving his evil twin behind, his good twin had emerged and taken charge immediately. He lay his father gently on the floor, checked the man's pockets for medication, then asked the waitress for water. While we waited for the ambulance, Jonathan sat caressing his father's head lovingly, as if caring for a baby. I heard him whisper "Dad" repeatedly while he wiped his father's brow with a dampened handkerchief that Mother had offered. The rest of the diners remained in their booths, mouths agape at the unfolding drama, food untouched and getting cold.

When the EMTs arrived moments later, Mother and I backed out of their way. I saw tears form in my mother's eyes as she stood a few feet from the ailing man. Grasping her hand, I pulled her over to another booth and sat her down. She'd recently lost three of her friends—two from the care center and one a longtime friend from her partying days—and each time the deaths had hit her hard. I wondered how much Stephen had come to mean to her in such a short time. And whether or not she could take another loss.

One of the EMTs questioned Jonathan about his father's previous condition, while the other gave Stephen oxygen and started an IV. Moments later the older man was lifted onto a stretcher and rolled out to the ambulance waiting at the curb.

Jonathan followed, giving me a quick glance on the way out. I nodded in return. After he disappeared into the back of the ambulance, I turned to Mother who had regained her composure. Together we listened, stunned, to the sound of fading sirens.

"Oh, Presley, do you think Stephen's going to be all right?" she asked, rising from her seat. "He's such a nice man. Oh dear." Again her eyes brimmed with tears.

"I'm sure he'll be fine, Mom," I reassured her. "The doctors will take good care of him. Let's get you home." My words felt hollow. I knew nothing about strokes, other than one of my stepfathers, Van, had died from one. I was only five at the time.

I held the diner door open and Mother shuffled through, clutching her Coach handbag as if it were a lifeline.

As we walked up the street, she kept repeating the word "fast." I could tell she was agitated when she rattled on like that.

"Mother, are you all right?"

"Yes, darling. I'm fine."

"You keep saying 'fast.' Are you in a hurry?"

"No, no. I'm just remembering what we were taught in our CPR class. The signs of a stroke."

"Fast?"

"Yes, it's an acronym, to help us remember more easily. I have trouble with my memory at times, you know." She held up a fist, then uncurled one finger at a time, counting off each letter in the acronym. "FAST: F for facial paralysis, A for arm weakness, S for speech difficulties, and T for time to act fast."

"Wow, I'm impressed."

"Yes, I got an A in that class. You should take it. You not only learn the signs, but you learn what to do. For example, if you suspect the victim has facial paralysis, you ask him to smile. If he's had a stroke, he can't smile easily and the mouth often droops on one side."

"Huh." I'd noticed a little drooping on one side of Stephen's mouth.

"For arm weakness," she continued, "you ask the person to raise both arms. He usually can't raise one."

I recalled Stephen's left arm dangling at his side.

"S is for speech difficulties. Many stroke victims slur their words or can't speak at all."

"And I assume 'time to act fast' means call nine-one-one," I offered.

She nodded. "Apparently there's a window of time when the victim can receive some medication that may increase his chances of surviving a stroke. Unfortunately, we didn't know all of this when Van died."

When we reached my mother's place, which she called her "hotel" rather than care facility, I escorted her to her room. She said she was tired and needed a midmorning nap after all she'd witnessed. I helped her slip out of her bright clothes and into a comfortable velour jogging suit, then tucked her into bed.

"I'll call you later, Mom," I said, standing.

She reached out and took my hand. "Presley?"

I squeezed it. "Yes, Mom?"

She looked up at me. "Will you do it?"

"Do what, Mom? Take the CPR class? Of course. Don't worry."

"No, not that. Will you take the job? For Stephen's sake?"

"Uh . . ." I stammered. "Under the circumstances, I doubt they'll want to—"

"Please, Presley. For me."

I patted her arm. "Okay, Mom. If it means that much to you—and *if* Jonathan still wants me—I'll take the job. But I'm guessing he's got more important things to think about right now, with his father on the way to the hospital."

Mother closed her eyes. "Thanks, darling. Now, would you turn off the light on your way out?"

I nodded, even though she wasn't looking at me. Flipping off the light switch by the door, I whispered, "Have a nice nap," and quietly shut the door behind me.

As I walked back to my car, I marveled at my mother's big heart. Hosting a party had always been her way of showing people how much she cared about them. For me, it was more of a business and a way to contribute to worthy causes. As much as I had initially disliked Jonathan, he'd stepped up when his father had fallen ill, and I admired him for that. But surely he wouldn't want to proceed with his party plans now.

And even if he did, I wasn't sure I still *had* a party business.

After all, my party stuff was currently locked up in a condemned building.

I only hoped it hadn't been hauled out and tossed into the nearest Dumpster.

Chapter 3

PARTY PLANNING TIP #3

To set the stage for your séance, you need to create an eerie mood. For example, unplug noisy appliances, darken the room, and light candles. And most important, turn off all cell phones. The dead still don't use them to communicate with the living.

I drove back to Treasure Island, my thoughts spinning as fast as my MINI Cooper's little wheels. So much had happened in a single morning. I'd been locked out of my office building (condemned!), nearly hired for a job (a séance?), hit on by an egomaniac (albeit a rich and good-looking one), and watched an old man suffer a stroke.

And it wasn't even eleven o'clock yet. What else could happen before lunch?

I pulled into the barracks parking lot and glanced at the front door of the office building as I gathered my purse. The chain and lock had been removed. Brad really did have magical powers. In more ways than one, I thought, remembering with a tingle the night we'd spent together recently.

I headed up the steps, then picked up the orange notice I'd wadded into a ball in a fury and uncurled it.

Placard of CONDEMNATION

City of San Francisco—Inspections Division
In accordance with Chapter 3, Section 5150 of the Building Maintenance Code of the City of San Francisco, the premises, building, and structure hereon located at:

_____Barracks B—Fifth & H Streets_____ are hereby condemned because

__It has been determined by the U.S. Environmental Protection Agency and the State Department of Toxic Substances Control to be dilapidated and unsafe, due to contamination with asbestos, plutonium, radium, and other substances, which are known to cause cancer.

Premises must be vacated within 72 hours, by __4/14_____

Housing Inspector's
Number___916-837-7089_____

Gripping the placard in my hand, I turned the knob—unlocked—and passed through the reception area on my way to my office. Maneuvering around several cardboard boxes, I noticed Brad had stacked a bunch near the door to his office. The rest of his room was stripped bare—except for Brad. Unfortunately, I thought, wickedly.

"You're already packed?"

"Yep," he said, adding one last box to a precarious pile. "We've got seventy-two hours to vacate. Found us some empty offices in the admin building, thanks to Marianne."

Instead of thank you, I said, "So how much is that going to cost me?"

"I got a deal. Promised to clean a few carpets and remove some mold now and then for a lower rent."

"That's great for you, but what have I got to offer in trade? Free balloons?"

Brad rubbed his chin. "About that . . ."

"Oh no. You didn't promise them an event!"

He grinned. "She's psyched!"

I crossed my arms, mostly to keep from slapping him.

"And guess what kind of party she wants," Brad continued, deliberately ignoring my fury.

"A hootenanny?"

He laughed. I got the feeling he enjoyed tormenting me. In fact, I knew it. "They want a mini Golden Gate Expo, like the one that was held here back in 'thirty-nine. The Island will be celebrating seventy-five years soon and she wants the public to come and visit the place. I think it's a great idea. And right up your alley."

"Of course you do. You don't know the amount of work involved in putting on a party of that magnitude."

"That's the point. You can deduct your time from the rent. At least for a while."

The anger left me as my mind started whirling, something it always does when a possible party plan pops into my head. Coming up with new ideas related to the theme was the most fun—the rest was work. But bringing back the "Magic City," as most had called it back then, would be a blast . . . *if* I could pull it off. I entered my office full of possibilities, and sat down at my computer.

Brad leaned in the doorway. "Shouldn't you be packing?"

"In a minute . . ." I said, preparing to do a search for details of the 1939 Golden Gate Expo. Instead, my eye caught on a local Yahoo! headline: "Man hangs himself at high-tech company." To the side was a photo of the man featured on the news that morning. I was certain I knew him. Curious, I clicked on the link. The information was sparse, but shocking.

"George Wells, a computer programmer at Hella-Graphics, apparently hanged himself over the weekend at the up-and-coming high-tech company. Details are being withheld by the San Francisco Police Department, pending a complete investigation."

George Wells. I knew that name. I pulled open a file drawer and searched the W's for the name. There it was. I yanked out the file and flipped it open on my desk.

I had given a party for George Wells—a surprise "Over the Hill" Sixtieth Birthday Party for him only a couple of months ago. During the planning stages, I'd gotten to know his wife, Teddi, well. She'd welcomed me into her grand Pacific Heights home, even invited me on their yacht.

He'd hanged himself? The news wouldn't compute and I sat holding the file, stunned.

Jonathan Ellington never said a word about it this morning. "Presley?" I heard my name called from what seemed far away. I looked up. Brad was standing right next to me. "Are you all right?"

I shook away the image of George Wells, a rope tied around his neck . . .

"Uh, yeah, fine," I said. "I just found out one of my former clients committed suicide over the weekend."

"The hanging?" Brad asked.

I blinked. "Yes, how did you know?"

"I cleaned up after it yesterday."

Oh my God. "You were at Hella-Graphics?" I asked.

"Did you know him pretty well?" Brad asked.

"A little. I know his wife. We just had coffee the other day. She was planning another party, this time for one of her daughters. I can't believe he hung himself." I looked down at the file. "You and Detective Melvin are tight. Did he have any theories on why George did it?"

"Nope. In fact, Melvin isn't completely convinced it's a suicide, but there was no evidence of foul play."

If Detective Luke Melvin, my nemesis at the San Francisco Police Department, was suspicious, perhaps there was a reason.

"Hmmm," I said. Jonathan Ellington hadn't said a word this morning about the death of his employee. But then, it wasn't exactly breakfast conversation. Still, he hadn't looked particularly affected.

"Hmmm, what?" Brad asked, sitting on the corner of my desk.

"I met his boss this morning at breakfast—Jonathan Ellington. And he didn't mention anything about it."

"What were you doing having breakfast with Ellington?"

There was an undertone to his voice—was it jealousy? Or something else?

"Oh, my mother has this idea about hosting a party for his new product. But with his dad in the hospital—"

"His father's in the hospital?"

"Long story," I said. "Anyway, it's moot at this point. I don't think there's going to be any party. Good thing, I guess, now that you've tossed me this Expo event."

"Yeah, well, my advice is, stay away from Jonathan Ellington. He's not the kind of guy you want to get mixed up with."

Before I could respond, Brad was out the door, leaving me totally confused . . . and a little curious.

While Brad started loading boxes into his SUV, I tried to continue my search for details from the Expo, but my thoughts kept returning to George Wells's wife, Teddi. I picked up the file, found her number, and punched it into my iPhone.

George's deep, disembodied voice came on the line, startling me.

"This is the Wells family. Leave a message or call back." Click.

Blunt and to the point. When I'd met him George seemed like a no-nonsense kind of guy. The type of guy to commit suicide?

I stumbled through a message, something about, "Sorry about George . . . If you want to talk . . . let me know if there's anything I can do . . ." then hung up, wishing there really *was* something I could do.

My phone rang—the theme from the movie *Halloween*—and I checked the caller ID. None—just a familiar phone number. The number I had just called.

"Hello?"

"Presley?" A woman's voice, weak and scratchy.

I felt a pang in my gut. "Teddi? Is that you?"

"Yes, sorry I didn't answer. I'm screening. I've had so many annoying calls from the press."

I hope I hadn't added to that annoyance. "I . . . I'm so sorry to hear about George. Is there anything I can do?"

"As a matter of fact, there is."

Her response surprised me. "Uh, sure. Anything. You name it."

"I'm certain George didn't kill himself. There's no way he would commit suicide. He didn't leave a note or anything. . . ." Her voice cracked, and I heard sniffles. She was crying. I wanted to reach out and hug her through the phone.

"Uh"—I didn't know how to respond—"are you sure?"

"I have no proof, if that's what you mean. But you offered to help. I know you've helped solve a couple of recent murders. I've been reading about you in the paper. I want you to look into George's death. Would you do that for me?"

"I—" I had no idea what to say. "I'm not a cop, Teddi. I'm sure they'll—"

She cut me off. "No one believes me," she sobbed. "I don't know what else to do. His life insurance is canceled if his death is ruled suicide. I'll be left with nothing . . ." She sniffled again.

I thought about her assets. If it came to that, she could sell her palatial home, the yacht. But this was not the time to tell her that. Besides, George had probably left a will that provided for Teddi and her girls.

"Teddi, it's going to be okay," I said, trying to soothe her.

"Listen, I know a detective. I'll see what I can find out, all right?"

I heard Teddi blow her nose.

"Thank you, Presley. Thank you. . . ." She hung up, leaving me still holding the phone to my ear.

"Parker! Let's go!" Brad stood in the doorway holding the last of his moving boxes. "I want to be out of here by the end of the day. Stop chatting on the phone and start packing."

I put my phone in my purse, closed the Wells file with a mental note to have a talk with Detective Melvin about George's death, then put it in one of the empty cardboard boxes, along with the rest of my files. I know most people have a hard time accepting that a relative would commit suicide. They either don't see the signs or they ignore them— until it is too late. But with the rate of suicides growing each year, it was not something to be ignored. Most were linked to mental illness or drugs and alcohol. And more men were successful at suicide, using "guaranteed" methods like gunshot or hanging, even though three times as many women attempted suicide. Was George one of the statistics?

His wife, Teddi, didn't think so.

"Presley?" Brad said, interrupting my thoughts. "You ready?"

I pushed George and Teddi Wells from my mind and tried to focus on the task at hand.

"Almost. What about the others? Delicia? Rocco? Raj? Berkeley?" I asked, referring to my office mates and part-time assistants.

Brad nodded toward the back offices. I walked down the hall, peering into the windows of each one. They were all empty. Everyone was gone. Vanished.

I looked at Brad, dumbfounded. "Where'd they all go?"

"Cleared out early this morning while you were at your breakfast date. They've already set up shop in their new digs. I got them offices at Building One, too."

"That's great. But doesn't Rocco need a kitchen?"

Brad nodded, shifting the boxes in his bulging arms. "There's one on the second floor."

"Raj?"

"He got the first office, behind the front desk. He'll be manning that desk when he's not patrolling the area."

"Delicia? Berkeley? Duncan?"

"Yep. They're sharing office space to save on rent."

"So we'll all be together!" I said as I returned to my office. I began pulling party supplies off the shelves and putting everything in boxes Brad had set out for me.

"I was hoping you'd say that," Brad said.

I stopped filling a box with ornate candlesticks I'd once used as props for a murder mystery party, and turned to Brad, still holding one of the candlesticks in my hand. "What do you mean you were hoping I'd say that?"

"Uh . . . you've got a roommate this time. Delicia."

He fled with his box before I could get a good grip on the candlestick. Don't get me wrong. I love Delicia and consider her my best friend, next to my mother. But that girl never shuts up. Without a wall between us, I wasn't going to get a thing done.

The Art Deco Administration Building, aka Building One, is the first of only a few structures remaining from the World's Fair that tourists see when they enter Treasure Island. In fact, they can't miss it. The concave half-circle design not only lures visitors to stop by, but it's probably the safest building on the island in the event of an earthquake. Tourists love to take pictures standing next to the large nude statues that flank the entrance and peek inside the heavy glass and brass doors at the huge dome inside. According to one of the many Treasure Island Web sites, "a security desk commands attention in the middle of the sweeping hallway and serves mostly as a courtesy to tourists who want to know more about this intriguing, anachronistic structure."

Currently, Raj Reddy, my favorite security guard on the island, manned the desk. Behind him, covering more than a dozen large wall panels, was a colorful mural illustrating the history of TI from its creation to the present.

Underneath the panels were doors to small offices, including one for the historical society museum. I wondered which of the remaining offices was my new party headquarters.

"Hey, Raj," I said, wheeling a cart towered with several boxes into the expansive hall. "I guess we're still going to be office neighbors."

Raj bobbled his head and gave a grin that revealed a small gap between his two front teeth. "Yes, Ms. Presley. Welcome to our new building. This is so much nicer than those old barracks. I'm so glad Mr. Brad got us a good deal."

I turned and eyed Brad who had followed me over, wheeling his own stack of boxes.

"So, which one is mine?" I asked him.

I needn't have bothered to ask. My former office neighbor, Delicia Jackson, popped her head out of a door on the right marked "104" and waved.

"Presley! Don't you love it? It's divine! And we're roomies! Come see!"

Delicia was a mostly out-of-work actress who spoke in exclamation marks punctuated by dramatic inflection. When she wasn't auditioning for commercials or small theater productions, she helped me out with my party business, doing everything from making decorations to appearing as a Disney princess. Petite, with latte-colored skin and long dark hair, she caught the eye of most men in her path, and had broken many a heart in her search for her Prince Charming.

I waved back and wheeled my cart toward her.

She pushed the door wide-open and ushered me in with a sweep of her hand. Most of the space in the tiny office was taken up by two face-to-face desks, one metal and covered with theater bills, ragged scripts, and head shots of Dee. The other, wood, stood pristine, waiting for me. The two walls behind the desks were lined with shelves, empty for the most part. It wouldn't take me long to fill them with everything from paper party hats to murder mystery weapons.

Brad unloaded the boxes while I began filling up the shelves. Dee kept busy hanging posters from *Wicked*, *Rent*, *Hairspray*, and *Beach Blanket Babylon*. When she finished, she helped me organize my party paraphernalia, albeit with nonstop narration. By working through the noon hour we were more or less settled in and ready for business by midafternoon.

"Looking good," Brad said, appearing suddenly like a ghost. He glanced around, nodding. "How do you like it?"

I had to admit, it was a lot nicer than the decaying barracks. And sharing space with Dee would probably save money. I just hoped she wouldn't be too distracting. With ADHD, I didn't need any more distractions.

"It's really great. Thanks for arranging this. Where's your office?"

"Next door. Just rap on the wall if you need me. Better than an intercom."

I'd miss being able to spy on him through the office windows in the barracks, but it was nice to know he was so close.

"Shall we grab an early dinner?" he asked. "I missed lunch."

My cell phone rang. I glanced at the screen. No name, just a number. Not familiar.

"Killer Parties," I said, holding up a finger to Brad in response to his question.

"Presley?" said the male voice on the other end.

"Yes, may I help you?"

"This is Jonathan."

I tried to conjure up all the Jonathans I knew.

"Uh . . ."

"Jonathan Ellington. I met you this morning at the diner?"

"Oh yes." I shot a guilty glance at Brad but he was busy swiveling in Dee's empty chair. "Hi. How's your father?"

"Holding his own. Thanks," Jonathan said. "At least, as well as can be expected. He's completely paralyzed on his left side. After the first stroke he had some movement there, but this one was a lot worse. Luckily he can still talk, but his words are slurred, and he's repeating himself a lot. Still, the doctor is hopeful."

"I'm so sorry, Jonathan. Is there anything I can do?"

Brad shot me a look when I mentioned Jonathan's name.

"As a matter of fact, there is."

I paused for a moment, surprised at his response. I couldn't imagine there was anything I could do to help him or his father, with such a serious medical condition.

"Really? Uh, what?"

"Can you meet me?"

"Where? At the hospital?"

"No. At the Winchester Mystery House. I want this party more than anything. For my father's sake."

Stunned, I stammered, "Are—are you sure?"

"Yes. While I was at the hospital, he kept repeating 'séance' and 'Winchester' over and over. Obviously he really wants me to do this."

"Uh, all right . . . umm. When would you like to meet? Next week sometime?"

"Tonight. Can you be there, say, seven?"

"Oh, I don't think . . . I have a lot of work left to do. How about tomorrow?"

"I'd really like to get going on this—for my father's sake. And I'd like you to see the place at night, when it's dark. That's when we'll be hosting the party."

I checked my watch, then said, "Uh . . . I suppose I could make it."

"How about dinner first?" he added.

I glanced at Brad. "Oh, I'm sorry. I already have plans."

"Then seven it is. I look forward to it."

"Okay, I'll see you there," I said, and hung up.

I tucked the phone into my purse. Something was bothering me about his request. Was he really doing this for his father—or did he have another motive? My mother would have called me a pessimist, always looking for the dark side, but I'd learned to trust my gut. And my gut was sending out an alarm. Especially in light of George Wells's death. Still, with my mother, Jonathan, and his father all pressing me to host this event, there was no way I was getting out of it. I would just have to stay on my toes. And perhaps I could gain some insight into why George committed suicide.

"Who was that?" Brad asked after I hung up.

I shook my long bangs out of my eyes. "Uh, Jonathan Ellington. He wants to go ahead with the party. A séance at the Winchester Mystery House to showcase his new computer product for investors. Something called 4-D Projection."

"How cool!" Dee squealed as she entered the room. "Can I play the medium? I go to psychics in the city all the time!"

Before I could answer, I caught Brad shaking his head.

"I know. It seems odd, what with his father in the hospital with a stroke. He says he's doing it for his dad. Did you meet Jonathan while you were there . . . cleaning up?"

"Yeah. He showed up. He told me to keep my mouth shut, like I was one of his employees or something. It's like a cult over there—his employees are fiercely loyal. No wonder, with all the perks they get working there."

"Really? Like what?" I asked.

"You name it," Brad said. "And everything's state of the art. He's got people working such long hours, they don't get much time outside of the office. So to keep them there—and keep them happy—he's installed a gym, a spa, a screening room, a video game room, a cafeteria . . . He's even hired personal trainers, a gourmet chef, and a masseuse for his drones."

I heard the disgust in Brad's voice. Or was it jealousy?

"Why don't you like him? Sounds like he's awfully good to his employees." Except George?

Brad gave a hollow laugh. "Employees? More like slaves. They have no life, other than working there."

I couldn't tell if Brad had a legitimate grudge against him—or if it was something else.

"Well, I'm only doing an event for him, at the request of his father. And for my mother."

"Your mom?" Brad looked surprised.

"Apparently she met Jonathan's dad, Stephen Ellington, at the care center and has a thing for him. She practically begged me to take the job."

"You're a sucker for your mom, you know?"

"Can't help it. Besides, if Jonathan is really that loaded, my fee should pay the rent here for a few months. And I'm going to need it," I added, glancing around the new office.

I picked up my purse and backpack that contained my notebook and party planning sheets. "I've got to run," I said to Dee. I wasn't sure she heard me; she was busy trying on a blond wig I'd recently used at a Cheerleaders and Jocks party.

"Want company?" Brad asked.

"Seriously?"

"Why not? We could grab dinner along the way."

"Don't you have any blood to clean up or maggots to . . . to . . ." I didn't have an ending.

"Nope. Maybe I could help you with the party."

What was he up to? "Brad, I realize you have a lot of hidden talents and secret knowledge, like how to break into locked rooms and send untraceable e-mails, but don't tell me you know how to conduct a séance or conjure up a three-dimensional spirit."

"Maybe," he said mysteriously, crossing his muscular arms like a freed genie.

I silently pondered his offer. I could always use help. And there was something about Jonathan Ellington that bothered me. If he was a slave driver, taking advantage of his employees, making them work long hours at low wages, I wasn't sure I wanted to be involved in his plans. And I didn't relish the thought of fighting off his advances either.

"All right, but—"

My cell phone rang again. I checked the caller ID, then answered.

"Hi, Mom."

"Presley! I just heard the news."

"What news?" Had Jonathan's father taken a turn for the worse?

"And I want to come along."

"Where? What are you talking about?"

"The Winchester Mystery House. I hear you're meeting Jonathan there tonight. It'll help take my mind off Stephen."

Great. Now I had an entourage, made up of my mother and a crime scene cleaner.

What more could a party planner want?

Chapter 4

My MINI Cooper is just right for me, but when you add a well-muscled guy over six feet tall and a mother who's two inches shorter than my five ten and who once rode in limos to society events, things get crowded fast. If I continued to have chaperones, I was going to have to get a bigger boat, er, car.

Or get rid of the extra baggage.

"This is going to be so much fun!" my mother said from the tiny backseat. I was sure she wasn't referring to the ride over to the Winchester Mystery House, located about forty to sixty minutes away—depending on traffic—in the nearby city of San Jose. But there was no way Brad could fit in the backseat, so my mother, being the good sport she is, climbed into the rear and curled up. She sat on the right side behind Brad, with her long legs extended into the area behind my seat. Her authentic designer bag filled the rest of the space, leaving barely enough room in the car for our three to-go coffees (mine a latte, Brad's an espresso, and Mom's a non-fat, decaf cap, extra dry, with whip).

As was her habit when we visited a place together, Mother lectured about the history of the site, filling in with exaggeration and rumor when the facts grew scarce. Although I'd been to the foreboding Winchester mansion when I was a Girl Scout, Brad had never toured the place and ate up the tidbits of information that Mother fed us on the ride over. For me, the details reminded me of how much the place still haunted me since that initial visit.

"You know, Bradley," my mother said, tapping Brad on the shoulder to make sure he was listening, "the Winchester House is supposed to be haunted."

"Oh yeah?" Brad said, tossing the words over his shoulder. "Do you believe in ghosts, Ms. Parker?" Although my mother has been married a number of times, she's kept the last name of her first husband.

"Me? No. Not really. Well, sort of. You never know."

Brad glanced at me and raised a questioning eyebrow.

"Don't look at me. No way am I superstitious," I told him. I hoped I was convincing . . .

"Anyway," Mother continued, "Sarah Winchester, the owner of the house, was told by a medium that she had to keep building the place to appease the spirits of Native Americans that had been killed by her husband's rifles. So she did, for thirty-eight years." If Brad had heard the stories, he didn't let on, seemingly absorbed in my mother's narration. "That must have cost a bundle," he said.

"Back then, about five and a half million," Mother stated. "Today it would be more like seventy million."

Brad whistled.

"She did most of the architecture planning herself, using the backs of napkins and scratch paper. The house is Victorian in style, but she added a lot of things that make no sense, plus a lot of psychic symbols everywhere. Can you imagine?"

I marveled at my mother's ability to recall so many specific details, when she had trouble remembering what she'd done the previous day or where she'd last put her purse. The more I learned about Alzheimer's, the more puzzling it became.

Brad grinned. "Like what?"

"The number thirteen," Mother said. "It was thought to ward off haunted souls."

"A lot of people are superstitious about the number thirteen. But it sounds like she was more than a little 'off,'" Brad said.

I saw Mother shake her head in the rearview mirror. "I think she was just overwhelmed by the deaths of her young daughter and then her husband. She went to the medium hoping to contact them, but the medium told her she was cursed, and that the spirits wanted vengeance—and a place to live. Sarah was told that if she kept building her house, she'd live forever."

And keep the medium in plenty of money, I thought. "Apparently that wasn't true," I added, "since she eventually died."

Ignoring me, my mother continued. "After all that construction, the house became a maze, with twists and turns, dead ends, and doors that lead nowhere. She figured the spirits would get lost in the house and never find her."

I was stunned at the lengths Sarah Winchester went to, all based on something her so-called "medium" told her. I doubted if anyone would believe such nonsense today— although we had plenty of psychic hotlines and palm readers on every corner of the city. But back in her day, psychic readings, mediums, and séances were all the rage, and common parlor entertainment.

We arrived at our destination in time to have a quick bite of dinner at Santana Row, one of those live-where-you-work-and-shop neighborhoods kitty-corner to the mansion. Passing up high-end shops like Gucci, Salvatore Ferragamo, Anthropologie, and Tommy Bahama, we stopped in at Maggiano's Little Italy and had pasta with a nice Chianti. As we headed to the Winchester Mystery House, I couldn't help but notice the unlikely juxtaposition of a rambling old Victorian set in the midst of high-tech Silicon Valley. A sign claimed the house was OPEN EVERY DAY EXCEPT CHRISTMAS. Judging by the cars still in the parking lot, the place attracted large numbers of curious tourists from all over the world.

Brad and I got out of the MINI, and he popped the seat handle to free my mother from her tiny prison. She managed to step out gracefully. We all gazed up at the turreted Victorian house, lit up by old-fashioned gas-type lanterns and moonlight.

"There used to be seven stories," Mother said, "but the 1906 earthquake knocked down three. Now there are only four."

I searched for evidence of the lost floors of the Queen Anne Victorian, but even at four stories, the house was imposing because of its utter vastness, odd angles, and bizarre history. The turrets, towers, cupolas, cornices, and spires all added to the castlelike appearance.

"There are one hundred and sixty rooms, forty bedrooms, thirteen bathrooms," Mother said. "Plus there are six kitchens, forty-seven fireplaces, seventeen chimneys, forty staircases, two ballrooms, and one séance room."

Brad blinked at the numbers Mother had thrown at him. How did she retain all that minutiae with her disease?

I did remember that Sarah Winchester, for all her eccentricities, kept abreast of the "new technology" of the times. She had been one of the first to install a hydraulic elevator in her home, use steam and forced-air heating, and indoor plumbing, all rare at the time. She'd been ahead of her time in terms of science and industry, yet hampered by superstition.

I checked my watch and glanced around for Jonathan Ellington. I caught a glimpse of him striding over from his late-model Mercedes. He'd parked in a red zone near the front, apparently unconcerned about breaking the law or getting a ticket. For all I knew, he could be rich enough to buy the old mystery house and discard the ticket.

"Hi, Presley," Jonathan said. "Ms. Parker, what a nice surprise!" He reached out to shake our hands. Brad had wandered off a few steps, but returned when he noticed Jonathan had joined us.

I spun around to introduce Brad. "Jonathan, this is my friend Brad Matthews. He . . . helps me with some of my events. I hope you don't mind my bringing him and my mother along." I decided not to mentioned that Brad had been at Hella-Graphics yesterday, cleaning up after one of his employees. Maybe Jonathan wouldn't recognize him.

"Not at all," Jonathan said, although his tiny frown said otherwise. "Nice to meet you." He shook Brad's hand, then stopped. "Have we met before?"

Brad said nothing, but pulled his hand out of Jonathan's grip. I interrupted before things got uncomfortable. "I can't wait to see the place again."

Mother touched Jonathan's arm. "How's your father, Jonathan?" Her eyes pleaded for a positive response.

"He's holding his own," Jonathan said, placing a hand over hers. "Thanks for asking. As I told Presley, he's lost use of his left side, but the doctors are optimistic. With physical therapy, medication, and perhaps a motorized wheelchair, Dad should be up and around and back at the care home soon."

Mother let out a breath. "I'm so relieved." The others probably didn't notice, but Mother's eyes had clouded with tears. She blinked them back as she turned away.

"Well," Jonathan said, rubbing his hands together. "Shall we get started? The last tour ends at seven so we'll have the place to ourselves. I've arranged for the manager, Mia Thiele, to give us a private tour. She's excited about the prospect of a Séance Party here at the house."

We followed Jonathan as he led the way, ducking under the low roofline that must have been just right for the diminutive Sarah Winchester. At four feet ten inches tall—I remembered that only because I was taller than she was by the time I was in junior high—she could apparently maneuver the narrow hallways, staircases, and doorways with ease, while Brad, Jonathan, and I, at five ten and over, would have to watch our heads at every entrance, elevation, and turn. Mother just had to watch her bouffant hair.

We entered the gift shop and Jonathan knocked on the door nearly invisible to shopping tourists. Without waiting for an invitation, he opened the door and led us inside. The tiny space was cluttered with a small desk and a table filled with a computer, printer, shredder, and other electronic equipment. They all seemed completely uncharacteristic for the setting. What had I expected? A butter churn and a printing press?

An attractive fortysomething woman with wavy shoulder-length auburn hair, manicured nails, and big green eyes looked up at us from the desk and gave a lip-glossed smile.

"Mr. Ellington, I présumé?" the woman said, rising to her feet. She was dressed in black slacks and a "Winchester Mystery House" T-shirt with the image of a skull superimposed on the outline of the house. She held out a hand.

Jonathan shook it firmly. "Ms. Thiele?" Was that a glint in his eye I saw as he looked the woman over?

"Please," she said, smiling as she returned to her seat, her face flushed. "Call me Mia." She tore her eyes from Jonathan and glanced at the rest of us.

Jonathan gestured a hand toward me. "This is Presley Parker, the premiere party planner I told you about."

"Event planner," I corrected, reaching for her extended hand. "Nice to meet you."

"And this is Presley's charming mother, Veronica Parker, a very close friend of my father's."

Mother nodded and blushed. She wasn't much of a hand shaker.

When it became quickly evident that Jonathan didn't plan to introduce Brad—perhaps he'd just forgotten his name?—I said, "This is my . . . coworker Brad Matthews. He'll be helping me with the event." I hoped that wouldn't be as a crime scene cleaner.

Mia took his outstretched hand and held it—a little too long for my taste. There was an unmistakable sparkle in her eyes when she smiled at Brad, much like the one she'd given Jonathan. I made a mental note to stab her at the first opportunity.

What an interesting party this was turning out to be, full of intrigue and mystery, with a side of possible romance. And I hadn't even sent out the invitations yet.

"So I understand you want to host a party here, with a séance theme—is that right?" She spoke mostly to Jonathan.

Jonathan took the reins. "Yes. It's my father's idea. He thought it would be a great way for me to showcase my newest product for investors. I'd like to get a ballpark figure for renting out the place and . . ."

My attention lagged at the financial details, and I quickly became distracted by some of the photos and news articles Mia Thiele had framed and displayed around her small office. There were enlarged but blurry black-and-white snapshots of the house from every angle, along with snapshots of the once-plentiful acreage where Sarah Winchester grew orchards of apricot and plum trees. Her property was apparently self-sustaining, and she'd harvested, canned, and sold her own fruit, even though she certainly didn't need the money.

But my gaze caught on the large portrait of the woman herself, hanging behind Mia's chair. Petite, dressed in a long full skirt, hat, veil, and gloves, she sat in a carriage, almost oblivious to the camera. With her small closely set eyes and pale white skin, she looked as frail as a child. Mia caught me staring at the portrait.

"That's the only known photo ever taken of Sarah Winchester after she moved out West. She had a fear of having her picture taken and wore a veil to keep prying eyes away."

I nodded at another one of Sarah Winchester's eccentricities.

"So, what's it cost to clean this place?" Brad asked out of the blue.

Everyone stared at him, surprised at the question, but Mia took it in stride, and brightened her smile as she replied. "Plenty. We have a full-time cleaning staff that dusts, sweeps, cleans fingerprints, and so on. And we have the place repainted throughout the year. It takes roughly twenty thousand gallons of paint, working every day for a year, to finish the house. By then, it's time to start over."

"Whoa," Brad said, under his breath.

"What about the number thirteen?" my mother asked. She'd been standing quietly listening until now, but apparently felt the meeting had opened up to random questions. "I hear it's everywhere throughout the house."

Jonathan sighed and I sensed he was becoming irritated at going off topic.

"That's true," Mia said patiently. Obviously she'd heard all these questions before, but she seemed to enjoy sharing the quirky details of Sarah Winchester's house. "You'll find the number thirteen throughout the house, along with spiderweb motifs. These symbols were especially important to Mrs. Winchester—she thought they would protect her from the unhappy spirits. The chandelier holds thirteen candles, the hooks on the walls are in groups of thirteen, and the spiderweb-patterned stained-glass windows have thirteen stones. There's even a topiary tree in the garden shaped like the number thirteen."

Mother's eyes widened. She loved this kind of folklore.

"Shall we begin the tour?" Jonathan asked, obviously anxious to get started. No wonder he was CEO of his own company, with leadership skills like this.

"Right this way," Mia said mostly to Jonathan. She squeezed past us, and we followed her, one by one, out the door toward the inner sanctum of the so-called haunted house. Just after I exited the room, I heard a loud thump, followed by a whispered curse, coming from behind me. I whirled around to see Brad rubbing a red spot on his forehead.

"You all right?" I asked, grimacing in sympathy.

"Yeah, fine," Brad grumbled.

If bumps on the head portended bumps in the night, I had a feeling we'd just received our first "warning."

Chapter 5

PARTY PLANNING TIP #5

When gathering participants for your Séance Party, invite those who are willing to suspend disbelief and are open to possibilities of a world beyond. Or at least those who won't laugh out loud.

"Sarah Winchester never slept in the same bedroom two nights in a row, to confuse the evil spirits. This is the bedroom where Sarah Winchester passed away from heart failure, on September 4, 1922, at the age of eighty-three," Mia said, nodding reverently toward the heavy dark-wood bed on the intricate parquet floor. In fact, everything about the room was heavy—the lavender velvet drapes, the needlepoint-cushioned chairs, the woven Oriental rug. "She'd just had a session in the séance room with her psychic."

We'd spent the last thirty minutes winding our way through the hundred-and-sixty-room mansion, which had more twists and turns than Lombard Street in San Francisco, also known as the "crookedest street in the world." Mia had led us past hidden rooms, up low-rising staircases, and through secret passageways that Nancy Drew would have loved. Mother leaned over and whispered in my ear, "Some people call this the 'Dead Room.'"

"It's true," Mia said, who'd apparently overheard her.

"Have there been any . . . ghost sightings?" Mother asked. A longtime fan of the occult, she'd been obsessed with the reincarnation recordings of Bridey Murphy, the predictions of Edgar Cayce, the hypnotizing techniques of Anton Mesmer, and films like *The Haunting*.

"I mean," Mother continued, "if there are such things as ghosts, this would be the place to see one, right?" She glanced around, no doubt looking for floating white sheets, flickering candles, or fiery red eyes.

Mia smiled indulgently. "A few strange events have been reported. As you can imagine, lots of psychics tour the place and, of course, they're always convinced that spirits still wander aimlessly around the mansion. Some of our tour guides claim they've heard footsteps, banging doors, whispered voices, strange lights, doors that close by themselves or creak when they open—the usual. Some even say they've seen the ghost of Sarah Winchester."

"Awesome!" Jonathan nearly shouted with excitement. "That'll add to the atmosphere of the party we're planning."

"I hate to disillusion you," Mia continued, "but nothing's ever been documented. We mostly leave it up to the imaginations of our visitors."

"How did she die?" Brad asked, scanning the room. No doubt he was imagining the cleanup involved.

"Nothing too dramatic. She died quietly in her sleep, in spite of the continual construction." Mia paused dramatically, then said in a lighter tone, "If you'll follow me, I'll show you the séance room."

"How did she sleep through all that noise?" Mother whispered to me. I shrugged, then lingered a few moments after everyone left the bedroom to see if I could get a sense of the woman who had lived—and died—here. But all I felt was sadness for her obsessive-compulsive disorder and superstitious nature. I caught up with the others as they turned another corner.

"What was Sarah Winchester like?" I asked, curious about the enigmatic woman.

We shuffled up a narrow stairway, all the while keeping an eye out for lost spirits. "From early newspaper reports," Mia replied, "she appeared to be quite pretty, in spite of being only four feet ten inches tall. Men found her charming, quite the belle of the ball." I reflected on the only surviving picture of Sarah Winchester that hung in Mia's office, taken by a gardener who would have surely been fired on the spot if he'd been caught. That snapshot was of an elderly, wizened woman—nothing like the "belle of the ball" Mia had just described.

"She had money and social position," Mia continued, "and eventually married William Winchester, the son of the wealthy rifle manufacturer . . ."

Mia fell into her tour-guide mode, repeating a speech about the Winchester rifle that she'd obviously given hundreds of times in the past. My mind drifted as I imagined what Sarah's life must have been like back in the mid-1800s. Piano recitals. Ballroom dances. Elegant parties . . .

". . . four years later she gave birth to a daughter, Annie,"

I caught Mia saying, "but the baby became ill with a disease called marasmus and died nine days later."

"How sad," my mother said softly.

Mia nodded. "And worse, she lost her husband to tuberculosis in 1881. At that point she was a forty-two-year-old widow with a twenty-million-dollar inheritance and nearly fifty-percent ownership in the Winchester Repeating Arms Company. That gave her an income of about a thousand dollars a day."

"Holy crap," Brad said.

"Yes, a lot of money at that time—even today," Mia confirmed. "But it didn't do much to ease her pain."

I shivered. Must have been a draft in the room we'd just entered. Mother moved closer to me and tucked her arm in mine.

"This is . . . the séance room," Mia said, with a sweep of her arm.

The area was so small, I had a feeling you couldn't swing a dead cat, let alone a dead body, without hitting something. It felt crowded even though there were only five of us. I looked up to see sprinkler pipes webbing the ceiling. On one side of the room was an unfinished closet, with wood slats and remaining bits of plaster—and no floor. Not much in the room suggested "Ghosts meet here."

I pulled out my iPhone and snapped a couple of pictures to use as a guide for party decorations—although there was no way we could fit many guests in the tiny room.

"We're at the very center of the house, where Mrs. Winchester regularly met with a medium to commune with the spirits and contact her deceased husband. And receive guidance for constructing the house."

"She seriously believed in this stuff?" Brad said.

"Oh yes," Mia replied. "Spiritualism was very popular during that time. People held regular séances claiming they were another form of scientific inquiry. Even Mary Todd Lincoln held séances in the White House in hopes of contacting her own dead child."

Mother tightened her hold on my arm. "Losing a child . . ." she started to say. I saw tears rimming her eyes.

"She often came up here," Mia continued, pointing toward a wall behind us, "using that secret doorway. If you look down through the opening there, you can see how she spied on her servants working in the kitchen below." Mia indicated the spot and we took turns peering out of Sarah's lookout point. "She used secret passages much the same way, not only to escape the spirits, but to spy on her help. There are hidey-holes all over the place."

"She spied on her servants?" Mother asked, shaking her head at the idea.

Mia smiled, enjoying Mother's reaction. "Not only did she watch them, but she also listened in on their conversations throughout the house."

"She'd have made a great spy. How'd she do it?" Jonathan asked, obviously intrigued.

"She'd had listening tubes installed."

"Listening tubes? Never heard of them," Brad said.

That surprised me. I thought he'd heard of everything having to do with espionage.

Mia pointed out what looked like one of the plumbing pipes that was exposed on the ceiling. But this one was narrower, and part of it ran halfway down the corner of the room. "Initially they were added so Mrs. Winchester could call her servants from wherever she happened to be. But she also used them to listen in on her servants' conversations."

"Paranoid, eh?" Brad summarized.

Mia shrugged. "She was a frail old woman, alone in the house except for her servants—and her spirits. I'm sure she just wanted to protect herself. No doubt the servants found her eccentric, and perhaps not all of them were completely honest."

"The same could be said for many other types of employees," Jonathan said.

I shot a look at him. Was he speaking of his own employee George Wells?

Mia continued. "Now, follow me to the Daisy Room, the second-most-famous room in the house after the séance room."

We did as she instructed, trailing behind her up some stairs she called "Goofy Stairs" because of the way they wound back and forth on tiny steps. Mia explained the "easy risers" were built because of Sarah's severe arthritis. After several dozen steps, we found ourselves in a brightly lit, cheery room filled with colorful stained-glass windows with daisy motifs. I had a feeling the windows were magnificent when the sun shone through them, but since it was dark out, I could only imagine them lit up.

"What a lovely room," Mother said, admiring the detail in one of the windows.

"You might not think so if you'd been here the night of April 18, 1906."

"The earthquake?" Mother's eyes went wide.

"Yes, indeed," Mia said. "Sarah Winchester was sleeping in this very bedroom when the earthquake struck, a little after five in the morning. She found herself trapped here for several hours, unable to get out. The rest of the house suffered major damage. The top three floors had collapsed, and this room essentially shifted, blocking her exit. She was lucky to be alive, but she was terrified, as you can imagine, certain this was a sign from the spirits who supposedly suspected she was nearly finished building the house."

"Poor woman," Mother said. Most of us native Californians just roll with the occasional quakes. But Mother was terrified of them, having experienced several over the years. She glanced around the room. "How did she get out?"

"At first the servants had trouble finding her because, like I said, she tended to sleep in a different bedroom every night, in an attempt to escape the spirits," Mia said. "They finally heard her screams and were able to clear the rubble and debris. They got her out, but it took hours, and she never really recovered from the scare. She boarded up the front thirty rooms in an attempt to trap the spirits forever. Then she added more bedrooms, more chimneys, and continued new construction."

I shivered again. Granted the house was chilly with no heat and I had my black leather jacket on, but this room in particular creeped me out, in spite of the bright and colorful windows. I was also feeling a little claustrophobic. Time to wrap up the tour, I thought, and made a show of checking my watch.

"Well, I've seen enough," I said. "What do you think, Jonathan?"

Jonathan looked lost in thought. "What happened to her fortune after she died?"

It figured. He was all about the money.

"Sarah had spent a good deal of it by then, with the continuous construction. There were rumors that she'd hidden a fortune in a secret vault, but when it was opened, all they found were mementos from her life, including a lock of her baby's hair."

"How sad," Mother said, still focused on the death of the baby. We followed Mia out of the Daisy Room and down the stairs.

"But the property? Surely that must have been worth a fortune," Jonathan said.

"Most everything was sold off—furniture, personal belongings, even materials from the house itself. Then some investors bought it and turned it into one of the most popular tourist attractions in the state. It's been declared a California Historical Landmark and it's registered with the National Park Service."

"Boy, they must really rake it in," Jonathan said. I could practically see his eyes rolling dollar signs like Scrooge McDuck.

We found ourselves back in the gift shop at the end of Mia's tour. While Mother shopped for souvenirs and Brad snooped around, Jonathan and I chatted with Mia.

"So," Jonathan said, straightening his tie, "what's it going to cost me to put on a séance here? Name your price, Ms. Thiele."

She did.

I tried not to gasp.

Jonathan barely blinked. "Great! I'll write up a contract and have it sent here tomorrow." He turned to me. "One for you too, Presley. I'd like to set the date. How about four weeks from Saturday. Are you in?"

Sweat broke out on my forehead. How could I possibly host a Séance Party—something I'd never done before—in that tiny room, for a bunch of bigwigs—in just a month?

"I'll need to check my calendar—I have some other events coming up—if the date is clear, I suppose that would work." Then I named my ludicrous price, with the stipulation that an additional ten percent be donated to a worthy cause. Raising money to support research and cure diseases was the main reason I'd gotten into this business.

"Do you mind if I choose where the donation goes?"

I didn't have anything currently in mind. I'd already raised money for the Alzheimer's Association and for Autism. "I suppose . . ."

"How about the American Stroke Association?" Jonathan suggested. "In honor of my father."

"Of course," I agreed instantly.

Jonathan reached out to shake my hand.

I took his hand, wondering if this whole thing would come back to haunt me, and we sealed the deal.

He held on to my hand and looked intently into my eyes.

"'S'up?" Brad said, startling me from behind.

I jerked my hand from Jonathan's and felt my face grow hot.

"Nothing! I . . . uh, just agreed to do the séance event for Jonathan. He's going to pay my price and donate a percentage to the Stroke Association." I wiped my palm off on my jeans. Why was I suddenly feeling so flustered?

And guilty?

Jonathan frowned at Brad. "You know, you really look familiar . . . What's your name again?"

"Brad Matthews," he said, meeting Jonathan's gaze.

"And you work for Presley?" Jonathan asked.

Brad shrugged. "I help her out sometimes."

"I— We'd better get going," I stammered, looking at Brad for backup.

The two men continued staring at each other. Neither one said anything in the growing silence.

"Okay, so, I'll start planning the details and—"

Jonathan cut me off and waved a finger at Brad. "Wait a minute!"

I frowned at him, irritated at his rudeness in interrupting me.

"I know who you are."

Suddenly the color drained from Jonathan's face as he said, "You're that janitor. The one I caught snooping around my employee's office."

Chapter 6

PARTY PLANNING TIP #6

When hosting your Séance Party, create a "spirit circle" by gathering twelve people. Then be sure to leave a single chair for the visiting spirit—also known as the Thirteenth Guest. Or Ghost.

"I wasn't snooping in his damn office," Brad snapped. "And I'm not a janitor. I'm a crime scene cleaner."

"Then what were you doing going through his stuff?"

"I wasn't going through his stuff. I was cleaning up after your ex-employee who supposedly committed suicide in his office."

"Supposedly?" Jonathan said, his hands balling into fists.

Before the two puffed-up roosters' feathers went flying, I moved between them. I felt the heat coming from both their bodies.

"Brad!"

"What? He started it . . . " he began, then no doubt heard how silly he sounded and stopped.

I turned to Jonathan. "I'm sorry about this. Why don't we talk about the details tomorrow?" To Brad I said firmly, "Would you please escort my mother to the car? I want to ask Mia one last question." He frowned, still staring at Jonathan. "Please?" I added, softly.

He tore his gaze away and met my eyes, his face visibly softened. "Yeah, sure. I'll meet you there." Shooting a last look at Jonathan, he strode off to collect my mother, who was paying the cashier for a counter full of Winchester Mystery House souvenirs: an illustrated book detailing the house, some postcards, a miniature replica of the mansion that served as a salt shaker, and a T-shirt that read "The House that Fear Built!" that glowed in the dark. What was she going to do with all that stuff at her care center?

"What a jerk," Jonathan said under his breath as Brad shuffled my mother out of the gift shop.

I bristled at the comment, but said nothing. I wasn't going to get involved in their pissing contest. This gig would pay me a lot of money and benefit a great cause. I didn't want to lose the opportunity.

Jonathan reached out a hand and touched my arm. His touch gave me a chill, but not the good kind. "I'll call you tomorrow," he said, "to set up another meeting. Then we can discuss the details." He squeezed my arm.

I wanted to jerk it out of his hand, but resisted. Instead, I took a step back, slipping out of his grasp. "Sounds good," I said, and headed toward the exit. "I'll talk to you then," I called back.

During the return drive from San Jose to San Francisco, Brad said little. Mother did most of the talking, recounting the tour and sharing her excitement about the upcoming Séance Party. We dropped her off at her care facility, then headed to Treasure Island, leaving the city and its twinkling lights behind as we approached the Bay Bridge.

"So what was that all about?" I asked him, finally breaking the silence between us.

He turned toward me. "What?"

"What do you mean 'what'? That whole thing with Jonathan."

He shrugged and looked out his side window again at the dark water below.

"You're acting like a kindergartner."

"He's a jerk," he mumbled. "I don't trust him."

I was tempted to say that Jonathan probably felt the same way, but didn't want to make things any worse than they were. After all, the three of us would be working together—if Brad didn't change his mind and bow out.

Not that I really needed him.

Because I didn't.

Seriously.

Okay, now I was being the kindergartner?

"What do you know about Jonathan Ellington?" he said, still staring out the window.

"Not much. But then, I'm just hosting an event for him. What do I need to know?"

Brad said nothing, but I could feel his eyes on me as I approached the exit from the bridge.

"Do you seriously think he had something to do with his employee's suicide?" I asked.

"I don't know. All I know is, when I was there to clean up after the body had been removed, Jonathan came into the guy's office and started going through his desk and filing cabinets. When he found what he was looking for—a bunch of papers—he left in a big hurry."

"He claimed you were the one snooping through the guy's desk."

"I was checking it, making sure I didn't miss anything. Jonathan's paranoid."

"Are you sure you didn't say anything to him?"

"Look, the guy seemed . . . furtive. You know, like he was sneaking in and taking things that maybe he shouldn't have."

"He does own the company," I said. "What exactly did he say to you?"

"He asked me what I was doing there, although I thought it was fairly clear."

I drove down Macalla, into the parking lot of Building One, and turned off the engine. "Didn't you say George hung himself? So there wouldn't necessarily be any blood to clean up, right?"

"No blood."

"Then what exactly did you clean up?"

"You don't want to know."

I had an idea what he was talking about and dropped that line of questioning. "Okay, what else did you two talk about?"

"He said something like, 'What are you doing here?' I told him I was cleaning up the room. He made a face, like my words didn't compute; then he went to the guy's desk to look for whatever he was so anxious to find. He probably thought I was just some random custodian."

"You must have said or done something to upset him," I insisted.

"Nope. The guy was acting weird—not like a concerned boss who'd just lost a valued member of his company. He was acting more like a guy who was anxious to find something."

"You sure you aren't being overly suspicious? Maybe you've been hanging around Detective Melvin too much," I said. Neither of us moved to get out of the car. Finally I asked, "Anything else?"

"No." He paused. "Well, I might have given him a look or something."

"Or something?"

"Okay, I may have said something as he was leaving."

"Oh God. What exactly did you say?"

"You know, something like 'Sorry about your loss.'"

I raised a suspicious eyebrow. "That seems harmless enough. Are you sure that's all?"

"Yes. Then he stopped on his way out the door and asked me what I'd just said."

"And?"

"I repeated my condolences."

"That's it?"

"Mostly. I might have added something like, 'Find what you were looking for?'"

"Oh my God, Brad!"

"You should have seen his reaction. Grinding his jaw. Balling his fists. I thought he was going to slug me."

"But he didn't?"

"Nope. He got up in my face though, and said something

like, 'Just do your job, shut up, and quit snooping around.' Then he left. That was it."

Jonathan Ellington seemed to be a very controlling guy, I thought, as I opened the car door. He's used to being the boss. Or was it something else?

"My gut says he was up to something," Brad said after he got out and closed the passenger door. "I don't trust him and I don't think you should either."

"But you don't really know him, do you?"

"No. But my gut is usually right, Presley. I don't think you should be alone with the guy."

I looked at Brad in disbelief, certain he was overreacting. "You're kidding, right?" While I saw Jonathan as a player, I didn't think he was truly evil. After all, he cared about his father.

"I'm just saying . . ." Brad added, "that guy has got secrets."

Brad and I went our separate ways home. Neither of us was in the mood to get together—I resented Brad's implication that I couldn't take care of myself, and he'd made it clear he didn't want me working with Jonathan Ellington. I got back in my car and drove to my condo, while he took off in his SUV. It was a long night without him, but my cats kept me company and I finally fell asleep reading a book on the history of the Golden Gate Expo.

The next morning, Brad's SUV was missing from the parking lot. I entered the office I shared with Delicia and found a note on the "In/Out" board she'd hung on the wall. Next to her name she'd written, "At vintage stores looking for séance costume accessories." With Dee playing the part of the medium, I knew I was in good hands. I couldn't wait to see what she came up with. I erased "At Winchester House" next to my name, and left the space blank.

I sat down at my desk and swiveled in my chair for a few minutes trying to decide what to do first. After sifting through a stack of pending party forms, I let them flutter back onto the desk like giant confetti, and turned on my laptop. But instead of dealing with a couple dozen waiting e-mails, I Googled the name "George Wells" and "Hella-Graphics." The screen lit up with an obituary bearing his name.

WELLS, GEORGE

San Francisco—George Wells, 60, died unexpectedly on Sunday, April 2. Wells was credited with developing one of the first three-dimensional projectors for Jonathan Ellington, CEO of Hella-Graphics. "This is a tragic loss to Hella-Graphics, to the world, and to me personally," Ellington said in a press release.

Really? I thought, because it sure hadn't seemed like it. I read on.

Born in San Francisco, Wells earned an electrical engineering degree from Stanford University, which he parlayed into developing state-of-the-art software. He felt he was on the verge of another exciting product.

Wells is survived by wife, Teddi, and three daughters, Susan MacLeod, Sandra Spellman, and Kathleen Mahn. "George was a kind man who loved to tinker in his garage workshop when he wasn't working at Hella-Graphics," his wife of thirty-eight years said. A private memorial is planned at the Wells home next Sunday. Donations may be made to the George Wells Engineering Scholarship Fund, c/o Stanford University.

I sat back, digesting the information about a man I had seen just a couple of months ago. But the obit left a lot of unanswered questions. And there was no mention that he'd hanged himself in his office.

I reached for my phone to try Teddi again, but it trilled, announcing a text message. I didn't text much, except to respond to Dee's texts. My mother preferred to communicate by old-fashioned telephone, my clients by e-mail, and Brad in person. I picked up the phone and read the texts from Jonathan Ellington.

Great meeting last night, Presley! Glad you're on board. Details coming via e-mail attachment from my VP, Stephanie Bryson. LMK if you have questions. Let's meet again this afternoon at the mansion.

Several more texts followed.

I think party should start around 8. Want it to be dark enough outside . . .
Expect to have 20–25 guests . . .
Invitations! Need to get those out ASAP . . .
Working on a script for Sarah's ghost . . .

I had a feeling I was going to regret giving Jonathan my contact information.

I checked my e-mail and found three more messages from Jonathan waiting, plus a detailed list of suggestions forwarded by his VP. It looked like he was going to be one of those micromanaging clients that drove me nuts.

I responded to half of his messages, then watched a dozen more pop up. If I hadn't agreed to plan this party for him, I'd have sought a restraining order and filed harassment charges. I just hoped all the hassle was worth the money.

Forgetting all about calling Teddi, I spent the morning researching séances on the Internet, hoping to give the event some authenticity. After reading about spirit circles, incantations, psychic energy, and the like, I worked on possible designs for invitations using invisible ink to write the party details on mini Ouija boards. The more I read, the more excited I got about the event. I couldn't wait to get started on the decorations and create a spooky atmosphere for the séance, using mood lighting, flickering candles, antique brass candlesticks, smoky crystal balls, and a reproduction of Sarah Winchester's only portrait.

This was going to be fun . . . if nothing went wrong.

Meanwhile, I also had to deal with communiqués from Marianne Mitchell, my new landlord, who was already pressing for details on the anniversary of the Expo celebration she'd envisioned for Treasure Island—and gently reminding me of her generosity in terms of my rent. The event would be at least six months away, but already Marianne wanted her stamp of approval on everything from invites to favors. Now I was contending with two micromanagers.

Feeling a little overwhelmed, I went in search of my part-time crew and delegated some of the initial tasks for the Séance Party—appetizers from Rocco Ghirenghelli, video-taping by Berkeley Wong, extra security by Raj Reddy. I stopped by Brad's office again, but he still hadn't come in. I missed him, but there was no way I was taking him along to my meeting that afternoon with Jonathan. No sense disturbing the spirits with Brad's animosity.

After a lunch of blueberry yogurt and a latte, I wrote on the message board, "Gone to Mystery House. Be back soon." Dee still hadn't returned from costume shopping, nor had Brad from wherever he'd been. I left Dee a note to check out some palm reading business that seemed to be on every street corner in the city, then grabbed my purse and headed out to meet Jonathan Ellington.

In spite of Brad's warning, this time I was going alone.

Chapter 7

"Presley!" I heard my name called as I entered the Winchester Mystery House gift shop.

Jonathan waved to me from the small adjoining café, where amateur ghost hunters could take a break from the hour-long tour and grab a hot dog and a soda in a Winchester Mystery House "keepsake" cup. He wasn't alone. He sat at a round table, between two women. On the right was an attractive, twentysomething blonde with pink pouty lips and big breasts, which nearly spilled out of her low-cut tight tank top.

On the other side was a severe-looking thirtysomething woman, dark hair in a tight twist, glasses, and heavy pancake makeup, wearing a gray business suit with the classic

Burberry scarf. A large crystal dangled from her neck. A balding, double-chinned, and overweight man sat across from him, wearing a loose-fitting and faded "We're Hella-Good" T-shirt, and baggy jeans. If he wasn't the cliché of a computer geek, I'd eat a Winchester hot dog.

Jonathan rose to greet me with an uncharacteristically brief handshake rather than his lingering grip. I sat down in the space available between the geek and the suit. I glanced down as I pulled my chair in and caught a glimpse of his ratty sneakers with missing laces and no socks.

Jonathan nodded at him.

"Presley, this is Levi Webster, our newly promoted product developer. You'll be working with Levi on the presentation of the 4-D Projector." Levi, bent over his hot dog, grunted a short, unintelligible greeting and returned to his food.

Jonathan gestured to the multihighlighted blond woman next to him. She looked more like a Victoria's Secret model in the tight black Bebe tank and rhinestone-studded white capris than one of Jonathan's employees.

"This is my wife, Lyla. She's a former model with a real eye for design. I've asked her to help out with decorations for the party."

Oh goody. Just what I needed. Assistance from arm candy.

Lyla lifted her blue eyes from the rhinestone-studded—or were they real diamonds?—cell phone she held and wiggled her French-manicured fingers at me. "Nice to meet you, Priscilla."

"It's Presley," I said.

"What an . . . interesting name," she said, her pouty

mouth forming an O. "Anyway, I have some fabulous ideas for the party room. I was thinking we'd hang up posters of Casper the Friendly Ghost and his girlfriend Wendy on the walls, and put a big crystal ball in the middle of the table, filled with smoke. And then we'd have spooky music playing in the background, like that theme from *Halloween* or whatnot." She said all this to me without taking her eyes off the text message she'd just received.

Great, I thought. Can't wait.

Finally he turned to the suited woman on his other side. "And this is my right-hand man, my VP who handles just about everything at Hella-Graphics, Stephanie Bryson. She'll be working with you on many of the details of the party."

Stephanie gave a tight smile and reached out her hand to shake mine. The woman would have been pretty if she'd have lightened up on the heavy makeup that covered her skin. I instantly felt for her, working with a man like Jonathan. Had she been the one he'd spoken to so brusquely on the phone at the diner? I wouldn't have let anyone talk to me like that.

"Would you like something to eat?" Jonathan asked.

"I'll just get some coffee," I said, and headed over to the counter to order a prefab latte. Jonathan followed me, whipping out his wallet.

"I'll get this," he said grandly to the cashier, then turned to me and placed his hand on my arm. "I'm so glad we'll be working together." He stole a quick glance at the table where his wife was busy tapping on her cell phone, then squeezed my arm. "Did I tell you you have such beautiful green eyes? Like your mother. I can understand what Dad sees in her."

Caught off guard by the compliment, his strong minty breath, and his sleazy come-on in front of his wife, I flushed and turned toward the clerk, using the movement to pull away from his tightening grip. I took the souvenir Winchester Mystery House mug of coffee and returned to the table while Jonathan gave the young counter clerk ten dollars. "Keep the change," he said.

When he sat down at the table, I could swear he winked at me.

What a player.

I sipped the lava-hot liquid while Jonathan started the informal meeting.

"Levi, why don't you explain the 4-D holograph to Presley?" he said.

Levi smiled, revealing something green stuck in one corner of his mouth. Relish? Stephanie typed something on her notebook computer, and Lyla continued to tap out messages on her phone's tiny keyboard.

Levi cleared his throat.

"Ahem. Okay, well," he said, shooting a glimpse at Jonathan. Jonathan tapped the corner of his own mouth to alert Levi. Levi grabbed a napkin lying on the table and wiped the green stuff away. "Uh, let's see if I can make this simple enough for you, Miss . . ."

"Call me Presley."

"Yeah. Well, Hella-Graphics is on the cutting edge of 4-D technology with the new holographic-slash-projection display unit. Unlike 3-D projection of the past, this unit can be constantly reprogrammed for 'situational awareness' in seconds."

I tried to look fascinated and not daydream while he continued his jargon-filled explanation. Apparently my glazed eyes didn't fool him. "Okay," he finally said, "so what that means is, you can use the unit in any situation without those funny glasses you wear in the movie theater. All you need besides the unit is a cell phone."

I recognized that word. "A cell phone?" I repeated.

"Yeah. I'll explain that in a minute. But let me finish. You know the little hologram on your Visa card?"

I nodded like a schoolchild, feigning interest in a dull classroom lecture.

"Well, this is nothing like that. Our 4-D is dynamic, 'alive,' if you will. Imagine walking into a store and seeing a large-as-life, three-dimensional product display, like a car, or even a person." His eyes danced with excitement as he spoke. "How it works is, there's a piece of special plastic film in between two pieces of glass, which are coated with a transparent electrode. The photo-refractive polymer uses laser beams and an externally applied electric field . . ."

A group of tourists wandered into the café, and I wondered where they were from, what they thought of the mansion, where the woman had gotten her knockoff handbag . . .

"That's fine," Jonathan said, interrupting Levi's speech and my distracted musings. "Presley really doesn't need to know all the details of how it works. We don't want to give away any secrets and have her end up making one of her own, do we?" He laughed at his little joke. Stephanie frowned. Lyla ignored him. "Just explain how it applies to our upcoming event."

Levi licked his lips. "Uh, okay. Basically this is a holographic movie that can be viewed from any angle and created in any size. It looks like a physical object—it actually makes you want to reach out and touch it—but of course, there's nothing actually there. It's just a very realistic image. And you can have it respond to an individual by using that person's cell phone signal."

Jonathan took over. "This thing is going to be big, Presley. Imagine. You can use it to view a medical technique, a house addition, a military weapon—just about anything."

"Sounds cool," I said, wondering how this applied to the party I was supposed to plan. Did he plan to remove an appendix or fire an AK-47 at the event?

"The point is, Hella-Graphics R and D—research and development—has come up with a low-cost realistic way of imaging that will change the world as we 'see' it." He put finger quotes around the word "see." Apparently he loved to use finger quotes.

"So your plan is to re-create a three-dimensional image of Sarah Winchester, then invite her to the séance during the party," I said, trying to clarify my role in all of this.

"Not just *invite* her," Jonathan said. "Have her actually *communicate* with specific guests at the table and explain the product to them personally, by using GPS technology, along with individual cell phones." In his excitement, he slapped the table, startling his wife, who shot him a look when she nearly dropped her own cell phone.

"Really cool," I said, summarizing my reaction.

"Stephanie and I will be working on the script," Jonathan continued, "and Levi here will program the display so the words appear to be spoken by Sarah Winchester. It's going to knock the boxers off those big boys in the movie biz."

"Don't forget me," Lyla spoke up, offering a full-lipped but fake pout.

Jonathan patted her arm. "Yes, honey, you're in charge of decorating. I'm sure Presley will welcome your wonderful ideas, won't you Presley?"

I kept my mouth shut so I wouldn't say anything I'd regret and just nodded noncommittally.

"Now, here's what we're going to do."

Jonathan explained the details of his plan while both Stephanie and I took notes. I shook my head internally at the overwhelming number of specific instructions he spewed, while Stephanie just seemed to take it in stride. Levi offered nothing more as he finished the remnants of his hot dog, but Lyla kept interrupting with off-the-wall decorating suggestions—glow-in-the-dark eyes around the room, trick candles that wouldn't extinguish, sounds of howling animals in the background. Between the pawing CEO, the meddling trophy wife, the robotic VP, and the socially inept programmer, I was in party planning hell.

"All right," Jonathan announced, placing his hands on the table and standing up. "I think we're done here. Honey, why don't you look around the gift shop for things to use at the séance? Levi, you can stay here with your laptop and work on that glitch you mentioned. Stephanie, get started on the guest list—names, addresses—you know." Jonathan turned to me. "Presley, why don't we go view the séance room again, and talk more about the logistics of the party?"

After offering an air kiss near her husband's lips, Lyla headed for the gift shop. Levi settled into his laptop, and Stephanie began working on her notebook computer. Although I didn't relish being alone with Jonathan in the creepy house, I followed him out as he headed for the séance room. Even with the map Mia had given us, the room wasn't easy to find and we hit several dead ends before locating the right place. I just hoped we didn't have a big earthquake or we might never get out again.

We stepped reverently inside the séance room, and after a moment of silence trying to envision two dozen or more people in the tiny room, I suggested we consider using the ballroom instead. Jonathan was reluctant to transfer the party out of the séance room, but once we entered the elaborate ballroom, we both knew it would be a much more appropriate setting for the party and would easily fit the guest list. The room was spacious, with parquet floors, intricately carved wood walls, shelves, alcoves, and ceiling, crystal chandeliers, and a well-used brick fireplace.

It was my favorite room in the Winchester mansion. While the séance room had a spooky, spiritual history, the ballroom was rich, ornate, and offered a cryptic message that Sarah Winchester had installed, which had fascinated me as a kid. After touring the place with Mia, I'd done more research and learned the ballroom had secrets that Mia had not shared with us.

"See those two stained-glass windows?" I pointed them out to Jonathan.

"Yeah." He studied them a moment. "What is it—a poem of some sort?"

"They're quotes from Shakespeare's works."

He read the words aloud: " *'Wide unclasp the tables of their thoughts.'* What's it supposed to mean?"

"I found a site on the Internet that suggests they're clues into Mrs. Winchester's bizarre life."

"How so?"

I pulled out my notebook where I'd placed a printout of the lines in their context. "It's from *Troilus and Cressida*. That section goes:

> *There's language in her eye, her cheek, her lip,*
> *Nay, her foot speaks; her wanton spirits look out*
> *At every joint and motive of her body.*
> *O! these encounterers, so glib of tongue,*
> *That give a coasting welcome ere it comes,*
> *And wide unclasp the tables of their thoughts*
> *To every tickling reader, set them down*
> *For sluttish spoils of opportunity*
> *And daughters of the game.*

"Still don't get it," Jonathan said, shrugging.

"The guy on the site thinks they reflect what Sarah Winchester believed—that she was misunderstood. He says the Shakespeare play begins with a romantic view of love and war, then ends with violence and death. He thinks maybe it expresses her feelings of grief and loss, and growing bitterness."

Jonathan shook his head. "Or maybe she just liked Shakespeare."

I ignored him and turned to the other window. "This one is from *Richard II*." I read it aloud.

> *These same thoughts people this little world,*

Jonathan frowned. "So what's she talking about in that one?"

"Again, you need the context." I read the computer printed words from the second play.

> *I have been studying how I may compare*
> *This prison where I live unto the world:*
> *And for because the world is populous*
> *And here is not a creature but myself, I cannot*
>   *do it; yet I'll hammer it out.*
> *My brain I'll prove the female to my soul,*
> *My soul the father; and these two beget*
> *A generation of still-breeding thoughts,*
> *And these same thoughts people this little*
>   *world*

"I get it. She feels like a prisoner in her own house," Jonathan summarized.

"Maybe. According to the site, King Richard II was imprisoned and created his own world, populated by his thoughts. But if you put the two quotes together, you supposedly get an image of an isolated, grief-stricken woman who blames herself for the deaths of her loved ones. And yet she's determined to create a new life—in her mind."

"You sound like my English teacher. I fell asleep during that class."

I folded my notes and put them away, with a twinge of disappointment. It appeared that Jonathan wasn't interested in exploring Sarah Winchester's past and motives. He only wanted to use her for his own means.

"You know, you're as smart as you are pretty," he added, moving closer to me. He took my hand and leaned in as if to kiss me, but I slipped out of his grasp, whirled around and escaped through the ballroom door.

Maybe Brad was right about Jonathan Ellington after all.

Back at the gift shop, we found Jonathan's wife, Lyla, standing at the cash register, handing over a gold credit card. Two staff members were wrapping logoed mugs, plates, salt and pepper shakers, miniature mansions, and other tacky knickknacks. It looked as if she'd bought out the place.

Levi spotted us from the café table and began packing up his laptop. Stephanie followed suit, and as soon as Lyla had her packages, we all walked to the parking lot.

"I think we're on the same page now," Jonathan said, after opening the car door for his wife. Stephanie and Levi got into the backseat of the beige Mercedes. "Let's touch base tomorrow and hash out a few more details, now that we've moved the party to the ballroom."

I hate jargon. I wanted to say "Roger that" or "10-4," but bit my tongue. I seemed to be doing a lot of tongue biting for this party.

"I'll call Mia and let her know we want the ballroom," Jonathan added.

As I stepped away from Jonathan's car to head for my own car, I heard the screech of tires coming from behind me. I turned in time to see a late-model BMW driving right at me. Before I could even think about fleeing, the car swerved to the side at the last second, hitting the Mercedes's rear bumper and knocking the car several feet forward.

My heart was beating like a frightened rabbit as I stood frozen to the spot. Letting out my breath, I realized I would have been killed if the BMW hadn't veered at the last minute. Jonathan came flying out of his car, his face red, his hands in fists.

"You asshole!" he shouted at the driver of the other car, which had come to a stop several feet away. Not bothering to check on the condition of his wife or employees, Jonathan stormed over toward the BMW, waving his fist, spittle flying from his mouth as he screamed obscenities.

Before Jonathan could reach the car, the driver of the BMW reversed, jammed on the gas pedal, and sped away on screeching tires, leaving burned-rubber skid marks on the parking lot pavement.

"Oh my God," I said when I got my voice back. "That guy almost killed me!"

Jonathan shook his head as he watched the car disappear down the street. "You were never in any real danger, Presley, believe me."

My jaw dropped at his arrogance. Did he think by yelling a few profanities at the guy, he'd saved my life?

"But he was headed right toward me!" I insisted. "Didn't you see him?"

"No, he wasn't," Jonathan said, cocking his jaw. "It was me he was trying to kill."

Chapter 8

My heart was still racing from my near-death experience when the mansion security guard arrived moments later. Apparently he'd heard the crash and the ensuing commotion and come running.

"What happened?" he said, puffing a little after his sprint to the parking lot. Fortysomething, he wore dark clothes instead of a classic uniform. His name tag read MARK PHILIP. Behind him I caught a glimpse of Mia striding toward us, looking bewildered.

"Nothing. It was just an accident," Jonathan explained.

I stared at him. "But you said—"

He shot me a look. "The driver probably lost control of

his car," he continued, interrupting me. He gestured toward the back end of his car, where Lyla now stood talking on her cell phone. Levi was hunched down, examining the fender. Stephanie had remained in the car. "He clipped my bumper, then drove off. Luckily everyone's okay."

"Maybe *you* are . . ." I started to say. Jonathan shot me another fierce look. What was wrong with him?

"Looks like a hit-and-run," the guard said, stating the obvious as he glanced around.

"Mark, notify the police," Mia ordered.

"No!" Jonathan said loud enough to wake the dead. He softened his tone. "No, really . . . it's fine. Besides, I don't have time to wait around for the cops to take a useless report. My insurance company will cover it. And like I said, we're okay." He turned to his wife. "Right, sweetheart?"

She nodded absently, still talking to someone on her phone. Levi, on the other hand, looked pale, as if he'd seen Sarah Winchester's ghost. The permanent crease in his brow was now cavernous and dotted with sweat.

Jonathan didn't bother to ask me how I was. He checked his watch and turned to Mia. "I've really got to run. Presley and my VP will fill you in on our new plans."

"Are you sure you don't want to file a report?" the guard asked.

Jonathan shook his head and motioned for his passengers to get back in the car. He climbed into the driver's seat and with a wave drove off, leaving me in the parking lot, puzzled and a little angry.

I checked my watch: a little after three p.m. Instead of returning home, I pulled up directions to Hella-Graphics on my iPhone GPS app and drove back to the city determined to talk to Jonathan about the parking lot incident. Why had he lied to the guard about the hit-and-run? He'd told me he thought the driver of the other car had aimed for him. If that was true, wouldn't he have wanted to involve the police? And why had Levi looked so spooked—as if he'd seen an apparition—while Lyla seemed entirely unaffected?

I barely noticed the fog softly rolling in until I reached the Presidio address of Hella-Graphics. I passed a statue of Yoda, surrounded in the mist and looking as if he'd just stepped out of his swampy home. Behind him was one of George Lucas's buildings where movie magic was made. He'd moved his company to the former army base and established his state-of-the-art filmmaking company, Industrial Light and Magic, there. Aside from a *Star Wars* museum that was open to the public, most of the ILM campus was off-limits to curious tourists, Luke Skywalker fans, and nosy party planners.

Jonathan's company, Hella-Graphics, was located in a similar white clapboard building that looked as if it might have been officers' quarters at some point. Like the other buildings nearby, it sported only an address; nothing that would indicate what was inside.

I parked the MINI in a free space next to a rack packed with bicycles and trespassed my way up to the front entrance, passing mostly BMWs and Priuses. I noticed Jonathan's Mercedes parked in a reserved space close to the building, still sporting the damage from the "accident" at the Winchester Mystery House.

Stepping up to the double glass doors, I tried the door handle. Locked.

I spotted a buzzer on the side of the entryway and pressed it. A voice came over the intercom: "Yes?"

No greeting. No mention of the company. No doubt their way of discouraging drop-bys and looky-loos.

"Uh, this is Presley Parker, from Killer Parties. I'm here to see Jonathan Ellington."

Silence, except for some faint hissing. Then, "Do you have an appointment?"

"Uh, not exactly, but I'm working with him on an upcoming event and have a few questions."

"I'm sorry. You'll have to make an appointment."

"Look, I was just talking with him a short time ago and . . ." I paused. The faint hissing of the intercom had ceased. The woman who'd been speaking to me was no longer listening.

Great.

Now what?

I stood on the doorstep, pulled out my iPhone, and punched in Jonathan's number.

Great.

Voice mail.

Time for a little industrial magic of my own, I thought, and quickly Googled the main number of Hella-Graphics. An automated voice answered, requiring me to punch in the first three letters of the last name of the person I wished to speak to.

Damn. What was Levi's last name? Strauss? Nope. Jeans maker. Stubbs? No. Former Idol contestant. Levi . . .

I'd forgotten. Or maybe Jonathan had never mentioned it. Great.

I was about to give up when a woman in a tailored gray

suit, Burberry scarf, and a crystal dangling from her neck came walking up to the door from the direction of another building on the campus. It was Stephanie, Jonathan's VP.

Without looking at me, she swiped the pass card that hung around her neck over a small metal square next to the intercom.

"Stephanie?" I asked.

"Presley!" Stephanie seemed to light up at seeing me. "What are you doing here?"

Before I could answer, she went on. "Jonathan just thinks you're the greatest party planner on the planet! He wouldn't stop talking about you all the way back to the office."

"Oh, well, I'm flattered. I'm glad he's happy with the plans so far. Not that we have many yet. That's why I'm here. I still have more questions. Would it be possible to see him? I can't seem to get my foot in the door without an appointment and I can't reach him by phone."

"No problem," Stephanie said. "I'll escort you in." She slid her card over the metal square again and the door clicked open. "Security is tight around here, as you can imagine. We get mostly tourists who are curious about the Presidio campus, but you can never be too careful. Believe it or not, there are industrial spies everywhere, and they'd kill to get hold of one of our prototypes. Especially the one Zach—I mean Levi—has been working on."

She held the door for me and I entered a wonderland of fantastical 3-D images. On one side of the lobby stood a large clear container on a pedestal that held what looked like mice. These mice, however, were multicolored and the size of cats, and they were standing upright, dancing. On the other side an identical container housed what could only be described as miniature people, no bigger than the cat-sized mice across the room. Tinted red, blue, green, and yellow, they nevertheless looked human, all talking or interacting with one another.

"These are amazing!" I said, feeling like one of those touristy looky-loos she mentioned. "I had no idea 3-D effects could be so realistic."

"You ain't seen nothin' yet," Stephanie said. "Want a quick tour? We might find Jonathan along the way. He doesn't spend much time in his office."

"Sure." I had heard how great these young companies were to work for and was looking forward to seeing the place.

I followed Stephanie through the lobby to the receptionist at the front desk, no doubt waiting for the next doorbell ringer to try to break into the Hella-Graphics fortress. Twentysomething, wearing a Roxy T-shirt, she had short black hair, stylishly cut, with supershort, precision-straight bangs.

"You're gonna have to sign in first with Maile," Stephanie said, indicating a sheet filled with names and times. I signed my name and added my arrival time, then stuck on the sticky badge that read VISITOR the receptionist had handed me.

"Follow me," Stephanie said, and I did, through the warren of building wings. She ticked off each room, describing them as if she were a tour guide in a mystery mansion.

"First of all, we're green."

At first I took her literally, then realized she meant eco-friendly. "Solar-powered, recycled materials, stuff like that. We try to keep the carbon footprint to a minimum."

I thought about the Winchester House and how energy

deficient it must have been. I wondered how many trees it had cost to keep that monstrosity fed.

"We have about five hundred people working for the company—some here in the building, some from home. HR gets something like a hundred résumés a day, if you can believe that, from electricians and gardeners to Ph.D.s in computer science and engineering. Everyone wants to work here—if they can't get a job at ILM, Pixar, or Stereo-Scope Graphics."

We headed down another corridor, this one painted to look like an undersea world. I kept wanting to hold my breath.

We turned another corner and into a spacious workout area, filled with exercise equipment. "This is our state-of-the-art gym," Stephanie said, "where our employees can work off stress, stay in shape, swim, shower, or enjoy the spa."

At the moment the place was empty. Was everyone too busy to use the gym?

Before I could comment, Stephanie went on with her tour speech. "Hella-Graphics also offers haircuts, laundry services, child care, a masseuse, a pool table, video games, and a physician for checkups. All free."

Okay, I could be happy here.

I followed her as she led me down another corridor. "We also have a dog park. Many of our employees bring their dogs to work."

What, no cat park? I'm outta here.

"What's that?" I asked, spotting what looked like a broad tube spiraling down from the floor above.

"It's exactly what it looks like—a slide. Jonathan wants his employees to have fun at work—and it's more fun to go from floor to floor using a slide! We also have firemen's poles and rock-climbing walls that lead to an upper floor. Hella-Graphics is not without whimsy."

OMG.

"And this," she said, stopping at a doorway that led to a large room full of tables, "is the café. We have our own chef, Rodney Worth, who used to be at the Peasant and the Pear. The café offers a salad bar, sandwich bar, dessert bar, a mix-and-match pasta bar, plus fresh gourmet meals, a DIY taco station, and a French mini-café that serves fresh Starbucks and Peet's coffees, everything from plain black to fancy Frappuccinos. Would you like a latte or something?"

I nodded, trancelike, and watched as she ordered my drink, along with a Caramel Frappuccino for herself.

"We're about done with the tour. I can't take you to R and D—research and development. That's under tight security, but each R and D employee has two or three computers and screens, a massage chair, and a cot in case they need a power nap or work late and just want to stay over."

I wondered if they could use a full-time party planner and was about to ask for an application when Stephanie said, "And, here we are."

I was standing in front of a corner office on the ground floor, with a door plaque that read: JONATHAN ELLINGTON, CEO, in gold letters. She tapped on the door, then tried the knob. Locked. She pulled out a key and opened the door.

"Jonathan?" she called, stepping in.

No sign of him.

Stephanie walked over to his desk, sat down in his chair,

and opened his computer screen. "It looks like he's in a meeting right now," she said, then tapped a couple more keys and stood up. I peeked in and saw a highly polished cherry-wood desk, black leather executive chair, and matching leather couch, creating a masculine, powerful feeling. On his desk was a three-foot statue I instantly recognized as the *Creature from the Black Lagoon*—one of my all-time favorite horror movies. On the wall were posters of other 3-D films—*Thirteen Ghosts*, *House of Wax*, *Jaws 3-D*—movies I watched with those red-and-blue-lens glasses. She returned to the door, closed it, and made sure it was locked. The scent of mint and cologne swept out on a waft of air.

He'd been here recently.

"Hey, maybe I can answer some of your questions. We've talked a lot about the party. Come over to my office and we can chat until Jonathan's free."

Stephanie's office, adjacent to Jonathan's, was half the size of her boss's, and not so richly appointed, but still impressive. Her desk was covered with papers—all neatly stacked. Instead of a couch for guests, there were two chairs, one behind her desk, and one for a visitor. I sat down in the comfy padded chair and looked around while she sat and checked her messages. There were no family pictures in view, no collections of ceramic cats or Smurfs, only a large framed canvas that looked like a chart of the skies, along with signs of the zodiac.

"This is nice," I said, lacking anything more complimentary to say about her office.

"I like simplicity. I came up through the ranks, you know, so I still relate to the other employees as well as the boss. Beside, Jonathan likes us to keep our offices neat. At least, the ones that visitors see. R and D is a rat's nest. I don't see how they can work under such messy conditions."

I could relate more to R&D than the administrative offices. I suppose my Killer Parties office could be called a rat's nest, but to me it was organized chaos, and I knew where everything was.

"Beautiful artwork," I said, indicating the heavenly circle on the wall.

"That's my birth chart," she said. Her hand went to the crystal that dangled from her neck. "I had it done a few years ago. It looked like a work of art to me so I had it framed and hung on the wall."

She saw me eying her necklace. "It's a healing crystal. I wear it to enhance creativity and for protection."

"It's stunning," I said.

Stephanie sat down and folded her hands on her desk. Her red nails were perfect and the only bright color in her gray ensemble. She wore no rings on her left hand, but sported an elegant pearl necklace around her neck and matching pearl earrings. She seemed relaxed and confident, while I felt stiff and a little out of place.

"So," she began, "have you recovered from that little incident with Zach?"

"Excuse me?" I said, shaking my head.

"Zachary Samuels. Jonathan said it was Zach who tried to run him down in the parking lot."

Zach Samuels? Jonathan hadn't mentioned a name to me. If he knew who had hit his car, why hadn't he told the security guard—or contacted the police?

"Is he a former employee?" I asked. I wanted to know

more about this guy who'd nearly killed me—even if he hadn't meant to.

"Yes. He's been harassing Jonathan ever since he was let go. Keeps showing up unannounced at places where Jonathan happens to be—restaurants, clubs, even his home."

"Why was he fired?"

"He started demanding more money for the work he was doing here. Everyone gets a salary, plus a bonus at the completion of a project, not to mention all the perks that go along with working here. But Zach wanted more." She sighed and shook her head at the memory.

"Can't Jonathan stop Zachary from harassing him?"

"He's tried, but Zach's brain doesn't seem to reboot all the time. He's one of those weird scientist-types you hear about. A genius, but not too savvy when it comes to the real world."

"What was he working on?"

She hesitated. "Uh, let's just say he was claiming to have invented one of our new products, which is ridiculous, of course. It was a team effort, along with Levi Webster and a few other R and D guys. But Zach keeps making accusations of intellectual property theft."

"Was it the 4-D Projector?" I asked, taking a wild stab.

She looked down at her hands. "I . . . really can't say. But I can tell you this: Zachary Samuels enjoyed stirring up trouble for Jonathan and he should have been fired a long time ago. I just hope he leaves Jonathan alone. God forbid if anything should happen to him, knock on wood." She actually knocked three times on her wooden desk. "Anyway, let's not talk about him. Let's talk about the party!"

Stephanie peppered me with questions for the next twenty or so minutes, things like what kind of food we should serve, who would be playing the medium, and what kind of favors did I have in mind. Finally, with still no sign of Jonathan, I told her I needed to get back to my office and get to work on the party plans.

Stephanie escorted me to the front entrance, then shook my hand. "It's gonna be great working with you, Presley. This Séance Party will be so much fun!"

I stepped outside, then had a sudden thought and turned back quickly, catching the door before it closed. "Stephanie?"

"Yes?" she said.

"The man who . . . died . . . here recently—George Wells? Was he working on the 4-D Projector as well?"

Stephanie glanced around as if looking for those spies she'd mentioned earlier. She slipped out the front door, letting it close behind her. I followed her glance at a corner of the building and spotted a tiny video camera.

"I'll walk you to your car," she said. When we were a few feet away, she took a deep breath, then said, "I suppose word is getting around about Wells. That was just an unfortunate . . . tragedy. I heard he was suffering from depression, money problems, relationships gone awry . . . you know. I guess he just couldn't take it anymore. Jonathan tries so hard to make sure everyone at Hella-Graphics is happy working here, but some people are unhappy for reasons other than the job."

She seemed to know a lot more about George's state of mind than his own wife. But then, that was often typical.

"I'm sorry about your loss," I said lamely, unable to come

up with something more appropriate. I stopped at my car and thanked her again for the tour and the chat.

On my drive through the fog back to Treasure Island, all I could think about were a seemingly deranged ex-employee named Zachary Samuels, a despondent suicide victim named George Wells, and the strange CEO of a successful company named Jonathan Ellington—who seemed to be trying hard not to be tainted by a recent death and an attempted murder.

Not the most auspicious beginning for a party.

Chapter 9

PARTY PLANNING TIP #9

The ideal time for your séance is midnight, which is fine if your guests are night owls. If not, they may be too tired to channel their energy and could doze off before the spirits arrive.

Séance Party time was upon me before I knew it. The last month had gone by like a let-go balloon. In between prepping for Jonathan's gig, I'd hosted a Twins party for the world-famous San Francisco Twins, Marian and Vivian Brown. Guests, including former mayor Willie Brown, current mayor Davin Green, and a number of A-list guests were required to bring a date and dress as twins. When Marian and Vivian appeared in their identical snappy outfits, colorful hats, and perfectly coiffed hair, they brought the house down, as in the Mark Hopkins Hotel.

As for the séance, there was simply too much to do and not enough time to prepare. Luckily, I wouldn't have to deal with Marianne's Golden Gate Expo party until after the

Winchester Mystery House party. I just hoped she didn't evict me in the interim. I caught her flirting with Brad several times and had a feeling if she found out Brad and I were "together," she'd send me back to the condemned barracks.

The Séance Party invitations had gone out three weeks ago. Jonathan suggested using a picture of the Winchester Mystery House on the cover of the card, with a superimposed 3-D holograph of Mrs. Winchester, who seemed to blink on and off the page, depending on how you held the card. I whipped up a prototype, he approved it, and off they went, with the party details, and promise of a "surprise" visit from a "special guest." The invitation was apparently intriguing. In spite of the short notice, positive RSVPs streamed in. Jonathan was going to have a full 160-room house.

While the invitations went smoothly, the rest of the party planning wasn't so stress-free. Jonathan kept changing his mind about who would lead the séance, how the ballroom would be set up, and what to serve as appetizers.

His wife, Lyla, was worse. She seemed to think the event was a reflection of her, rather than a showcase for her husband's 4-D Projection. She insisted on hiring the chef from Hella-Graphics, Rodney Worth, instead of using my caterer, which didn't make Rocco happy. We compromised by having both—Rodney in charge of appetizers, Rocco doing dessert. I just hoped it wouldn't turn into the Battle of the Diva Chefs.

As for decorations, Lyla found a magic shop at Pier 39, and for some reason thought props and tricks from the store would provide the perfect atmospheric touches during a séance. "And they'll make great party favors, Priscilla," she said, still calling me by the wrong name. "After all, a séance is really nothing more than a magic show, right?"

At that point I gave up on trying to control the planning. This was essentially Jonathan's party—and apparently his wife's—and I was just there to choreograph the event. My only concern was his insistence on secrecy about everything from the guest list to the food. And the hope that Zachary Samuels—the guy who'd tried to run us down in the Winchester Mystery House parking lot—didn't crash our killer bash.

When the day of the event dawned, I woke up from a nightmare where I was being chased by a faceless man in a black BMW. As I stood at the edge of a cliff, watching the car speed toward me I realized there was nowhere to go—but down. When the image of Sarah Winchester appeared hovering over the abyss, I jolted awake, drenched in sweat. My startled cats leaped off the bed as if being chased by a rabid dog, and hid.

"It's okay, guys," I said, trying to reassure Thursby, Cairo, and Fatman. At the sound of kibble tinkling into their bowls, they came running from their various hiding places. Full bowls of gourmet cat food seemed to help calm their nerves, but mine were still on edge.

I peeked out of the kitchen window while waiting for my latte to brew. Touches of spring were evident in a couple of neighbors' flowerpots, but the fog was thick, making it a great day for a haunting. I've become somewhat of an expert at identifying different types of fog in the San Francisco Bay Area, since I've lived with it all my life. Plus it impresses the tourists.

The most common is Radiation Fog, which sounds scary, and simply means there's a layer of moist air near the ground. It's also called Valley Fog but I call it Blanket Fog because that was what it looks like—a big blanket covering the ground. It usually goes away when the sun comes up.

Checking my watch for party countdown—fewer than twelve hours before the first guests would arrive at the Winchester House—I jumped into the shower to wash off the sweat from my nightmare. I dressed in torn work jeans and a "Will Teach For Food" T-shirt left over from my days teaching abnormal psychology at San Francisco State University before I was downsized. Slipping on my black Vans, I grabbed the long black dress and black Mary Janes I'd be wearing at the party, then stuffed some makeup, costume jewelry, and other necessities into a backpack. With a blueberry bagel in one hand and a latte to-go in the other, I said good-bye to my cats, hopped in my red MINI Cooper, and drove the short distance to Building One to gather a few last party items.

"Oh my God! You look fantastic!" I cried, as I entered the office I shared with Delicia. She was dressed in a red-and-purple velvet skirt, a billowing white blouse, with a knitted silk shawl around her small, slim shoulders. Her fingers, hands, and chest were laden with noisy costume jewelry. She'd wrapped a colorful scarf at the top of her long black hair. Black ballet slippers covered her tiny feet.

"Snap!" Berkeley Wong appeared in the office, snapping his fingers.

"Did you help her with this?" I asked him, indicating Dee's costume.

Berk grinned proudly. "James is into vintage costumes,"

he explained. James was Berk's new love interest. They'd recently moved in together, which I thought was rather sudden, since they'd only met a few weeks ago. Talk about drama—the stories Berk shared about his new guy were better than an episode of *Celebrity Housewives in Rehab*.

Dee twirled around to give me a 360-degree view of the stunning creation. "Half of this stuff was James's! The rest we got at Vintage 1920 in the Mission."

"You look awesome—just like a medium. I think Jonathan will love it. Speaking of the devil, we need to get over to the mansion ASAP, before Lyla turns it into the Magic Castle with all her Houdini stuff. Berk, you've got your video camera?"

He saluted me as if I were some kind of dictator. Which I wasn't.

I turned to Delicia. "Dee, you better change into your work clothes. I'll need you to help me set up before you morph into the role of medium."

She was already removing her scarf by the time I was done speaking.

"I've got to check on Rocco. Be right back." I stepped out of the office door, tried Brad's door—locked—then backed up. "By the way, has anyone seen Brad?"

Dee and Berk exchanged an odd look.

"What?"

Dee shrugged and Berk shook his head. "Nope, no, huh-uh. Haven't seen him," he added.

I eyed them for a long moment, then headed for the kitchen on the second floor of the building to see how Rocco was coming along with the desserts. A large tray of little meringue ghosts greeted me as I entered. Their dotted chocolate eyes seemed to follow me as I made my way over to Rocco, who was carefully piping red flames atop miniature marzipan candles.

"Adorable!" I squealed like a little girl. "You're amazing! I love the ghosts, and these candles are to die for!"

I regretted saying that the minute the words came out. At one of my other parties, someone had injected poison into some chocolates that Rocco had made. Luckily, Rocco didn't seem to notice my tactlessness. He looked up at me from the delicate work he was doing, a streak of yellow frosting on his cheek. Tall, thin, and balding, he looked nothing like the cliché of the chef who ate all his own food. How he managed to stay so slim was a mystery to me.

"The wicks are licorice, so the whole thing is edible," he said. "But getting the frosting to stick to the licorice is driving me nuts."

"Can I help?" I asked, my mouth watering for a finger full of what looked like a bowl of chocolate frosting sitting idly by.

"Yes. By leaving me alone to finish these." Never one to mince words—only garlic—he went back to his painstaking work. He wasn't being rude; he was just being Rocco, the temperamental chef. That was part of what made him so good at his job—his attention to detail, his perfectionism. He'd pouted a little after learning he was doing only desserts for the party, especially when a competitor he loathed was handling the appetizers, but when he heard the amount of his paycheck, he bounced back quickly.

"Will you be ready to go over to the house soon?"

He grunted, and I made my escape.

On the way back to my office, I swung by the front desk

where Raj sat reading a copy of *Us* magazine. Apparently it was a slow day in the world of island security.

"Raj?"

He set the magazine down and straightened up. "Yes, Ms. Presley. What can I do for you?"

"You still available to help out at the party tonight? Make sure everything goes according to plan?"

He grinned, revealing his widely spaced white teeth. "Oh yes, I'm ready to come and make sure no one steals anything."

"I doubt theft will be a problem. But I'll just feel more comfortable if you are there, keeping an eye on . . . things." Ever since the run-in with Zachary in the parking lot, and hearing more about him from Stephanie Bryson, the Hella-Graphics VP, I'd found myself looking over my shoulder. If the disgruntled employee from Hella-Graphics decided to show up at the séance, at least I'd have some backup with Raj there.

Raj nodded, a kind of yes-no combination head shake.

"Thanks, Raj. Whenever you get finished here is fine. I'll e-mail you the directions. Raj?"

Raj was no longer looking at me. His eyes were focused on something behind me. I turned around to see Brad entering the building. He was holding the door for a woman dressed in a long madras skirt, a chemiselike purple blouse, and Birkenstock sandals. She was laughing and holding a white paper bag.

Marianne Mitchell, the building manager.

"Thanks for breakfast," she said to Brad, touching his arm.

"My pleasure," he replied, and watched her move toward

the staircase at the far end of the vast lobby, her wispy skirt swaying. With the Séance Party taking up so much of my time, I hadn't seen a lot of Brad in the past couple of weeks. Apparently he hadn't missed me. Not with that cougar around.

"Presley!" he said, grinning. I was sure he'd caught me staring.

I turned back to Raj. "Thanks again, Raj. See you at the mansion."

I started back to my office, when Brad caught my arm. "Hey."

"Hey," I said, trying to sound casual.

"I hardly see you anymore, Pres. Not since you took that séance job. How's it going?"

"Great," I said lightly. "How's it going with you?"

"Busy, too."

I glanced at the staircase where Marianne had disappeared. "I noticed." I took another step for my office.

He laughed. "You're not . . . jealous, are you?"

"Don't be ridiculous!" I huffed.

"How's what's his name?"

"Jonathan? He's fine," I said, glancing away as I remembered his lunge for me in the ballroom.

The tension between us was thick enough to cut with a machete. And all I had was my razor-sharp sarcasm.

"So, when's that party?"

"Tonight." I checked my watch. "I'm on my way now."

"Wow, I completely forgot it was tonight. Need any help?"

"It's not a crime scene . . . not yet, anyway."

"How about someone to blow up balloons? Or make scary noises in the background? Or channel a spirit or two?"

He brushed a hair out of my face and I just about melted on the spot.

"Already taken care of."

Brad looked a little hurt at my lack of enthusiasm for his offers. I softened and said, "Sure. I always need last-minute help when everything goes wrong."

"Great. How about I drive you and all your stuff? I can fit a lot in my SUV."

I wondered how a Crime Scene Cleaners vehicle parked out front of the Winchester House would look. Might add some atmosphere.

"All right. Are you ready to go now?"

He gave my arm a squeeze. "I'll go clear out some space."

I turned around and headed for my office, when I saw Delicia standing in our office doorway, and Berk standing in his. They immediately disappeared inside.

What was up with them?

My entourage and I arrived by caravan at the Winchester Mystery House around eleven. The fog had lifted—or we'd left it behind in San Francisco—and the day was turning out to be sunny and warm with a light breeze. As usual there were plenty of cars in the parking lot of the tourist attraction; I recognized Jonathan's Mercedes, minus the ding. Apparently he and his own entourage had beaten us there.

We entered the gift shop and I spotted Lyla, dressed in obscene black Spandex pants and a bright red tube top that defied gravity. She was talking on the phone, while another woman—young, pretty, also with long blond hair—stood nearby with a large shopping bag from Houdini's House, the magic shop. She introduced herself as Violet Vassar, Jonathan's administrative assistant. She hardly looked the admin type, but then Jonathan seemed to surround himself with attractive young women, all practically clones of his wife.

Mia arrived from her office, wearing a short blue skirt and a tight maroon top, a contrast to her previous business attire. I was stunned at the change, which included more eye makeup (blue eye shadow) and dangling earrings (blue stars). Her tennis shoes had been replaced by open-toed high heels.

"Welcome," she said. "Jonathan's already in the ballroom. If you're ready, I'll take you there. We have to take the back way to avoid the tour groups."

We followed her through yet another secret passageway to the lavish ballroom, where I spotted Stephanie Bryson sitting in a folding chair, her electronic notepad in her lap. She looked up, waved, and smiled, then returned to the tiny computer. On the other side of the grand room I saw Jonathan, who appeared to be in a heated discussion with Levi, pointing and gesturing as he spoke to the bespectacled balding guy.

I put my crew to work. Rocco unloaded his goodies in the adjoining butler's pantry that led to the kitchen. Berk scouted for a place to set up his video camera. Raj took a tour of the ballroom and neighboring rooms to check security. And Brad helped set up the large round séance table that had been delivered by a party supply company.

I set down the box of candlesticks I was carrying and headed out for more supplies, hoping I didn't get lost. On my way back, as I entered the ballroom again, I thought I saw something white dart across the butler's pantry opening.

A ghost, I thought, amusing myself.

I knew there was no such thing. But the little hairs on my arms didn't quite believe me. I glanced around to see if anyone else had noticed the fleeting vision, but everyone was focused on their tasks. Only Brad had stopped what he was doing to look over at me.

"Did you see that?" I asked him, setting down a box of candles and pointing toward the pantry.

"See what?" he said.

I shook my head. "Nothing."

I returned to the entryway and studied the pantry opening. Supposedly it led to the kitchen. I decided to take a look. Following a narrow hallway that ran parallel to the pantry, I arrived in the vast kitchen, where I found Rocco cursing under his breath.

"Rocco, did you see—" I started to say.

"What?" Rocco snapped as he removed a couple of meringue ghosts that had broken on the ride over.

"Uh . . . never mind."

I started to return to the ballroom—I had work to do—but out of the corner of my eye, I saw another streak of white move past a window on the other side of the kitchen. Dashing out, I zipped down the hall and caught a glimpse of someone—or something—disappearing around a corner.

"Wait!" I called out.

No response.

I moved around the corner and followed the passageway around until it came to a pair of paneled, sliding doors. The smell of onions and garlic wafted through the crack. I slid one door open and found myself in another kitchen.

And there stood my ghost: A man, thirtysomething, dressed in loose white pants, a white shirt, with black patent-leather shoes that matched his jet-black hair, black mustache, and black-rimmed glasses. He was bent over a plastic container filled with something pungent that made my mouth water.

"Who are you?" I asked.

The man straightened up and turned to me.

"I'm . . . Joe Thornton. Who are you?" he returned, smoothing down his mustache.

"Presley Parker. I'm the event planner for the Séance Party tonight. What are you doing here?"

"Working," he replied, shoving his glasses back on his face and returning to the bowl of what had to be roasted garlic and onions. In a few seconds, I was going to need a napkin to wipe off the drool.

"Where's Rodney, the chef Lyla hired to make the appetizers?"

"Here," a deep, scratchy voice said from behind. I turned to see a burly man wearing chef's whites and a once-white apron, holding a large pot. "Rodney Worth, at your service. Joe is one of my waiters tonight. What can I do for you?"

I reintroduced myself. The chef nodded, only half listening, as he peered over his waiter's shoulder and into the open container. "What are you doing?" he said to Joe.

The bewildered waiter took a step back. "Nothing. Just checking it." He smoothed his mustache again. The guy seemed to have a lot of nervous tics.

"Leave it alone," Rodney barked. "I told you to bring in all the supplies, not open containers and check them. Where have you been? There's a bunch of stuff still in the van I need. Now."

Joe nodded in acquiescence, but his eyes narrowed and I

could see his clenched jaw before he headed out to do his boss's bidding.

"He's new," Rodney said with a sigh. "My sous-chef got him from craigslist or somewhere. Spends more time wandering around this place or talking on his cell phone than working. When will I learn."

"Well, I'll get out of your way. Let me know if you need anything."

"Some competent help would be nice," he said. "These cheese and crab *amuse-bouches* aren't going to make themselves."

I ducked out of the room before he put me to work—I had enough on my plate as it was. And that séance table wasn't going to decorate itself either. Heading back, I must have taken a wrong turn, because I found myself at a dead end. I was about to retrace my steps when I thought I heard faint voices coming from the wall.

Great, Presley. First you think you're seeing ghosts, and now you think you're hearing them.

More indistinct mumbling. Coming from the wall.

I followed the sound. The voices grew louder. I heard a woman's voice.

Coming from . . . where?

I looked around for the source, but all I saw was an old rusted pipe on the ceiling, that ran the length of the wall. It turned down in one corner, then dead-ended halfway to the floor.

Suddenly it dawned on me. A listening tube.

Mia had pointed out a couple of these pipes on our tour of the house. Mrs. Winchester had had them installed throughout the house so she could call on her servants from various rooms whenever she needed them. Or listen in on their private conversations.

I stepped over to the tube in the corner and saw an opening where it dead-ended. I put my ear up close and listened.

"Oh yes. It will be the surprise of his life," the female voice said. I recognized it immediately: Lyla Ellington, Jonathan's wife. Was she planning some kind of surprise for him at the Séance Party?

"You're sure this is going to work?" a male voice said. This one I didn't recognize.

"I'd bet my life on it," Lyla replied. "So don't let me down."

The man mumbled something I couldn't make out.

"Here he comes!" Lyla hissed. A pause. Then louder: "Coming, darling!"

Lyla hadn't taken the tour with us. I had a feeling she was unaware of the listening tubes. And the discussion I'd just overheard had sounded secretive.

What was the surprise Lyla had referred to?

Whatever it was, I just hoped it didn't ruin the party.

Chapter 10

By the time guests started arriving at the Winchester Mystery House, a little after eight, the grand ballroom had been transformed into an atmospheric séance room. In the middle stood a large round table, covered in a black cloth and surrounded by thirteen vintage chairs. At each place was a brass candlestick, with black unlit candles inserted. A crystal ball stood on a brass stand in the middle of the table, thanks to Lyla, who'd insisted, "It's not a séance without a crystal ball!"

When all but two of the thirty or so guests had arrived and were gathered in the guest-reception room with drinks labeled "Bloodred Wine" in hand, Mia, the Winchester House manager, took everyone on a modified tour of the eccentric mansion. George Lucas from ILM, Phil Tippett from his studio in Berkeley, and Spaz Cruz from CeeGee Studios on Treasure Island were the most recognizable guests. The others included their plus-ones, a few high-tech investors, and some of Jonathan's staff—Stephanie, the VP; Violet Vassar, his administrative assistant; and Lyla, his wife. Mother, who'd already toured the house, stayed back with Stephen Ellington, who had arrived in his wheelchair via limo, thanks to Jonathan. Unfortunately, the house wasn't wheelchair accessible. Brad, who'd been keeping a low profile around Jonathan, seemed to have completely disappeared behind the scenes.

I hadn't seen Levi Webster, Jonathan's programmer, since late afternoon. He was sequestered in an adjoining room, preparing to bring Sarah Winchester "to life" when cued. He'd spent the first half of the day installing numerous tiny cameras, projectors, and other over-my-head pieces of equipment in the ballroom. Now that it was showtime, he'd made himself as invisible as a ghost.

I checked on Delicia, tucked in another room off the ballroom, rehearsing the speech Jonathan had prepared for her. Confident there was little more I could do, I caught up with the guests touring the house, and stayed at the back of the group to make sure no one wandered off or got lost. Mia led us from room to room, sharing details of Sarah Winchester's life and pointing out quirks and curios of the mystery house. Berk videotaped the guests as they reacted to the oddities— the doors that opened to walls, the spiderweb stained-glass windows, the number thirteen hidden throughout the unfinished construction.

By the time we reached Sarah's séance room, the crowd was duly impressed, and immersed in the heavy atmosphere.

So far, so good.

"We're now entering the original séance room," Mia intoned, "where Mrs. Winchester made contact with the spirits through her medium . . ."

As Mia narrated her story, the guests gathered shoulder to shoulder in the small room, *ooh*ing and *ahh*ing.

Suddenly, the lights flickered.

"Uh-oh," she said, a split second before the room was plunged into complete darkness.

Feet shuffled. A couple of women gasped. A few whispered. Someone giggled.

A glow began to emanate from the middle of the room. A swirl of white light, like wispy curtains, fluttered and grew in intensity, until an image the size of a child slowly took shape.

Mrs. Sarah Winchester had arrived.

Not quite in the flesh, but very lifelike, albeit nearly transparent. She stood in the middle of the room, dressed in a long black skirt and a puffy white blouse, with a dark knitted shawl wrapped around her shoulders and a netted veil over her face. She looked just like her picture on the wall in Mia's office.

Before we could blink—or scream—the apparition disappeared as mysteriously as it had appeared.

More gasps and giggles as the lights came up, softly illuminating the room.

"That was awesome!" someone said.

"Where'd she go?" whispered another.

"Oh, she'll be back," Mia said with a secretive smile,

right on cue. "Now if you'll follow me . . ." She opened a secret door to the next room and led the group onward as they buzzed with growing excitement.

Act One, the preview of Sarah Winchester's ghost, had been a great success, whetting the ghost-hungry appetites of the guests.

On to Act Two.

Shortly thereafter the guests found themselves in the ballroom turned séance room, where Jonathan awaited us, flanked by his father on one side and his wife on the other. He looked undeniably handsome in his tux and shiny black loafers—I was used to seeing him dressed more casually— and he seemed eager to get on with the show. Lyla wore a low-cut blue-sequined gown and matching sequined shoes with lethal-looking heels. She was so striking and drop-dead gorgeous, I wondered if even a ghost could keep the men away from her.

"Welcome, everyone!" Jonathan said, opening his arms grandly. "Thank you all for coming tonight! We have quite an evening planned for you, an evening you're not likely to forget. We'll be starting the séance in a few minutes. But first, enjoy some appetizers by Chef Rodney and wine from the Napa Valley."

The waiter I'd spotted earlier appeared with a tray of puffy-looking things, skewers of fishy-looking things, and lettuce cups filled with meaty-looking things. His tray wobbled in his hands, and he approached the guests without smiling or lowering the tray. At one point he nearly dropped a platter, and it made me wonder where he'd worked before. In spite of his awkwardness, still, the appetizers were gobbled up quickly and the wine flowed easily.

While Jonathan worked the crowd, shaking hands and patting backs, I checked on Delicia, hidden in the small room off the ballroom, to make sure she was in her costume and ready for her close-up.

"How's it going?" I asked, as she dotted on a beauty spot just above her upper lip. Her eyes were thickly lined in black and contrasted with her bright red lips. The heavy jewelry, bright head scarf, and multicolored outfit only added to her exotic appearance. The truth was, she looked fabulous no matter what she did. But then she could wear a housecoat and hairnet and still look amazing.

"Great, so far. I just hope that Levi guy is ready with his bag of tricks. I heard him cursing to himself in the other room."

I heard the ring-tap of a wineglass coming from the ballroom and left Dee to finish her toilette.

Jonathan was already speaking to the crowd as I sneaked back into the festive room.

". . . and I've selected twelve of you to participate at the table. Please look for your place card and take your seat. The rest of you may stand behind and observe quietly. I only have one request—please leave your cell phones on, but silence them."

The guests circled the round table, searching for their spots. One by one, members of Jonathan's A-list sat down in the twelve seats, leaving the thirteenth open. They included the media stars Lucas, Tippett, and Cruz; two investors; Jonathan's wife, Lyla; his VP, Stephanie Bryson; and his admin, Violet Vassar. To my surprise, Mia was invited to join the group, as was another of Jonathan's staff, his driver, another young, beautiful blonde. One of the expected investors and his wife were no-shows, so Jonathan gave the last seats to his father and my mother, removing a chair for Stephen Ellington and wheeling him in. The one remaining seat stood ominously empty.

Raj, Brad, and I stood in the background to keep an eye on things, while Berk continued to videotape the event.

Moments later I dimmed the room lights, leaving the room in a soft, shadowy glow. A door a few feet behind the empty place opened and Delicia entered with a swish of her skirt, a jangle of jewelry, and a regal turn of her head. She swept into the available thirteenth seat with an air of majesty and mystique, and rested her multiringed hands on the table. The guests grinned at both her dramatic arrival and her theatrical appearance. I could tell they were enjoying every minute of this exotic event. My butterflies were starting to subside.

"I am Madam Delicia . . ." Dee began, dragging out the syllables of her name—Dee-lee-cee-ah—in a low, heavily accented voice that sounded Transylvanian. "Velcome to ze Vinchester Mystery Houze. Ve're here tonight to contact ze spirit of Zarah Vinchester, because ve believe she has zomezing important to zay. But first, you must light ze candles in front of you."

Dee lit a match that had been placed next to her candlestick, and touched it to the wick. An eerie glow from the candlelight danced on her creamy face. She removed the lit candle from the brass candlestick and passed it to the person on her left—Jonathan. He took Dee's candle, lit his own with hers, then passed it on to his wife, Lyla. Everyone waited quietly as the candle was ceremoniously passed around the table. When it arrived back at Dee's spot, she replaced it in her own candlestick. That was my cue to turn off the ballroom lights completely. I was just about to turn the dimmer when I caught a glimpse of the waiter standing in a far corner, watching.

Brad elbowed me, reminding me to finish the task at hand, and I turned off the light, leaving only the flicker of candlelight in the semidarkened room.

"Now, free your minds," she continued in her bizarre accent, "relax your bodies, and join hands to form a continuous, unbroken spirit circle."

Grinning at her entertaining persona, the guests joined hands and rested them on the table. I was impressed with Dee's acting chops. I almost believed Sarah Winchester—the real Sarah Winchester—might surprise us with a visit.

Candlelight flickered on the table.

Floorboards creaked beneath the feet of the observers.

Dee closed her eyes, tilted her head back, and began to chant: "O spirit of Zarah Vinchester, ve zummon you to our table. Please join us now."

Nothing happened.

Great.

What was Levi doing in his hidden room? Sleeping?

A few minutes passed. Dee repeated her incantation, but the guests began to stir, and murmurs grew in the room. I decided to slip out and check on Levi, but before I could move, a light suddenly appeared inside the crystal ball that sat in the middle of the table. It began as a tiny three-dimensional wisp of light, then quickly grew in size and began to take shape, slowly morphing into the ghostly apparition of an old woman.

Sarah Winchester was back from the dead.

I relaxed as delighted gasps and hushed murmurs swirled through the room. The faint figure filled the space. Sarah Winchester hovered in the center of the table, all four feet ten inches of her, semitransparent but fully formed.

"Oh my God!" someone whispered.

"She looks so real," said another.

It was true. Jonathan's new 4-D Projection technology proved to be incredible. I wanted to reach out and touch the figure.

Sarah's image slowly turned around. She looked down at each person at the table, pausing for a moment. When she arrived at Dee, she stopped—and began speaking.

"Why have you summoned me, Madame Delicia?" Although somewhat scratchy and high-pitched, the voice was familiar. Dee had tape-recorded Sarah's "voice" using one of her many theatrical dialects. This one was a cross between Glinda the Good Witch and Granny from the Tweety Bird cartoons.

I noticed the hand-holders tighten their grips as they witnessed the "spirit" come to life. They seemed to be especially impressed by Sarah's ability to focus on Delicia and address her by name.

"Zarah, ve believe you have zomething to share vith us." Dee said this as if she talked to spirits every day.

"Why, yes, indeed. I've come here to tell you about an amazing new discovery that has brought me back to life," the image said. She turned and faced Jonathan, gesturing toward him with a lace-covered arm. "Jonathan Ellington has created a new dimension in 3-D, which he calls 4-D Projection. As you can plainly see, he's gone way beyond 3-D of the past, and without the aid of cumbersome glasses."

The speech Jonathan had written for Sarah sounded more like an infomercial, I thought. Sarah Winchester would no doubt be turning over in her grave at the showmanship.

"How is this possible?" Dee asked.

Sarah Winchester slowly turned in a circle as she spoke, gesturing as naturally as a real human being. "Thanks to Jonathan's group of engineers, Hella-Graphics has broken through a technological barrier and has moved three-dimensional holographic displays light-years ahead. Simply stated, a special plastic film is used, along with laser beams, transparent electrodes, and an electric field. The exact formula is top secret, of course, but you can see the results as I stand here talking to you."

Sarah kept spinning as she talked, seemingly making eye contact with each guest in turn. "In other words, this isn't your grandmother's credit card hologram. Hella-Graphics's 4-D Projection offers 'situational awareness'—like I'm using now—that can track the progress of microscopic surgeries, show pilots upcoming hazards in their airspace, or give emergency response teams nearly real-time views of disasters in progress."

Even in simple terms, most of this went over my head. I was still in the mind-set of the kind of 3-D where giant hands lunged out from the movie screen to grab the audience and make them toss the popcorn. I hoped those seated were a little savvier than I.

Sarah's image turned and focused on one of the investors at the table. "Think about the possibilities beyond the movie business. 4-D Projection could eventually replace MRIs and CAT scan monitors, improve military intelligence, and sell products on a whole new level. Imagine going into a store and seeing Matt Damon open a can of Coke, pour it into a glass, and drink it—all while standing right there in front of you. Now, instead of limited viewing angles, we can view three hundred sixty degrees in all directions. And I'm, well, 'living' proof, as you can see." Sarah's image actually formed air quotes around the word "living." Jonathan's input, no doubt.

Even without fully understanding this new technology, I was blown away. If Sarah were really alive, I had a feeling she would be blown away too. I knew that the eccentric woman was one of the first to get an electric elevator, indoor plumbing, and other "new-age" technology.

I glanced over at Brad to see his reaction. Instead of raised eyebrows or wide eyes, he was frowning at the image. I glanced back at Sarah and noticed a glitch in the image, as if there had been a split-second interruption in the transmission.

Sarah turned again. I wondered who she'd address next? But instead of stopping, she kept circling, slowly at first, then more rapidly. Her arms began flapping up and down, frantically. Dee's mouth dropped open and she, too, looked at Jonathan, who was frowning deeply, obviously alarmed.

Suddenly, Sarah began to speak again, but this time her voice was distorted, as if she were a talking doll low on batteries. This voice didn't sound like anyone in Delicia's repertoire of characters.

"Jonathan, Jonathan, Jonathan," the voice repeated in a singsong tone as the image twirled madly on the tabletop.

Even in the dim candlelight, I could see the color fade from Jonathan's face as Sarah chanted his name.

"Jonathan, I have a message from George Wells. You remember George? He killed himself in his office last month."

Jonathan jerked his hands from Lyla's and Violet's grips. He glared at Dee. "What are you doing?"

Dee let go of the hands she was holding and held hers up. "Nothing! I swear—"

Jonathan rose up, knocking back his chair. He turned and faced me. "Stop this at once!"

I stood frozen to my spot.

"Jonathan . . ." came the distorted voice again. "Jonathan . . . did he kill himself because you were having an affair with his wife?"

Lyla gasped and looked at Jonathan.

He shook his head. "No! No—"

"Was it even suicide?" the voice continued. "Maybe you made it look that way when George found out about all your affairs . . . You're up to about a dozen now, aren't you? Almost as many as Tiger Woods. Let's see—there's your secretary, Violet"—at this point, Sarah Winchester's image turned to Violet and pointed a finger at her—"your receptionist, Maile, your personal trainer, Gina, your driver, Courtney, your accountant, Melissa, the barista, Jennifer. Even your latest conquest"—the image turned again—"Mia, the manager of this very mansion."

Mia gasped and tried to cover her shocked look with her hands.

"Is there anyone you haven't done, Jonathan?" Sarah continued. "Was George going to expose you for what you really are—a lying, cheating scumbag?"

Lyla suddenly stood up. Her face burned with anger and embarrassment, her eyes filled with tears. She picked up the brass candlestick propped in front of her and swung it at Jonathan. He pulled back just in time to avoid a blow to the head. Grabbing her arm, he tried to snatch the candlestick from her grip. She let go, then clawed him across the face and fled from the ballroom, disappearing through the exit door where Dee had materialized as a medium.

"Lyla! No!" Jonathan yelled. "Levi, that bastard. He's ruined everything. Lyla! Wait!" He stopped and glanced around the room, suddenly aware that everyone—his staff, peers, and possible backers—was watching him, eyes wide, mouths agape.

Still holding the candlestick he'd wrestled from Lyla, he ran out after his wife, leaving the rest of us stunned into silence.

So much for Act Two.

Chapter 11

PARTY PLANNING TIP #11

Expect the unexpected at your Séance Party, but try to maintain control. If things start getting out of hand, end the séance by thanking the spirit, breaking the circle of hands, and extinguishing the candles. You really don't want to piss off the spirits.

Whoa. What just happened?

Sarah Winchester had gone berserk.

Jonathan Ellington had been accused of having multiple affairs.

And Lyla Ellington had tried to kill him with a candlestick.

This party was definitely over.

I stepped to the wall and brought up the lights.

After swallowing a hefty mouthful of wine, I rang a wineglass to attract the buzzing crowd's attention. "Listen up, everyone," I said, then had another gulp of wine before continuing. "Uh, it seems our host . . . uh, is indisposed. I want to thank you all for coming tonight, and for donating to the American Stroke Association. Feel free to have more wine. My chef, Rocco, has made some wonderful desserts for you. And when you're ready, we, uh, have some nice gifts for you to take home . . ."

I looked around for Brad but he had disappeared too. I shot a look at Dee, who immediately headed for the gift table by the exit door and began handing out bags filled with magic tricks, tarot cards, and crystal ball key chains that Lyla had put together. "Thanks again for coming, and good night."

It wasn't much of a parting speech, but then, for ad-libbing, it wasn't bad. Everyone else was as stunned as I was, so it probably didn't matter what I said, as long as I emphasized the wine, desserts, and parting gifts.

"You okay?" Brad asked, sidling up and wrapping an arm around me.

"Sure. Fine. Where have you been?"

"I went looking for Jonathan but didn't find him."

"Would you give everyone a few minutes to have their desserts and then help me get them out of here?"

He gave me a squeeze, then ambled over to Raj and Berk, who were helping Rocco serve the meringue ghosts and marzipan candles. It wasn't long before they slowly herded the bewildered crowd out of the ballroom and out of the house, gift bags in tow.

Mother came striding over, a look of empathy on her face. "Darling, what on earth happened?"

"Good question, Mom. I'm not sure. You know about as much as I do."

"Stephen is devastated. I don't know what to tell him. Are you going after Jonathan?"

"Brad tried to find him, but Jonathan's apparently disappeared. I suppose I could look for him . . ." I was a grand example of indecision, standing there glued to the floor.

"Please, dear. Find Jonathan and see if he's all right. Stephen wants to see him."

I figured no one would miss me for a few minutes while I looked for the missing host. The last I'd seen him he was swinging a heavy brass candlestick and had stormed out after his wife.

I headed through the door where he and Lyla had made their escape, and did a quick search of the room where Dee had been before the séance started. Dee's clothes were still in the room, along with her purse, makeup case, and cell phone. Aside from that, the place was empty.

I moved on to the adjacent room, where Levi was manning the computer. This time the door was locked.

I knocked.

No answer. Alarm bells went off.

I knocked again, wondering if I would have to get Mia to unlock it.

The door cracked open an inch.

"What?" Levi peeked out. With his sweaty face and rapidly blinking eyes, he seemed distraught.

"Whew, you're here," I said, relieved. "Uh . . . I'm looking for Jonathan. Or Lyla."

"Yeah, well, they're not here." He started to close the door.

I pushed out my hand to stop him. "Wait a minute! What happened out there?" I pointed back to the séance room. "What was all that about Jonathan sleeping around? Or cheating on Lyla? Why did you have Sarah say those things?"

Levi left the door open and abruptly returned to his computer. Plopping into his chair, he began typing frantically on the keyboard.

I waited. When no explanation came, I said, "Levi?"

He whirled around, his face red, spittle on his lips. "What! Can't you see I'm trying to figure out what happened! Now leave me alone!"

Whoa. This was a side I hadn't seen from the quiet computer nerd. "So, you have no idea why the image started saying all those things?"

"No. It wasn't supposed to happen like that."

"How was it meant to happen? And whose voice was it? It didn't sound like Delicia."

"I told you, I don't know! I don't know!" He was back at the keyboard, fingers flying.

I didn't want to make things worse than they already were so I decided to stand down. "Okay, well, uh, will you let me know when you do?"

No response.

"Levi?"

"Yes! Okay!"

"And let me know if you see Jonathan or Lyla."

He shooed me away with a single wave of his hand. I backed out of the room, leaving the door open a crack. I could hear him beating his fingers against the keyboard as I moved along and hoped he'd soon be able to explain to me what had happened. He seemed to be as clueless as we all were about the glitch that had ruined the party. But who else could have hacked into it and made such a change?

I headed for the kitchen and found Chef Rodney cleaning up his utensils and packing up his stuff. Two waiters were helping him with the cleanup, but the clumsy waiter—what was his name?—was nowhere in sight. The last time I'd seen him, he'd tucked himself into a corner of the ballroom and was watching the séance.

I returned to the ballroom where I found Mia talking with Raj about security. She wouldn't meet my eyes, obviously embarrassed about what "Sarah" had said about her having an affair with Jonathan. Dee, Berk, and Brad were busy taking down decorations and packing them into boxes. Mother sat in a chair next to Stephen, her hand on his, obviously consoling him. I went over to them.

"Sorry about all this, Mr. Ellington," I said, pulling up a chair. "It's not what I'd planned—that's for sure."

He looked down at his knees and shook his head. "I knew this would happen one day."

I glanced at Mother. She was as wide-eyed as I was. "What? You mean, you knew Lyla had a violent temper?"

"No, no, not that," he grumbled. "Jonathan. All those women. He's a sex addict, or whatever you call it."

How about slimeball? I thought.

"Can't keep his hands to himself," Stephen continued, "even when married to a beautiful woman like Lyla."

"You knew about the . . . affairs?" I asked Stephen gently.

He nodded slowly, not looking up. He seemed to be taking on Jonathan's shame. "A couple of years ago, I caught him . . . you know . . . doing it . . . in the limo right outside my home. With his pretty young driver. I guess he figured no one would see them through the tinted windows. Nor did they expect anyone to come bursting in, like I did."

"How did you know about the others?" I asked. Mother sat mutely in her seat, eyes as big as crystal balls. I was sure this wasn't going over well with her. She was a serial monogamist—one man at a time—and she didn't cheat.

"I caught him again, making out with his secretary in his office. For being such an intelligent guy, he was an idiot when it came to women. He could have at least been discreet."

"And there were more after that?"

"I found a hotel bill in one of the jackets he'd lent me and confronted him. He tried to lie his way out of it, but he finally gave up. He knew I knew. He swore he was going to stop."

"But he didn't."

I was surprised Stephen hadn't caught on sooner. I guess people don't see what they don't want to see.

Stephen sighed. He seemed more defeated than embarrassed. Mother rubbed his arm. "Like I said, he's whatcha-call-it—an addict. I know he loves Lyla, but he can't keep his tool in the toolbox."

I wanted to laugh at the metaphor but it just wasn't the right time.

"Any idea where he is now?" I asked.

Stephen shook his head. Without looking up, he began wheeling his electric wheelchair toward the exit.

"Wait, Stephen," Mother said, running after him. "I'll go with you." She turned to me and said softly, "Jonathan's driver brought us. She's waiting outside in the limo."

I gave her a sympathetic smile and a little wave, and headed over to face Mia.

"Listen, Presley, about what you heard . . ."

I waved her words away. "That's none of my business, Mia. What's important is that we find Jonathan and Lyla.

They could be anywhere in this house, and you're the one who knows it best."

"I'll do whatever I can," she said, biting her lip. "I'm sorry . . ."

"Just take a look around. Maybe get your security guard to look for them. I checked the room where Dee changed clothes and where Levi was manning the computer. And the kitchen. No luck."

"Will do," she said, then paused. "Presley, honestly, I didn't know he was married. That first day you both came to see me? He came back to the office, said he forgot to ask something. We got to talking and . . . he was so charming and good-looking. When I found out he was married, I broke it off. . . ."

In the short time I'd known Jonathan, I knew how charming he could be—but also what a player he was. How could she have not seen that? "Just see if you can find him—or Lyla—all right?"

She nodded, signaled the security guard, and together they left the ballroom.

What a mess, I thought, surveying the pile of decorations, the overturned chair, the empty wineglasses, the appetizer skewers.

Literally and figuratively.

"Let's call it a night," I said to my tired staff after they'd removed and packed away most of the decorations. "I'll finish the rest of the cleanup tomorrow. Hopefully Jonathan will have turned up by then and I can get the money he owes me. And then I'll pay you all," I added.

For the last fifteen minutes we'd all been sitting around

talking about the unexpected twists and turns of the event, waiting to see if Jonathan turned up, and eating as many of Rocco's leftover meringue ghosts as we could stomach. We told ourselves we didn't want his carefully crafted goodies to go to waste—and I wanted to appease Rocco for the last-minute rush. But mostly I needed something to go with the several glasses of wine I'd consumed while lamenting the upcoming end of my career. I mean, how many party fouls can an event planner make before her business balloon bursts?

Mia and her security guard returned moments later, after searching most of the house, including the sections that weren't locked to the public. They'd found no sign of Jonathan or Lyla anywhere—not even a candlestick. Brad and I headed for his SUV, while the others drove off in their cars. I checked for Jonathan's Mercedes but by the time we left, it was gone, along with most of the other cars in the lot, except two cars parked in reserved spots and a red Prius badly in need of a car wash. I figured Mia and the security guard had the prized parking spots. But it was the license plate that had caught my eye. It read HELAGEK.

"Brad, look." I pointed to the car.

"What?"

"I wonder if that's Levi's car. Do you think he's still here, working on that glitch?"

"Don't know. I didn't check on him before we left. Did you?"

"Not after I saw him the first time. He must still be there." I thought a moment. "Do you think Jonathan would leave without making sure his precious and expensive 4-D Projector was safe?"

"Maybe he told Levi to take it with him," Brad suggested.

I trailed him to his car, stealing a last glance at the Winchester Mystery House as it loomed in the shadows of moonlight—the classic haunted house.

I shuddered.

Maybe raising the dead wasn't such a good idea for a party theme after all.

Although it was late, I invited Brad in for sobering lattes—his decaf, mine caf, which took my excitement down a notch. Exhausted but wired, I knew I wouldn't be able to sleep for a while, and caffeine actually soothed me. We rehashed the party again while sitting on the couch, discussing how it had gone so horribly, horribly wrong, and what I could do to salvage my Killer Parties reputation if word got out.

After we'd concluded that Jonathan was a liar, a cheat, and a scoundrel (my words), that Lyla had to be an airhead not to see past Jonathan's false charm (Brad's assessment), and that someone—who? Levi?—had taken the opportunity to expose Jonathan's peccadilloes in the most embarrassing way possible, we declared the party officially over. The fat lady had not only sung, but probably had been choked to death.

"So," Brad said when we reached the end of our analysis. He looked at his watch. "It's getting late." He made no effort to get off the couch. Instead he put his arm around me, sending a jolt of electricity through my tired bones.

He leaned over and kissed me, practically electrocuting me with his tongue.

"I sure don't want to make that long drive home . . ." he said, when the lingering kiss ended.

"You mean all the way back to Yerba Buena Island? It's, what—five minutes from here?" Flat, man-made Treasure

Island connected to naturally hilly Yerba Buena Island in the middle of the Bay Bridge. They reminded me of fraternal Siamese twins, which I think is an oxymoron.

He laughed. "Yeah, I might fall asleep at the wheel, take a wrong turn, and end up in the Bay."

I elbowed him. "Thanks for reminding me." One of my competitors had ended up doing just that, after taking a bite of a poisoned chocolate I had served her.

He grabbed his rib cage in mock pain. "Oops. Sorry about that. But at your parties, people do have a way of ending up . . ."

"Dead?" I stood up. "Not this time."

He stood and wrapped his arms around me.

He wasn't going to get off teasing me so easily. "I think I have some of those leftover chocolates . . ." I gave him an evil grin.

"I'll pass." He kissed me again, longer, deeper this time.

"What about your cat allergies?" I whispered, noticing he hadn't sneezed once.

"Took drugs," he whispered.

I couldn't respond. My voice had lost its capacity for speech. All I could do was nod mutely, then drag him, not exactly kicking and screaming, into my bedroom.

As I lay on the bed, looking up into Brad's glistening brown eyes, I melted like chocolate in his arms.

This party wasn't quite over. The fat lady was about to sing an encore.

I woke up with a cozy, warm body next to my back. I rolled over. The body turned out to be Cairo, my orange scaredy-cat. Meanwhile Fatman, the fat white cat, had draped himself over my legs, and Thursby, my black attack cat who mostly attacked my feet, had slept at the head of the bed and was attacking my hair.

No Brad.

I bolted up and glanced at the clock. Eight fifteen! Damn.

I threw the covers off and jumped into the shower. The smell of lattes took over the scent of soap as I toweled off. Was there anything better than a night with an attractive crime scene cleaner? Yeah, a latte the morning after.

Brad sat at my little table, sipping his coffee and reading the *Chronicle*.

"Any news?" I asked as I joined him. Two blueberry bagels sat on a plate between us, one partially eaten. I snatched the other and took a big bite.

"Nothing about the party, if that's what you mean," he said, licking the coffee 'stache from his lips.

Those lips.

He folded the newspaper closed. "You going over to the Winchester House this morning?"

"Yeah," I said, then took a curative sip of my latte. "I've got a few things to finish up. I wanted to get there early before they open the place to the public but I overslept. I hope anything I left behind is still there."

"I'd join you but I've got a cleanup on aisle five this morning. Elderly couple found in Hunters Point, buried under a pile of their own floor-to-ceiling trash."

"Dead?" I asked, horrified at the thought that someone could have so much crap, it might actually cause their death. I glanced around my living room at the party catalogs, discarded clothes, empty bags of Cheetos, and stained coffee mugs, and recognized the beginnings of a similar fate if I wasn't careful. My three cats would only add to the frightful end I envisioned.

"Yep. Cops said it looked like the woman fell into the debris, and then, when her husband went to help her, he also fell. That caused a major landslide of old magazines, books, and other junk. They hadn't been seen for a week, but nobody bothered to check on them."

"That's awful!" I shivered. I promised myself that when I returned home this afternoon I'd do a thorough decluttering of my place. No way was I going to let Brad find me in a heap of stale chips, dirty underwear, and cat puke.

"Okay, well, I've got to run," I said, shaking off the image and remembering my priorities. I handed him an extra key I kept in my kitchen junk drawer. "Lock up when you leave. And thanks for the latte and bagel." I gave him a quick kiss, like a housewife headed for the dry cleaner, and flew out the door.

On the hour-long drive over to the Winchester Mystery House, my thoughts ping-ponged between memories of last night with Brad and visions of last night at the party. By the time I arrived at the mansion, Brad was winning the match.

I parked, dashed inside the front door of the gift shop, and knocked at Mia's door.

No answer.

A security guard I didn't recognize entered from another door. He appeared startled to see me.

"May I help you?" he asked, frowning.

"Yes, I'm Presley Parker . . ."

He glanced round. "How did you get in? We're not open yet."

"I'm the event planner . . . was, anyway . . . for the Séance Party held here last night. Mia showed me which door to use."

He crossed his arms as if waiting for a better explanation.

"I'm here early because I left a few things behind and came to collect them."

Blank look.

"Where's Mia?"

"She's in the ballroom with another lady."

"Oh great! That's where I need to go. Can you take me there?"

The guard pulled the walkie out of his belt and spoke into the squawky mic. I heard Mia's voice at the other end give permission for me to join her.

"This way." He led me along a winding path to the ballroom that was becoming more and more familiar to me.

"Hi, Mia," I said as I entered. "Sorry I'm late. I meant to get here earlier. Looks like I still beat the tourists. I just came to get a box of candlesticks I left behind—"

"Hey, Presley." Stephanie Bryson appeared from the doorway that led to Delicia's green room.

"Stephanie! What are you doing here?" I asked.

"I came to check on the 4-D Projector," Stephanie said. "Anyone seen Levi? He didn't come into the office this morning. He's always there early."

Mia and I looked at each other and shook our heads.

"What about Jonathan? Did he show up?" I asked.

"No sign of him either," Stephanie said.

Jonathan was still missing? Or was I jumping to conclusions? Maybe he was with Lyla somewhere, working out their problems—or battling them out.

Stephanie rapped on the door that led to Levi's temporary workplace. No answer.

"Mia," Stephanie called out. "This door's locked. Can you open it, please? Levi said he'd bring the projector into the office this morning, but he never showed. Jonathan will kill me if anything happens to it."

Locked? It had been locked when I went to see Levi last night. But I'd made sure it was open when I left.

Mia pulled out a ring of keys as she headed over. She found the one she was looking for and inserted it into the lock. With a quick twist of her wrist, she opened the door, then stepped aside to allow Stephanie to enter.

I was putting the last few candlesticks into a cardboard box when I heard a scream.

Stephanie appeared at the door, her eyes wide, her mouth covered by trembling hands.

"Stephanie?" I said, rushing toward her. Goose bumps had broken out along my arms. "What's wrong? Is the projector gone?"

She shook her head, her hands slowly sliding down from her face.

"It's Levi! He's . . . dead!"

Chapter 12

PARTY PLANNING TIP #12

*You may think your Séance Party is unsuccessful if no
actual spirits appear. But look for subtle signs of their
presence, such as the smell of perfume, an odd
reflection in a nearby mirror, or a participant's sudden
feeling of trepidation.*

Levi? Dead?

Please, no.

I rushed into the room—big mistake when there's a dead
body inside—and saw Levi Webster slumped over his computer keyboard. The back of his head was a mass of thick,
coagulated blood, dotted with bits of white matter. Blood
had dripped down the side of his neck and seeped into his
T-shirt.

My stomach clenched.

"What happened?" Mia said, following me inside moments later. She gasped when she saw Levi's mutilated head
and slumped body. Meanwhile, Stephanie had pulled back at
the door and stood cringing at the sight.

"Stephanie! Call nine-one-one!" I yelled to her. No response, just a glazed look. "Stephanie! Now!"

"Okay . . ." she whimpered, finally withdrawing her cell phone.

"Don't touch anything," I told Mia, who was reaching to pick up something from the floor. I glanced down. A large brass candlestick lay at the back of Levi's feet. The corner of the heavy end was covered in blood.

"The candlestick," Mia whispered, recoiling her hand and crossing her arms over her chest. "It's like a real game of Clue. What do you think happened?"

I took a deep breath, trying to get control of my nausea. When the dizziness passed, I glanced around, avoiding looking at Levi's wound directly, and said, "It seems pretty obvious. Someone hit Levi, probably from behind, then dropped the candlestick, and ran." I glanced outside the open door and yelled, "Stephanie? Did you call?"

She appeared in the doorway, calmer now, more like her controlled self. "Yes, the police are on their way."

"Oh dear," Mia said. "I hate the thought of a bunch of police cars out front. Not good for business, you know."

I shot her a look that said, "This is not the time to be worried about appearances." Out loud I said, "A man has been murdered, Mia."

She nodded and stepped out of the room, and pulled out her cell phone. In spite of my urge to throw up, I remained in the room a few minutes, checking for any clue as to who might have killed Levi. Lyla? Jonathan?

It had happened as a result of my party and the weapon was one of my party props. I felt somewhat responsible. I knew once the police arrived, I wouldn't get another chance to do much investigating of my own. And the last time something like this happened, I was nearly arrested as a suspect. I wouldn't let that happen again.

I studied the crime scene, quickly making mental notes. Levi appeared to have been working on the computer, probably still trying to figure out what had gone wrong at the séance. His right hand was on the keyboard, the left had dropped to his side. He'd been struck from behind—that was clear. The door we'd entered was on his left side. It had been locked last night when I knocked on the door, I'd left it unlocked. Then it was locked again.

The bloody candlestick lay on the floor behind him. Hopefully there would be prints on the weapon, but my guess was, probably not. Even the dumbest criminals knew to wear gloves or wipe off prints after they'd killed their victims.

Unless it wasn't premeditated, or the killer was forced to leave quickly.

I checked the computer screen. It was dark. What had Levi been working on when he'd been attacked?

I looked around for something to use to tap a key and bring up the sleeping screen. I spotted a pencil at the far corner of the desk and picked it up by the tip. I held it over the computer keyboard and tapped a key with the eraser end.

The screen came alive, filled with a bunch of numbers, much like I'd seen the night before. Must have been some kind of coded program for the 4-D presentation that Jonathan had requested. Had Levi finally figured out what had caused the glitch?

Or who had hacked into the program?

I heard the sound of sirens in the distance. The police

would be here momentarily. I didn't want to be accused of "tampering" with the crime scene, so I stepped back into the ballroom, got out my iPhone, and called Brad. Glancing around while I waited for him to answer, I spotted Stephanie still on her phone and likewise Mia on hers. I left Brad a short message—something along the lines of "Come quick!"— then waited for the police to arrive.

Two uniformed officers from the San Jose Police Department cordoned off the room, while one of two detectives asked the three of us—Mia, Stephanie, and me—to stay until he could question us. We'd been waiting nearly thirty minutes when Brad finally arrived.

"Thank goodness you're here," I said, rushing up to him. "You'll never believe what happened . . ."

But he didn't look surprised at all. "I know. Someone found a body. I heard it on the police scanner. You okay?"

Of course he did. "It was Stephanie—she found him. She was pretty shaken up, although she seems better now."

"You okay? Of course, it's not like you've never seen a dead body before, right?"

"Very funny."

"Brad!" the taller, better-looking detective called as he strode over. Odd . . . he looked familiar. But I'd never had any dealings with the San Jose Police.

"Hey, Lonnie." Brad grinned widely and gave the officer a vigorous handshake. "Long time, no see. How's your golf game?"

"Better than yours," the detective replied.

"We'll have to see about that," Brad countered.

The two of them threw a few more manly barbs at each

other. Finally Brad remembered I existed and turned to me. "Presley, this is Lonnie Melvin. *Detective* Lonnie Melvin, that is. Congrats on passing the exam, by the way."

"Melvin?" I repeated, shaking his proffered hand. "You're not related to Detective Luke Melvin of the San Francisco Police Department, I hope."

"My big brother." He grinned proudly.

Oh boy. That was all I needed—another Melvin cop in my life. That was why he'd looked so familiar. I could see the resemblance, in spite of the fact that Lonnie had auburn hair, light freckles, and green eyes, while Luke Melvin was blue-eyed, black-haired, and freckle-free. Not to mention, always on my case. Two cops in the same family? They probably came from a long line of police officers. Lucky me.

Brad followed Lonnie to the crime scene, while I finished filling another box with mini Ouija board key chains. At the same time, questions kept popping into my head like inflated balloons. Last night I had deliberately left Levi's door ajar when I finished talking with him. This morning it was locked.

Had Levi shut and locked it? Or the killer?

If it was the killer, when had he arrived? Soon after the party broke up? Or sometime early this morning?

Had I been the one who inadvertently let him in by not closing the door? Or did Levi know the killer and let him in?

Or did the killer have a key?

The questions were driving me crazy. It would take a medical examiner, a trained detective, or a real psychic to determine some answers.

Mia approached me as I closed the box of party props.

"Who do you suppose did this?" she whispered. "Someone from the party last night?"

I wondered where her concern lay—for the dead man? Or for the reputation of the Winchester House? And I also wondered if her brief affair with Jonathan played any part in this.

"I don't know," I said. "Whoever it was obviously went in some time after we left last night. The door was open when I left Levi, but it was locked this morning because you had to use a key to get in."

"You know that's not the only entrance to the room, don't you?" Mia asked.

I blinked. I'd not thought of a second door—and certainly hadn't seen one when I went in there.

Mia went on. "I told you, this mansion is full of secret doors and hidden passageways. It's like something out of a Nancy Drew mystery. Some of the doors only open from one side, some lock automatically when they close, and some are just facades."

"So you're saying someone could have gotten into that room from another entrance?"

"In that particular room, yes. There's a door inside the closet. But we keep that door locked, too."

Two doors to one room. One hidden in a closet. Both supposedly locked.

"You don't think . . ." Mia began, then pressed her lips together as if trying to keep the words from pouring out.

"What?"

"Well, Lyla and Jonathan were really upset last night. Remember how they stormed out of here? Do you think one of them might have killed that poor computer guy? I'll bet Jonathan was furious at Levi for exposing all his secrets."

Where were Lyla and Jonathan?

No one had seen them since they'd left the party last night. According to Stephanie, Jonathan had not turned up at work, and Lyla had not answered the cell phone that was practically glued to her ear. Both seemed to have disappeared . . .

A balloon popped inside my head. Could they have disappeared into the Winchester Mystery House? Were they still here somewhere? Trapped? Lost? Hiding? There were so many places a person could be in this 160-room mansion.

Brad and Detective Lonnie Melvin reappeared from the crime scene. A forensics team had arrived to do their CSI thing. Dr. Vicki Huynh, the ME, according to her name tag, was the last to arrive—a petite, slim woman with short dark hair. Melvin began talking with her, while Brad sauntered on over to me.

"Do they have any ideas?" I asked Brad.

"Not yet. Hit over the head from behind. Don't know exactly how the killer got in—both doors were locked. Nothing seems to be missing."

He'd apparently found the hidden door—the one I had missed. I mentioned to Brad that I'd left the door open last night, then asked, "The killer just left all that expensive, high-tech equipment behind?"

"Appears so. But Lonnie will have his computer guys take a thorough look. Although someone could have downloaded something using a flash drive and just walked off with it."

I hadn't thought of that.

Two technicians brought out the body on a gurney, wrapped in an opaque plastic bag, and wheeled him out the main ballroom exit. Luckily, I couldn't see the wound, but the memory of what I had seen made the room spin again.

"You okay?" Brad asked, grabbing my arm.

"Fine," I said brushing him off.

"You sure?"

"Yes, of course."

"Okay. Well, it looks like they're done, so I better get to work." He gave me a last squeeze, then returned to the room where Levi had died. The body had been removed, but the blood remained, and that was Brad's jurisdiction.

"Miss Parker?" I heard my name called and turned to see Detective Luke Melvin's brother standing behind me.

"Yes?" I said. My heart began to beat rapidly. I was always nervous talking to Luke Melvin, and apparently it would be the same talking to Lonny Melvin.

"I just want to ask you a couple of questions. You're the one who found the body?"

"No, that was Stephanie. Mia let her into the office, Stephanie went in, she screamed. Then I went in."

He had already talked to Mia and Stephanie, so I wondered if this was a trick question, an attempt to trip me up and— What? Confess? That was what Luke Melvin would have done.

Lonnie Melvin asked a few more questions, jotted down a few notes, then said if I remembered anything else to call him. He gave me his card and returned to the crime scene.

Left on my own, I thought about poor Levi. More questions bubbled up like sparkling champagne.

Who had access to the room? Just about anyone who was at the party—the guests, the staff, even the caterers. And waiters.

Who had access to the candlestick? Likewise—anyone. Well, that narrowed it down.

I thought about MOM—one of the many things I'd learned from hanging out with Brad. Determine the Method, Opportunity, and Motive. Retrieving my notepad from my purse, I sat down, and jotted down some facts.

I knew the method—the heavy brass candlestick. I wrote that down, then added "Fingerprints?"

I'd learn the opportunity—the approximate time Levi was killed—when the ME came back with her results. I left a question mark.

But what was the motive? Why had Levi been murdered? I did a little brainstorming and came up with some possible motives:

1. Jonathan was enraged at Levi for embarrassing him at his own function. That was a strong one. Jonathan carried the candlestick out of the room and could easily have used it on Levi.

2. Lyla could have been furious at Levi for exposing something she may have already known—that her husband was a philanderer of epic proportions. And she could have bashed Levi's head in. I remembered Lyla having some sort of conversation with someone about a "surprise" she had planned. What was that about?

3. Girlfriends: Jonathan had allegedly slept with a number of the women who had been present at the party, and Levi had named them—Violet, the administrative assistant; Courtney, his limo driver; even Mia, the manager of the mansion. Maybe one of them had been

mad enough to hammer Levi for dragging her name through the mud.

4. Someone else at the party who had had a grudge against Levi, like one of the filmmakers or investors.
5. Someone trying to steal Jonathan's 4-D technology—and Levi was in the way.

I closed my notebook and stepped over to the doorway of the crime scene, blocked by yellow police tape. Brad was on his hands and knees in his white jumpsuit, pressing a cloth into the bloodstained carpet. Detective Melvin had disappeared.

"How's it going?" I asked.

He looked up. "We'll see. This carpet is hand-painted. It's really old and very delicate."

I looked over the Victorian carpet, with faded cabbage roses in peach and forest green. "Did you find anything . . . unusual yet?"

"You mean besides blood?"

I gave him a you-know-what-I-mean look. I'd also learned from Brad that everyone has secrets and that things are not always what they seem. He knew this because he'd uncovered a lot of secrets cleaning up after horrendous murder scenes—and probably had a few of his own.

He grinned, then added, "Oh. You mean a clue?"

"I was sorta hoping you might have stumbled onto something."

"Not yet," he said, pressing a fresh cloth on the stain. "You thinking about playing detective again?"

"Well, it happened on my watch," I said. "I feel a little responsible. Wouldn't you?"

"Nope. This had nothing to do with me or you. Like I always say, everyone—"

"—has secrets. I know. So what kind of secrets do you think Levi had?"

Brad sat up and opened a plastic bottle filled with liquid. As he poured it into a plastic bowl, the strong smell stung my nose. Ammonia. I waved my hand in a useless attempt to fan it away.

"Phew."

"Probably," he answered, opening another plastic bottle. He poured blue liquid that smelled like a flower garden into a plastic bowl. Dish detergent.

I watched him work for a few minutes, fascinated, as he dipped a toothbrush into the blue detergent and began to scrub the stain. Knowing how to get blood out of a carpet would no doubt be helpful for an event planner like me.

"Don't you need a bigger brush?" I asked.

"Nope. That'll just spread the blood." He blotted the wet area again with a dry cloth, turning the cloth pink. Then he poured a small amount of ammonia on the spot and let it set a few more seconds.

"Why the ammonia?" I said, nearly nauseated by the smell.

"Blood is made up of iron and proteins. Coagulation makes it harder to remove a dried stain. This breaks down the blood." He blotted again, then repeated the whole process, starting with the detergent and toothbrush, then the ammonia and cloth.

"That's it?" I said, watching the stain slowly disappear before my eyes.

"Pretty much. Sometimes I use a shop vac to suck up the

stuff. But not on this antique carpet. This one's going to take time."

"It's going to reek of ammonia."

"Naw. I'll rinse it with soapy water when I'm done, then blot it again. If that doesn't work, there's always meat tenderizer."

"You're kidding. Meat tenderizer?"

"Yep. The crystals break down the collagens in meat. They're made of enzymes from tropical fruits like papaya, pineapple, and kiwifruit. Meat tenderizer works on swollen joints and sports injuries too."

What didn't this man know?

I figured Brad was going to be a while, so I told him I'd see him later. I picked up my boxes and started out of the ballroom. I nearly bumped into Stephanie entering as I exited the main ballroom doorway and almost dropped the boxes. She caught the top one and said, "Let me help you out with this."

"Thanks, Stephanie."

"Have they released the crime scene yet?" she asked, as she followed me to the parking lot.

"Not yet. Most of the officers are gone—I didn't see Detective Melvin—but Brad is still working in there."

"Do you think they'll question everyone at the party?"

I set my box on the ground and pulled my key from my purse. "Yeah, the detective asked for the guest list."

"What about the 4-D Projector? I need to get that back to Hella-Graphics or Jonathan will have my butt."

"I think the police took it. They impounded Levi's computer and everything else." I opened the trunk and took the box from Stephanie.

She dropped her hands. "What? They took it? That equipment belongs to Hella-Graphics. It's invaluable IP—intellectual property!"

I lifted up my box and set it on top of the first box, then closed the trunk. "Why don't you call the San Jose Police Department and check with them? I'm sure they're planning to return everything to the company once they've gone over it."

"I hope so," she said, checking her watch and fiddling with the band. "If they don't, I'll sic the company lawyers on them to make sure nothing's leaked."

"Have you heard from Jonathan yet?"

"No. I'm seriously worried about him. You don't suppose . . . I mean, it's just that he seemed so upset . . ." Her voice drifted off again.

"Okay, well, I better go," I said awkwardly, and opened my car door. "I'm sure Jonathan will turn up, and you'll get your equipment back."

Stephanie didn't appear to be listening to me. I didn't blame her. My words rang false, even to me, considering the circumstances. But she seemed genuinely concerned about her boss. A fleeting thought went through my head as I closed the car door and started the engine.

Was it possible Stephanie was also having an affair with Jonathan?

By the time I returned to my office, I had a whole scenario going about who killed Levi Webster. I'd decided it was the guy who'd been harassing Jonathan. The guy who, in fact, had tried to kill him with his car. The way I imagined it, this Zachary character had followed Jonathan to the Winchester

House, waited for a chance to get him alone, found him in the room with Levi, grabbed the candlestick, slugged Jonathan over the head, killed Levi since he was a witness, dragged Jonathan's body away, and, and . . .

Where had that wild scenario come from? Good thing I had party planning skills to fall back on. I'd never make it as a mystery writer.

As soon as I'd unloaded the boxes from the MINI into my office, I plopped into my chair and checked my iPhone messages. There were three. The first was from Mother asking if I'd found Jonathan yet. No, Mom, I told her in my head. That was not my job. I was a party planner, not a host finder. I hadn't even talked to Detective Melvin about George Wells's questionable suicide for Teddi.

The second call was from a blocked number. A whispered voice came on the line; I could barely hear it. I had to listen twice to make out the message. "If Jonathan Ellington isn't caught soon, he'll come after you next. Watch your back."

I hung up, feeling a cold sweat break out.

WTF?

Somebody had just threatened me! And I hadn't done anything!

With trembling hands I checked the third call, wondering if it would be the same voice with another ominous message. But this voice was warm and familiar.

"Presley," Brad said. "Got some news you might be interested in. Call me back ASAP."

I took a deep breath, trying to calm my nerves—and my hands—so I could punch Brad's number. I waited for him to answer, my heart beating double time.

"Hey, Presley," he said.

"Brad! I just heard the strangest thing."

"You heard already? Personally, I don't think it's so strange."

"Heard what? What isn't so strange?" I was confused.

"Oh, I thought that's what you meant. That you'd heard my news already."

"No, tell me! What? Did you hear from the police?"

"Yep. They got a match on fingerprints they found on the murder weapon."

"Oh my God. There were fingerprints on the candlestick? Whose?"

"None other than your party host—Jonathan."

Wow. Even though I'd sort of suspected so, it felt like a kick to the stomach. So Jonathan *had* killed Levi after all. For exposing his sex secrets.

"Yeah, although I'm not surprised. I knew that guy was trouble. Now they've got him. So, what were you talking about—you heard something strange?" Brad asked.

I'd almost forgotten about the disturbing phone message. Suddenly it didn't seem so frightening.

"Uh, nothing really. I got a phone call from someone warning me about Jonathan. But now that he's been caught—"

"What did you say?" Brad interrupted.

"I said, now that Jonathan's been caught . . ."

"Oh no, Presley. I didn't say that. He hasn't been caught yet."

Oh God. Jonathan was still free? And according to that phone call, he was supposedly after me? But why? Did he think I knew something? I didn't know anything! What was there to know? That he was Levi's murderer?

I felt prickles of sweat break out on the back of my neck.

"Brad, I need you to come back to the office, as soon as you can," I said, my hands trembling once again. "I may be in some serious trouble."

Chapter 13

PARTY PLANNING TIP #13

You may want to use a Ouija board, also known as a "spirit board" or "talking board," during your Séance Party. No special psychic "gifts" are required for using a board; however, in the wrong hands the board can be used to summon evil "demons" instead of friendly Caspers.

It took Brad nearly an hour later to get to the office. By then I'd had enough caffeine to keep a narcoleptic awake; except for me, it did the opposite and calmed my trembling hands. Unfortunately, it didn't keep me from looking over my shoulder for a killer.

"Thank God!" I said as he walked into my office. I grabbed him and pulled him in the door.

"Whoa!" he said, trying to put his arms around me. He was still wearing his white jumpsuit, but there were pink stains on the knees. He usually kept his uniforms ghost white. "What's up? You sounded weird on the phone. Has something else happened?"

My iPhone rang before I could reply. I checked the caller ID. Another "unknown."

"It's him!" I whispered, even though I had no reason to whisper. I hadn't answered the phone yet.

"Who?"

"That guy who called earlier." I hushed him, then answered the phone, putting the caller on speakerphone so Brad could hear.

"Hello?" I said cautiously.

"Presley?"

This voice I recognized immediately.

"Jonathan!" I glanced at Brad. "Where are you?"

"Take me off speakerphone," he commanded. Brad nodded, watching me intently.

"Okay." I punched the button and lifted the phone to my ear.

"Jonathan," I repeated. "Where are you? What's happened?"

"Presley, I'm in trouble. Someone is trying to frame me for murder."

I picked up a pen and starting scribbling Jonathan's side of the conversation for Brad to read: "Someone framing him."

Brad rolled his eyes and made a "Yeah, sure" face.

"Frame you for what?"

A pause, then, "Murdering Levi." I wrote it down for Brad to see.

So Jonathan knew. Well, of course he knew. He was most likely the killer.

"Jonathan, you need to turn yourself in. Your dad is worried sick—"

"Listen, Presley. I don't have much time. I didn't kill Levi." His voice sounded strained as he spoke.

"If you're innocent, why not tell that to the police?" I asked. "Why call me?"

"Because I'm innocent, not stupid. The police think I did it."

"How do you know?"

"I know some people. Listen, Presley, you're the only one I can trust at this point."

"Why me? I can't do anything—"

"My dad really likes you. He told me how you solved another murder."

"My mother talks too much," I said.

"So do you. Stop talking and listen. You're the only one because, well, my other relationships are . . . complicated."

In other words, he hadn't slept with me like he had so many of the others. I didn't write that down for Brad to see. Instead, Brad grabbed the pen and wrote, "Ask him where he is!!!"

I held up a finger, asking him to wait. "But what can I do . . ."

"Find out who's trying to pin this on me. I'm sure it's someone out for revenge."

"What about Zachary—the guy who tried to run you down in the parking lot?"

"I thought about that, but when I went to his apartment, he'd disappeared. Packed up his stuff and moved out."

"So what do you want me to do? I can't—"

"Find Zachary. He must have found out about the party. He's the only one besides Levi who could rig the 4-D with that other voice telling everyone about my . . . personal business."

"How am I supposed to find him if he's disappeared?"

Brad shook his head and underlined "Ask him where he is."

"Presley, if you won't do it for me, then do it for the money. I can't pay you until all of this is cleared up."

"That's blackmail, Jonathan," I said angrily.

Brad pointed to the sentence he'd underlined.

"Where are you, Jonathan? How do I contact you if I find out—"

"I'll contact you. Gotta go."

The line went dead.

I looked up at Brad. My hand was cramped from writing down Jonathan's words and I stretched out my fingers.

"Did he tell you where he is?" Brad asked.

I shook my head.

"But he wants your help."

"Apparently."

Brad's eyes narrowed. "And you're planning to help him?"

"I would, but I haven't a clue how," I said.

"Well, let me fill you in some more on Jonathan Ellington." From Brad's harsh tone, I could tell he was irritated by Jonathan's call and his request for my help. He began ticking off his fingers as he listed his reasons for having me back off.

"One, Motive. He's angry at the victim for humiliating him in front of everyone. Two, Opportunity. He went in the room where Levi was alone after we'd all left. Three, Method. The candlestick was covered with his fingerprints. San Jose PD has issued a warrant for his arrest, and if you do

anything to interfere with that—or help him in any way—
the cops will get you for aiding and abetting a suspect who's
wanted for first-degree homicide."

"Thanks for the lecture," I said, throwing my pen down.

"I'm just saying . . ." He held up his hands in a gesture of
surrender.

"You're saying I don't know how to think for myself. Listen, I'm not about to do anything stupid."

Brad said nothing. Good thing or I would have whacked
him with a candlestick if I'd had one handy.

My phone rang, interrupting our little spat. This time I
recognized the ringtone: "San Francisco, open your golden
gate . . ."

"Hi, Mother." I shot a look at Brad. His face relaxed when
he learned it was Mother and not Jonathan again.

"Presley, dear, are you all right?"

"Of course, Mother. How are you? And how's Stephen?"

"Oh, I'm fine, but Stephen's not doing so well."

"What's wrong? Did he have another stroke?"

"No, no, but he's terribly upset, what with all that's going
on with his son."

"I can imagine. You two haven't seen Jonathan by any
chance, have you?"

Brad sat up. His eyebrows rose in anticipation.

"No, and that's what's worrying Stephen so much. Jonathan either calls or comes by faithfully every day, but Stephen hasn't heard a word from him. And Jonathan's not
answering his phone."

I shook my head at Brad. He sat back in his chair.

I hesitated to tell her the news—that the police were looking for Jonathan to arrest him for murder. I decided to play dumb.

"Well, if I hear from him, I'll let you know."

"So he hasn't been arrested yet?" Mother asked.

Ah, she did know.

I sighed. "Not yet, Mom. But I'm sure they'll clear all of this up."

"Stephen insists that Jonathan is not capable of murder. Yes, his son has done a few things that Stephen isn't proud of, but he's certain murder isn't one of them."

Most parents felt that way about their kids—that they could do no wrong. I'm sure my mother would say the same thing if I'd killed someone. Not that I would. But still . . .

"Presley . . ."

"Yes, Mom."

"Stephen has a favor to ask."

Not another one. It was the "favor" of hosting a Séance Party at the Winchester Mystery House that had gotten me into this mess.

I sighed. "What is it, Mother?"

"Will you do what you can to find the real killer and clear Jonathan? It would mean so much to him—and me."

"Mother, I'm not a cop! I can't—"

"I know, dear, but you've helped the police before. I'm sure you can do it again. And I know Brad will help. He seems to have connections with that nice detective— What was his name?"

"Luke Melvin." My nemesis.

"Well, I'm counting on you. And I'm happy to help in any way I can. I enjoy being your sidekick."

OMG.

"I'll do my best, Mom."

"Thank you, dear. Oh, and something else that's very important. The next time you're at Nordy's, will you pick up one of those Lancôme gift specials for me? It's quite a bargain."

"Sure, Mom. I'll stop by and see you later, too."

I hung up.

"Your mother's putting you in charge of the case?" Brad asked, grinning.

"Of course. She thinks I can do anything."

"Well, if you want my advice, stay out of it."

I'd like to stay out of it, I thought, remembering the phone call warning me about Jonathan. But when I talked with him, he didn't sound at all threatening. Instead he sounded desperate and frightened.

Brad rose to leave.

"Did the police find anything else?" I asked.

"Yeah, I forgot to tell you. The system recovery guys at SJPD found evidence of some recent e-mails on Jonathan's computer that had been deleted."

"E-mails? Really? Jonathan said he rarely used e-mail, and that he preferred to text. What did they say?"

"They're still working on that, but I should hear from Lonnie soon. I do know that some of the e-mails were sent to someone named Dane Scott. But that's about all they have at this point."

Dane Scott.

I was sure the police had checked out the name by now, but that wouldn't stop me from doing the same. As soon as Brad left my office.

*　　*　　*

After promising Brad I wouldn't do anything stupid, I Googled "Dane Scott" the moment my office door closed behind him. The name turned up several hundred hits. I started at the top and clicked on the first link: Stereo-ScopeGraphics.com. A Web site with lots of bells and whistles. The name of the company—STEREO-SCOPE GRAPHICS—blazed across the top in giant red letters. Underneath were the words, "The Premiere 3-D Company." Next came a brief description of the company's products, things like RealD, 3DX, and TDV.

Scrolling down I found links to Future Developments, Conventions, Latest News, and so on. Finally, at the bottom in small print, were the usual business links: Public Relations, Product Sales, Job Opportunities, About Us, and Contact Us.

I clicked About Us. Up popped a series of color head shots of the company executives. Dane Scott was centered, grinning at the camera, with a brief bio underneath. He looked about Jonathan's age—thirtysomething—with dark curly hair, puffy cheeks, and a bronze complexion. I didn't recognize him as one of the guests at the Séance Party. I read over his bio, which included his title of CEO, his engineering and computer background, how his start-up company had expanded over the past couple of years, and his outlook for the future. At the end was an explanation of the company name. "Since Sir Charles Wheatstone invented 3-D in 1838, we've come a long way from the stereoscopes that delighted your great-grandparents at San Francisco's Playland at the Beach and the Cliff House's Musée Mécanique."

Aha. So this Dane Scott character was in the same business as Jonathan—a competitor who was also working on 3-D of the future. Jonathan had apparently sent him e-mails and then deleted them. Could he be mixed up in this?

I scanned down, checking out the executive VPs, then general managers, then managers, when my eyes caught on another head shot near the bottom of the company hierarchy under managers. This one looked vaguely familiar. It was a picture of a younger man, maybe twenty-five, clean-shaven, with short brown hair and round beady eyes. For a few seconds I couldn't place where I'd seen him.

I read a little more about the company on the Web site. Coincidentally, Stereo-Scope Graphics was also planning to launch a "revolutionary new product in the exciting field of 3-D." According to the latest press release:

". . . With our new product," Dane promised, "which we're calling SS-D, the people on your screen won't just pop out at you. They'll sit next to you, meet you face-to-face, and even give you a kiss. You'll feel like you're in the action, not just watching it. SS-D is the future of movies and television, and we're on the forefront of this exciting breakthrough!"

And then my memory cells kicked in.

With a mustache, glasses, and black wig, he suddenly became the clumsy waiter at Jonathan's Séance Party.

Chapter 14

PARTY PLANNING TIP #14

If, during your Séance Party, an unpleasant spirit appears and says things like, "You're all going to die," ask that spirit to leave. If that doesn't work, end the séance and perhaps begin an exorcism.

The impostor/waiter's name was Jerry Thompson. What had he called himself at the party? Joe something? According to his bio, he'd been a computer tech who had worked his way up to manager at Stereo-Scope Graphics. Sounded like he was on the fast track. Apparently his job description included corporate spy. In his ten-cent getup, Jonathan must not have recognized him at the party.

What had Dane Scott and Jerry Thompson hoped to achieve by infiltrating Jonathan's Séance Party? I'd heard Stephanie tell the police she was worried about the intellectual property.

Did they plan to steal the 4-D idea? Or the actual product?

And had Levi gotten in the way of that goal?

It was time to add Dane Scott and Jerry Thompson to my list of suspects, headed by Jonathan and Lyla. Maybe Jonathan wasn't lying and he really didn't kill Levi. Maybe the guys from Stereo-Scope Graphics were trying to make him look like the murderer. They certainly had motive—to ruin Hella-Graphics. Jerry Thompson had opportunity, being at the party. And the candlestick provided the means.

I reviewed my short list of suspects—Jonathan, Lyla, Zachary, Dane Scott, and Jerry Thompson. Now it was time to start scratching them off. It would be easier putting on a wine tasting for Alcoholics Anonymous than figuring out if Jonathan was really innocent.

Like I do when I've signed to do a party, I pulled out a planning spreadsheet. Actually my spreadsheet looks more like a family tree. When planning a party, I start at the top of the tree with the name of the event and the host. Underneath are branches for various aspects of the party—the invitations, decorations, costumes, games/activities, refreshments, and favors. Farther down are twigs for more details under each category, such as what kind of invitation, when they're sent out, who's on the guest list, the RSVPs, and so on.

This time, instead of writing the name of the party host at the top—Jonathan Ellington—I wrote Levi's name. In the row of spaces underneath, I filled in the names of the suspects, and under each I added details—their possible motives (competition, jealousy, humiliation, etc.), their relationships to one another (sex, friendship, employer), their secrets (multiple affairs, corporate spying, blackmail), and anything else I could think of.

I soon had a tree full of bad apples. But which one was rotten to the core?

I reviewed the sheet, trying to imagine why each suspect might have killed Levi.

Jonathan Ellington: revenge? Levi had exposed Jonathan's secret affairs and humiliated him. Or so it seemed.

Lyla Ellington: revenge? She was also embarrassed in public by having such a scoundrel for a husband, so perhaps she killed Levi to frame Jonathan. Question: Would she inherit the company if Jonathan went to prison for murder?

Zachary Samuels: revenge? He was fired and replaced by Levi, so maybe he wanted to frame Jonathan. Question: Would he benefit in another way?

Dane Scott/Jerry Thompson: greed? The CEO and his spy from Stereo-Scope Graphics might have wanted Jonathan out of the way so they could present their own cutting-edge 3-D product. Question: Or did they plan to steal Jonathan's 4-D Projector and claim it as their own?

I added a few more names to the spreadsheet.

Violet Vassar: revenge? Was she angry about Jonathan cheating on her and embarrassing her in public? Or did she have another reason, such as blackmailing Jonathan or she'd go public with his sex addiction? And what about the other women he'd seduced?

With a couple of spaces left, I added two more names—Stephanie Bryson, the VP of Hella-Graphics, and Mia Thiele, the manager of the mystery house—although their motives were weak.

Would Stephanie be next in line at Hella-Graphics if Jonathan was gone? And had she also had an affair with Jonathan that wasn't revealed at the séance?

As for Mia, did she kill Levi because he revealed her one-night stand with Jonathan? Or could she have had another reason?

Like I said, weak.

With party requests piling up and an urgent need for cash—now that I wouldn't be seeing a check from Jonathan anytime soon, I set my suspect tree aside and worked on my Killer Party business, even though it was Sunday. In the event-planning business, the hostess never sleeps.

Delicia came in to the office around noon to pick up some costume parts I kept handy. She was up for a part in a local commercial for the San Francisco Department of Tourism and was trying to win the job by getting Berk to videotape her wearing appropriate outfits at various popular sites. She'd planned to pose on Alcatraz in a black-and-white-striped prison uniform, dress up as Cinderella for the San Francisco Opera House, wear a Cable Car uniform on a ride up steep California Street, and sport a San Francisco Giants outfit while tossing a ball at AT&T Park. I was tired just watching her pick out the clothes.

When Brad popped by at five o'clock, I hadn't done a thing about proving Jonathan's innocence.

"Hungry?" he said, stepping inside. He'd exchanged his crime scene suit for jeans and a blue T-shirt, which outlined his muscular chest and set off his strong arms. For a moment, I didn't think he was referring to food.

"Starving," I said, coming to my senses. I saved my work and shut down my laptop.

"How about dinner at a special place I know. Heard the food is great, the view spectacular, and the ambience cozy and romantic."

"How could I resist that?" I gathered my purse and notes, and walked with him out to the parking lot. Working inside all afternoon, I hadn't noticed the fog had rolled in. I shivered.

Before we got far, someone called his name, "Braaaaddd!"

I turned to see Marianne, the TI administrator and person who held my rent fee over my head, hustling out of Building One to catch up with us. She wore what looked like a tie-dyed muumuu and sandals. Her shoulder-length brown hair was highlighted several shades of blond.

"Hi, Presley," she said to me, then turned her attention to Brad. "Glad I caught you, Brad. My computer just froze. Any chance you could take a look at it? You're so good with computers, and I'm desperate."

Brad glanced at me for permission. I blinked once for "Fine. Go do it."

"Sure, I'll take a look." To me he said, "I'll be right back."

Brad and Marianne returned to the building entrance and disappeared inside, leaving me standing in the parking lot alone. What was she doing here on a Sunday, running around in a cloud of tropical flowers and sandals? And what was up with the "helpless me" act?

Duh. Marianne was hot for Brad.

I decided to walk to the edge of the Bay, just across the street from the admin building. Staring out at the San Francisco city skyline, the tips of the buildings covered in fog, the lights beginning to sparkle, I started to think of ways to get rid of Marianne. That led me to thinking about Jonathan again—whether he was guilty, what I could do to help him if he was innocent. I was conflicted about his claims that he didn't kill Levi, and it had left me paralyzed and unable to start investigating.

A thought occurred to me as I sat on a large rock and looked down at the water: Almost all the motives I'd listed on my spreadsheet involved revenge. I knew revenge was a powerful motive for retaliation—and murder. I'd even been thinking of ways to off Marianne. Jonathan certainly could have wanted revenge for what Levi had done to him.

So how did George Wells tie into all of this? I was sure he was somehow connected to this family tree. But George Wells was an orange among apples. Still, I added his name to the list, reminding myself that I'd promised to help his wife, Teddi. I had to find out more about him.

My daydreaming was interrupted by a tap on the shoulder. Startled, I whirled around.

"You scared me!" I said, feeling my face flush at the sight of Brad.

"You were deep in thought," Brad said. "That kind of scares me too."

"Very funny." I took his proffered hand and rose up from the rocky seat.

"Shall we go?"

"You're finished? Did you fix her computer?"

He nodded innocently.

"So what was wrong with it?"

"Nothing. Too many open files caused it to freeze up. I just rebooted and it worked fine."

"I'll bet," I said under my breath. She probably did it on purpose.

The evening westerly was picking up and I pulled my arms in close to keep out the chill.

"You cold?" he asked. "My jacket's over there." He pointed back to the parking lot.

"I'll be fine in the car," I said, glancing around for his ride. "Where's your SUV?"

He pressed his lips together.

"Oh no, you didn't. You brought your *bike*?"

I spotted his motorcycle parked off to the side of the admin building. When we reached it, he pulled two black leather jackets from a sort of locked dashboard and helped me slip it on. He shrugged into his own jacket, then handed me a helmet.

Oh my God. By the time we reached the restaurant, my hair would be flat, my face would be red, and my hands would be too cold to open a menu.

"Hop on," he said, seating himself up front. I hopped onto the back, wrapped my arms around his tight waist, and hung on for dear life.

Marianne could bite me.

Before I could even get somewhat comfortable in my seat, we were zooming up Macalla Drive. Seconds later we crossed over to hilly Yerba Buena Island and practically flew around the hairpin curves. The smell of eucalyptus trees filled my nostrils, and I caught quick glimpses of colorful flowers as we whizzed by former military housing. How strange it was to go from bare flatlands to lush green hills in less than five minutes. YB was another world. Moments later Brad pulled up to a large white two-story house and killed the engine.

I got off the bike, unclasped the helmet, and looked up at the elegant home that once belonged to an Admiral Bryson, according to the name plate on the steps that led to the front door. "This is impressive," I said. "You live here?"

In all the time I'd known Brad—and granted that wasn't so long—I'd never been to his place.

Brad took my hand and led me up the steps to the porch. Across the top of the door and at the bottom were strips of yellow crime scene tape that read "Police Line—Do Not Cross."

I looked at Brad, waiting for an explanation. Was this building also condemned? Or had some kind of crime occurred here?

He stuck a key in the lock and opened the door. "That's just to keep nosy people away. I got the tape from Luke Melvin. You wouldn't believe the number of curious visitors who come snooping around."

He pointed to several other large homes close by. "I moonlight as the caretaker of these old historic homes. That one down at the end is where Admiral Nimitz used to live. Now they rent it out for special events. Meanwhile, I keep an eye on the place—and my rent is free."

I was quickly learning that Brad was quite the negotiator when it came to living quarters. After scanning the spectacular view of the Bay Bridge from his front porch, I stepped over the bottom stretch of tape and entered the front hall. On the right was a parlor, with a crystal chandelier, hardwood floors, and wainscoting on the wall. It was absent any furniture. On the left, a formal dining room was identical to the parlor except for a small table and a couple of folding chairs in the middle. I wanted to rush out and buy him some furnishings from IKEA until he led me to the back of the first floor. On the right was a huge kitchen, and on the left what may have been the admiral's study.

But Brad had transformed it into his own man cave.

A huge black leather couch and Papa Bear–sized chair occupied most of the room. A mega flat-screen TV dominated the wall facing the couch, flanked by a variety of entertainment systems—a DVD player, Xbox, PlayStation, CD player, and other electronic gizmos every man thinks he must have in order to survive.

Brad gestured for me to sit down on the couch and quickly poured me a glass of wine. He set it on the glass coffee table that held a laptop, some paperwork, and, oddly, some small toy cars. I picked up what looked like a race car and asked, "Do you play with these in your spare time?"

"No," Brad called from the kitchen. "Those are for—"

The doorbell rang.

"Just a sec." He sprinted for the door. Curious about who'd be calling at a home with crime scene tape covering the door, I followed him. In the open doorway stood a little boy of about five or six, big eyed, rosy cheeked, and holding a leash that led to a small furry ball of white fluff.

"Spencer! How you doin'? How was Bruiser today?" Brad knelt down and began petting the dog. When he saw me come up behind him, he stood. "Presley, I'd like you to meet Spencer Brien. Spencer lives next door with his mom, Sansa. He takes care of Bruiser while I'm at work, don't you, Spence?"

The boy nodded proudly as he handed the leash over to Brad.

Brad picked up the dog and cradled it in his arm. "Were you a good boy today, Bruiser?"

Spencer grinned, revealing a gaping hole where a bottom tooth had once been. "He was real good, Uncle Brad. We went to the park and he didn't run away or anything." Spencer couldn't quite manage his "s" or "r" sounds, which only made him even cuter. I wanted to give his buzz-cut hair a noogie.

Instead, I leaned over and noogied the dog. "Oh my God. This is Chou-Chou! Mary Lee's dog."

Mary Lee Miller had hired me to do a party at the de Young Museum recently. When she died under tragic circumstances, Brad had somehow ended up with her puffy purse poodle. I thought he'd unload the dog as soon as he could find a home for it. Apparently I was wrong.

Brad grinned. "His name is Bruiser now, not Chou-Chou. And yes, I still have him. I haven't found a place for him yet. Besides, Spencer is a great dog nanny. I pay him five dollars a week to watch Bruiser for me when I'm gone."

I laughed. "Well, this is yet another side to Brad Matthews I haven't witnessed. Maybe you could bring Chou—I mean, Bruiser—over for a playdate with my cats sometime."

"Are you kidding? Those cats would turn him into pillow stuffing before I could say 'bad kitties.'"

After Spencer left, Brad returned to the kitchen to finish preparing whatever it was that smelled so good—something garlicky. Chou-Chou/Bruiser seemed excited to see me, although I had a feeling he was always like that. Eventually he calmed down and took his spot on a small rug near the giant chair.

"Dinner is served," Brad announced, and I followed him into the dining room, where he dimmed the lights and lit candles. All we needed was a crystal ball to reenact the séance. The Crock-Pot chicken cacciatore turned out to be better than anything I'd ordered in the city's Little Italy district.

Avoiding the subject of Jonathan, I asked about Spencer.

"His mother, Sansa, is a single mom. She had a home business—she's a notary—and lives in one of the smaller units around the corner. Spencer loved Bruiser, so I asked his mom if I could hire him for doggy day care when I'm gone."

"I still can't believe you kept the dog. He looks—and acts—like a completely different dog! And he's not pink anymore. So how did you manage to cure his ADHD?"

"I don't think he liked having his fur dyed pink. Made him defensive. He's a lot calmer now."

"Didn't Corbin want it?"

"Mary Lee's son? Nope. Told me to do whatever I wanted with him." Brad cleared away the dishes and asked, "Dessert?" returning with two small cups of what looked like chocolate mousse.

Oh my God. This guy could cook a meal, fix a computer, break into a house, take care of an obnoxious dog, moonlight as a caretaker, and remove blood from an antique carpet. He also liked kids, tolerated cats (even with his allergies), and looked hot in a black leather jacket and black jeans.

What did I need with dessert?

Chapter 15

PARTY PLANNING TIP #15

If, during your Séance Party, a participant slips into a trance, do NOT attempt to awaken him. Let him return to consciousness gradually. Caveat: Beware of jokesters who think pretending to be in a trance is amusing.

I woke up to someone sloppily kissing my face. When I opened my eyes, I realized it wasn't Brad. The Dog Formerly Known as Chou-Chou was giving me a tongue bath. A little disoriented in the unfamiliar surroundings, I tried to get my bearings. I was in Brad's house, in Brad's bed, with Brad. And Bruiser.

Brad was snoring lightly, an arm draped across his eyes to block out the early-morning sun that streamed in from the upstairs bedroom window. I slipped out of bed, pulled on my jeans and T-shirt, and headed downstairs to the kitchen to make us lattes. I must have hit every creaky floorboard in the house.

Bruiser followed me down, either eager for a latte too, or hoping for something more doggylike. If he was anything like my cats, he'd want his bowl of food first thing. I found a bag of generic kibble food on top of the refrigerator, located a cereal bowl in a corner of the kitchen, and filled it up. He was gobbling up the bits before I finished pouring.

This was not the high-maintenance dog that had once belonged to a high-maintenance woman and traveled in a Coach handbag. What had Brad done to him? Taken him to obedience school? Given him Valium?

I petted the top of his curly white mop, which he ignored, too busy chomping down bits of food, then washed my hands.

Unlike mine, Brad's kitchen was fully stocked. I kept only enough sustenance to stay alive in emergencies, while Brad had stored enough food to feed the Donner Party for a year. After getting the espresso machine started, I cracked a half dozen eggs, whipped them in a bowl with some milk and shredded cheddar cheese, and poured the mess in a saucepan. I hoped the fragrant aroma of sizzling eggs would wake Brad so we could get this day started. I had a lot on my to-do list and it had kept me sleeping fitfully during the night.

I heard a creaking floorboard.

"Mmmm. I love the smell of burning food in the morning." Brad stood in the kitchen entryway in his blue velour bathrobe that came to just above his knees and did nothing to cover his broad chest. Wish I looked so good in the morning.

"Burned toast." I said. "The burned lattes are on the table. The burned eggs will be ready in a minute."

"Cool. I'll go put on some pants and get the fire extinguisher."

"Ha. Ha," I said. He didn't really need the pants, I thought, as I transferred the salvaged omelet onto a plate. When he returned, he was wearing jeans and his bloodred T-shirt with the logo: "Crime Scene Cleaners: Our Day Begins When Yours Ends."

After breakfast and more witty repartee, I excused myself to take a quick shower, then gathered up my things.

"Where're you headed this morning?" Brad asked, picking up Bruiser and tickling him under his chin.

"I thought I'd go over to Hella-Graphics, talk to some of the employees there. I think you're right about George Wells, the assumed suicide. He's tied to this somehow. I'm hoping to find someone who knows something—and will talk about it."

"How're you getting in? The security there is pretty tight. I even had trouble when I went over to clean up after Wells's death. I don't think they'll let you in with your 'balloon delivery' trick."

"Got a better idea."

"What's that?"

"I called Stephanie Bryson and told her I needed to talk with her about something. I'm meeting her there in an hour. Once I'm in, I plan to snoop around a bit." I headed for the door, then turned back. "See you later?"

"Sure. I'll come visit you in jail when you get arrested."

"For what?" I said, frowning at his little joke.

He grinned. "Corporate espionage? Illegal trespassing? Impersonating a police officer?"

I rolled my eyes and closed the door behind me.

*   *   *

I pulled up to the Hella-Graphics lot on the Presidio campus and parked the MINI in a visitor's space. The fog had lifted early, exposing a gently rolling lawn, a small waterfall that led to a stream, and lush landscaping throughout. The buildings looked more like college dormitories than former military housing and offices. Employees with badges hanging around their necks held to-go coffees as they headed for work. I glanced around at the nearly full lot and saw no sign of Jonathan's Mercedes among the numerous BMWs, Volvos, and Priuses. Not surprising, now that he was wanted on suspicion of murder. I wondered where he was hiding.

I was about to get out of the car when I caught a glimpse of a dirty BMW parked in a loading zone. I noticed it because a man in a baseball cap and sunglasses was sitting in the car, watching me. The car's right bumper sported a large dent.

I recognized it immediately—it was the same car that had struck Jonathan's Mercedes in the Winchester Mystery House parking lot.

The driver had to be the menacing and mysterious Zachary Samuels.

And he was looking right at me.

"Miss? Do you have business here?"

I about jumped out of my seat. A security guard was hunched over, peering in my window.

"Uh, yes. I'm here to see Stephanie Bryson at Hella-Graphics."

"You'll need a temporary parking permit. You can get it from their office."

"Thank you," I said, and watched him walk away. I

glanced back at Zachary. He, too, was watching the guard. As soon as the guard disappeared from sight, Zachary got out of the car, without giving me another look.

He hadn't been watching me after all. He'd been watching the guard.

I scooted down in my seat before he spotted me—not that he'd necessarily recognize me, but I didn't want to take a chance. Plus, I was curious as to what he was doing at Hella-Graphics, showing up so boldly like he was. Stephanie'd said he'd been fired, so I assumed he was persona non grata at the company. Was he planning to just waltz in?

In addition to the cap and sunglasses, he wore a dark green hoodie, jeans, and athletic shoes, and was carrying a bag. As he headed toward the building, I could read the lettering on the back of his hoodie: SUBWAY.

SUBWAY? As in sandwiches?

There was something off about the letters. While they were white and yellow like the official logo, they looked like standard iron-ons, not the SUBWAY font. Was he using this corny ruse to get himself into the building? And would it work? In such a simple disguise, wouldn't he be recognized immediately by the receptionist?

This I had to see.

I opened the door slowly, slipped out, and scrunched down behind my car, craning my neck to see where he was going. To my surprise, he didn't continue to the front entrance of Hella-Graphics. Instead, he pulled his cap down even farther, glanced from side to side, and walked briskly to the left side of the building.

It was time to take action. If I didn't keep up with him, I'd lose him. I followed him, keeping my distance and trying to look casual and to blend in among the several dozen people passing by.

Suddenly he stopped halfway down the side of the building and pulled out his cell phone. His thumbs moved rapidly over the display. Seconds later he stuffed the phone back into his jacket pocket and glanced around again.

I pulled back behind a tree and took out my own cell phone, trying to look occupied in case he spotted me.

Out of the corner of my eye, I caught movement and looked over. A side door had opened near where the man stood. I couldn't see who'd opened the door, and before I knew it, Zachary Samuels—if that was who it was—had sneaked inside Hella-Graphics.

Someone who worked there had let him in.

I stepped out from behind the tree, stunned at what had just happened. An innocent party planner like me couldn't get past the front door, and a possible killer just walked right in. I guess you had to know the secret knock.

I crossed over to the front entrance and rang the bell. A voice came over the intercom: "Yes, may I help you?"

"Presley Parker to see Stephanie Bryson," I announced, with a hint of entitlement in my voice. I wasn't about to be turned away at the gate this time. Not when I was expected by Jonathan's VP.

A buzzer sounded. I pushed open one of the double glass doors and slipped inside before the receptionist changed her mind.

"Sign in, please," she reminded me.

I performed the ritual with a flourish and set the pen down, meeting the receptionist's watchful eyes.

"I'll let her know you're here. Please have a seat." She handed me a visitor badge.

With a nod, I chose a chair opposite the little 3-D mice and watched them while I waited for Stephanie. Nearly thirty minutes later, I had read all my e-mail messages, sent out half a dozen of my own, added Zachary's suspicious entry into Hella-Graphics to my notes, cleaned out my purse, read the latest issue of *Computer Graphics* magazine, and counted the number of employees who passed by: forty-eight.

I thought about making a run for Stephanie's office—what would the receptionist do? Call security? Have me arrested? Instead, I rose and returned to the front desk.

"I'm sorry, but could you check on Stephanie Bryson? I've been waiting over half an hour for her."

The young woman, who had piercings through her lip, eyebrow, and nose, sighed, lifted the phone, and punched a number. "Stephanie, you have a visitor." She paused, then said, "Okay," and hung up the phone.

"She'll be right here."

I frowned at her, puzzled. That was what she'd said thirty minutes ago. Had she forgotten to call Stephanie the first time? I decided to loiter near the front desk rather than disappear into one of the comfy chairs, to make sure the receptionist didn't forget me again.

Seconds later Stephanie appeared from the company's inner sanctum.

"Hi, Presley," she said warmly, reaching out a hand. "Hope you haven't been waiting long."

I took her hand and shook it, a little surprised by her unapologetic greeting. "Uh . . . no . . . uh . . . a few minutes." I decided to let it go, figuring she hadn't gotten the original message that I was waiting for her. Stupid receptionist. What was her name? I'd have to remember her.

"Any news on Jonathan?" I asked, anxious to hear if he'd contacted her.

She glanced around sharply, then said, "Let's go to my office."

I followed her down the hallway, stealing glimpses into rooms filled with employee amenities and envious of all that Hella-Graphics had to offer. I really needed to submit an application. Surely they needed a party girl.

Stephanie closed the office door behind me and gestured toward a chair. She took her seat behind her usually pristine desk, now filled with piles of paperwork. I imagined Jonathan's absence had caused her workload to increase.

"So, any news on Jonathan?" I repeated, leaning forward.

She shook her head. "I'm really worried. The police have been here twice, but they don't have any news either. They're saying his fingerprints were on the candlestick that struck Levi, but I just can't believe Jonathan would do something like that. I think something's happened to him."

"What about Lyla? Has she turned up?" The way they'd behaved the other night had me worried about her safety too.

"Oh yes. She called me yesterday when Jonathan didn't come home. She thought he might be at the office—he's here practically twenty-four-seven. She hasn't seen him either."

I nodded. "Well, at least she's safe. Where is she, by the way—at their home?"

"Yes, she said she wanted to be there in case he showed up. The police searched the home but they found no sign of him. I just don't know what to think."

I sat back in my chair a moment, composing my thoughts. Lyla was back, but Jonathan was still missing. Interesting. I wondered if I should I share with Stephanie the phone call I'd received from Jonathan, or keep that to myself? At this point, I didn't know who to trust.

"Stephanie, do you have any idea why Levi did what he did—why he exposed all of Jonathan's affairs in front of everyone? Did he have some kind of grudge against Jonathan?"

Stephanie folded her perfectly manicured hands on her desk. "Not that I know of. Levi was an odd guy, granted, but then aren't all computer programmers?" She hinted at a smile. "Maybe he was jealous. He wasn't much of a social guy, unlike Jonathan. Maybe he had a crush on one of the women Jonathan had been . . . er, seeing . . . and figured that was the best way to get revenge. Who knows? I just hope they find Jonathan soon and get this all cleared up. We need him here. My work has grown exponentially." She glanced at the stacks of papers on her desk.

"When I talked with Levi after the party, he denied having anything to do with changing the recording. Do you think that's true?"

"Hard to believe, since he was the only one operating the 4-D," Stephanie replied. "There aren't too many employees who know how to operate it. It's certainly way over my head."

I took in a long breath and let it out slowly as I thought of the last time I'd seen Levi. He looked as if he were really trying to fix the machine rather than sabotage it. Was he just covering for himself? Or was he an innocent bystander?

"Do you know anyone else who might have wanted to kill

Levi—or ruin Jonathan by making it look like he murdered Levi? Did someone else have a grudge against him?"

"Oh, Jonathan had plenty of enemies. I suppose any of those women who were mentioned during the séance could have been angry enough to kill Levi for exposing them. Then again, maybe one of the guests had a problem with Levi—a former employer, maybe? Or maybe someone in competition with Jonathan—"

I sat up. "Like Dane Scott from Stereo-Scope Graphics?"

Stephanie pulled at the crystal around her neck. "How do you know about Dane?"

"The Internet," I said simply. Claiming the Internet as a resource was as easy—and believable—as it was vague.

She looked down at her desk, as if searching for an answer among the many papers that littered it. "Um, I . . . really can't discuss our competition. But, sure, Dane was always trying to find out what Jonathan had up his sleeve. He's as competitive as Jonathan. There was no love lost there."

"Do you know anyone named Jerry Thompson?" I asked.

She thought for a moment, then said, "I don't think so. No. Who is he? Another suspect?"

I saw no reason not to tell her. "He works at Stereo-Scope, too, as a manager."

Stephanie dropped the crystal and refolded her hands. "And how does he figure in?"

"I saw him at the Séance Party."

Her eyes flared. "What? Someone from Stereo-Scope? That's impossible."

"Well, he was disguised. He wore one of the phoniest

mustaches I've ever seen. Plus glasses. And I assume he used some kind of temporary color on his hair. I saw his picture on the company Web site. Once I looked closely, he wasn't hard to recognize, not with those beady eyes."

"How could he have gotten in? He wasn't on the guest list, and Jonathan knew all the invitees, at least by sight. There's no way—"

"He was hired as a waiter."

Her face colored and her voice rose. "You mean, your caterer—"

I held up a hand. "Nope. Not mine. The caterer Lyla used. Apparently Jerry Thompson was hired as a temp."

Stephanie sank a little in her chair. She actually seemed to shrink a little. "Oh my God," she whispered. "We never thought . . ." She didn't finish her sentence as the repercussions of the infiltration sank in.

I figured I'd learned all I could from Stephanie at this point and rose from my chair. I reached out to shake her hand, but she was too busy playing with her necklace and didn't notice the gesture. Maybe she was asking it for protection.

"I should get going. But I do have one more question."

She came out of her trance and met my eyes. I had a feeling she wasn't really looking at me, her mind still a million miles away. "Uh, what?"

"I thought I saw Zachary Samuels in the parking lot."

She blinked several times, as if she didn't comprehend my words for a few seconds. "You're kidding. When?"

I checked my watch. "Probably an hour ago." I decided not to tell her that someone had let him into the building. For all I knew, it could have been her. Although why would she risk giving a fired employee entrance into Hella-Graphics? Especially one who might be a killer.

Her hand shot to the phone on the desk and she punched three numbers. "Lisa, call security! We may have a breach. . . . I don't know where! Have them check the building!" She slammed down the phone, stood up, and said, "You'll have to excuse me, Presley." She walked me swiftly to the front doors of the building, and left me there, wondering if I should have spoken up earlier. Or had I said too much already?

As I headed for my car, I realized I still had on my visitor's pass. I ripped it off as I glanced around for a sign of Zachary. His dented car was still in the loading zone, unoccupied. I opened the door of my MINI, slid in, and stuck the key into the ignition.

An arm circled my neck.

"What the hell are you doing?" the low voice hissed.

I couldn't have told him if I'd wanted to. He was choking me to death.

Chapter 16

I saw spots before my eyes.

Blindly reaching up, I grabbed the assailant's arm and dug my short nails into his skin. I still couldn't breathe. I pinched some skin, twisted it, and he released his grip a little, freeing my airway.

I coughed, trying to catch my breath. The guy's hairy arm tickled my nose. I shoved his arm to my mouth and bit the hell out of it.

He cursed and let go.

I reached for the doorknob.

He grabbed my hair and jerked my head back.

"Ouch!" I screamed.

"Calm down!" he screamed back.

Yeah, right. A man was mugging me and I was supposed to calm down. I thrashed out backward, trying to hit him in the face with flailing arms, but couldn't make contact over the back of the seat.

"Calm down and I'll let you go!" he shouted.

I took a breath and tried to relax but it was nearly impossible under the circumstances.

Slowly he released his grip on my hair. As soon as I was free, I twisted around in my seat and came face-to-face with Zachary Samuels.

His eyes were red rimmed, his face drawn and sallow, and the deep ridges between his eyes looked like he'd been wearing that frown all his life. His collar-length hair was greasy and uncombed, and the T-shirt under his fake delivery jacket sported stains. It looked like he hadn't eaten, slept, or changed clothes in days. He certainly hadn't brushed his teeth. His breath smelled of sour booze.

"What are you trying to do—kill me?" I sputtered, my voice still ragged from being choked. I'd reacted in anger, but quickly realized this guy was a viable suspect in Levi's murder—and therefore dangerous. Plus, he'd tried to run down Jonathan with his car, nearly hitting me in the process. I regretted my choice of words.

"No!" he cried. "I just want to talk to you."

His hot, alcohol-infused breath hit my nostrils again and I backed up. "You attacked me! In my car!"

"I didn't attack you. I got you in a headlock and you overreacted. I needed you to keep quiet."

I suppose my ADHD had something to do with my fight-or-flight response. Nevertheless, I'm sure anyone else in my position would have reacted the same way. I looked him over and instead of a killer, this time saw a mostly sane, nerdy guy who seemed to be in trouble.

"So what do you want?" I tried to keep my tone neutral.

"I want to know where Jonathan is."

My jaw dropped. "How would I know that?"

"Because you're probably sleeping with him," Zachary said.

I choked out a laugh. "What? You've got to be kidding!"

I had no idea where this was going—or when it would end. Slowly, I reached for my purse on the seat beside me, planning to retrieve my iPhone without him noticing. At the moment he appeared calm, but there was no telling what might set him off again. I needed backup.

"There's no way I would sleep with Jonathan," I said, feeling the phone and easing it out slowly. "He's a pig."

Zachary sat back in the seat, rubbing his arm where I had bit him. I hadn't drawn blood, but I'd left a nice set of teeth marks.

"I can always tell when Jonathan has a new girl in his life," Zachary said, "because he's always hanging around them. And he's been seeing a lot of you lately."

"That's because I was planning a party for him! Not sleeping with him."

"So you have no idea where he is?" Zachary's shoulders slumped, his face fell. I was beginning to feel sorry for him. But he'd still attacked me. I clicked off the audio on the phone.

"No idea. The police are looking for him, but they haven't found him either."

"The police?" Zachary's eyes widened.

"Yeah. They think he might have murdered Levi Webster."

He pressed his lips together. "I heard."

I glanced down at the icons on the phone.

"Personally," I continued, feeling a little reckless now that I had the phone and was about to call 911, "I thought you might have done it."

"Me? Kill Levi? Why would I?" He seemed genuinely shocked. "You know nothing about me."

I pushed an icon and my e-mail came up. Wrong one.

"How about because Jonathan fired you from Hella-Graphics and replaced you with Levi. So you killed two birds with one stone. You murdered Levi and made it look like Jonathan did it."

I was tossing out motives like confetti, but what the hell. I touched the phone icon. Out of the corner of my eye, I saw the contacts screen pop up.

Zachary gave a harsh laugh. "What bullshit."

His reaction surprised me. I'd expected anger. "So Jonathan didn't fire you?"

"Well, yeah, he did . . ."

"But you didn't try to run him down in the Winchester parking lot?"

"That was an accident. . . ."

"So, you're completely innocent?" I raised an eyebrow, then glanced down at my phone and pushed Brad's number.

He reached out a hand. "Give me the phone," he said wearily.

"What?"

"I said, give me the damn phone." His tone was patient but firm.

There was no point in pretending any longer. I handed him the phone. He laid it on the seat next to him.

"To answer your question, yes," he said, "I was fired, but not for any real cause. Jonathan had accused me of planning to defect to another company."

"Stereo-Scope Graphics?"

His eyes narrowed. "How'd you know?"

I felt like I was getting the upper hand—and I wasn't about to stop and explain. "Go on."

"Anyway, I wasn't going to jump ship. And even if I did bolt, I wouldn't be caught dead working for Dane Scott. He's an asshole."

"Okay, so Jonathan fired you and replaced you with Levi. You must have been angry."

"Hell, yeah, I was. I wanted to kill the guy who got me fired."

"Jonathan?" I was getting confused.

"No!"

A light went on. "Do you mean George Wells?"

His eyes flared. "How did you—"

"Did you kill Wells and make it look like a suicide?"

He sat up, his face red. "No!"

"Did you do it to embarrass Jonathan? Or frame him?"

Zachary threw his hands up. "Shut up! I didn't kill anyone. I have no idea what happened to George. I didn't know he was suicidal. His death surprised me as much as anyone."

"Okay, so what *do* you know?"

"Listen, I'm asking the questions here." He bowed his head as if collecting his thoughts, then said, "Look. I'm the one who invented 4-D for Hella-Graphics. It took me years, but I came up with the original idea, built a prototype, and made it work. I figured I was worth something for that."

"Like more money?"

"Sure, more money. 4-D was going to make Jonathan and Hella-Graphics a hella lot of money."

"But Jonathan wouldn't pay you anything more, right? No bonus, no extra stock options, nada." The pieces were coming together. I just didn't quite have the big picture.

He nodded.

"And because you wanted more, you were fired?"

Zachary glanced out the window. "Not exactly."

"Why then?"

He shrugged, not meeting my eyes. "I told him he needed to pay me or I'd . . ."

"You'd what?"

"Tell."

"Tell what?"

"I'd tell everyone about his 'hobby.'"

"You're not talking about stamp collecting, I gather. Jonathan's affairs?"

"I had no choice," he said. "Besides, the guy was a jerk to women." His words and tone sounded both defensive and angry.

So Zachary was trying to blackmail Jonathan. A light went on in my head. "Zachary . . . were you the one who caused that glitch in the séance program, when Sarah Winchester's voice suddenly changed and she started telling everyone Jonathan's little secret?"

Zachary remained silent, staring out the side window at the Hella-Graphics building.

Thinking out loud, I said, "So when your blackmail scheme didn't work and Jonathan wouldn't pay you off, you got even by hacking into the program and having Sarah Winchester expose him. For revenge."

Zachary glanced at me. I saw a glimmer of pride in his eyes.

"How did you do it?"

"Simple. I created a separate workstation in another room in the mansion, hacked into the computer, took control, and made the old lady say what I wanted her to."

"You were in the house the night of the Séance Party?"

He shrugged noncommittally.

"So you got your revenge against Jonathan."

"Yes, but not by killing him, although believe me, there were times when I thought about it. And not by killing Levi."

I still wasn't convinced he wasn't a murderer, but he hadn't killed me yet, so I had to consider the possibility he was telling the truth.

"So what do you want from me?" I asked.

"I told you. I have to find Jonathan."

"Why go after him now? You've had your revenge. The police are looking for him. They'll find him. They think he killed Levi, so let them handle it."

"You don't understand."

I stared at him, waiting for the other shoe to drop. In this case, a ratty-looking athletic shoe.

"I was . . . having an affair with Lyla."

My jaw dropped again. Zachary Samuels hardly looked like the Lothario type. He might have been good-looking under all that dirt and behind that stubble, but why on earth would Lyla fool around with him?

He seemed to read my mind. "Lyla has a thing for smart guys. Brains turn her on," he said.

"So you screwed him a couple of ways," I said. "Did Jonathan know about you and Lyla?"

"I don't know. I have a feeling Lyla might have told him she was two-timing him with me after she learned about all his affairs."

"That still doesn't explain why you want to find Jonathan."

Zachary's face drained of color. "I think Jonathan killed Levi. And if he did, then he's capable of killing his cheating wife."

And Lyla could be in serious trouble.

"Damn it!" Zachary finally said after staring out the window a few moments. He seemed to be focused on the Hella-Graphics building. "Damn security guard. He's coming this way."

I turned to see a man in a khaki uniform headed toward us. I wondered if someone reported seeing a couple of suspicious-looking people sitting in a car in the parking lot.

"I'm outta here." He grabbed the handle on the passenger seat, pushed the backseat forward, and prepared to bolt the MINI.

"Wait!" I said, grabbing the back of his hoodie. I had one more question I'd almost forgotten to ask. "Who let you into the building?"

He jerked out of my grasp and ran, disappearing down a small hill. I glanced back at the security guard, who was talking on his walkie. He broke into a run, and gave chase, also disappearing out of sight.

I started the engine, wanting to avoid answering a bunch of questions when the guard returned. By the time I reached the street, I saw the guard in my rearview mirror, trudging back up the hill.

He was alone.

Chapter 17

PARTY PLANNING TIP #17

Up the suspense at your Séance Party by adding "spirit rapping." Give an accomplice a broom handle and have him hide in the basement. Let guests ask the spirits yes or no questions, and have the accomplice tap the ceiling of the basement with the broom handle in response: One rap for "Yes" and two raps for "No."

As I drove back to Treasure Island around noon, I thought about everything Zachary had said. Had he been telling the truth? Or was he just a good liar? He and Lyla seemed like a bizarre pair, but then so were Drew Barrymore and Tom Green, Julia Roberts and Lyle Lovett, my mother and a number of her husbands. Who knew what attracted one person to another? Apparently, in Zachary's case, it wasn't always love, but revenge.

One of the many questions he hadn't answered was who had let him into the Hella-Graphics compound via a side door. I ruled out Jonathan, although he could be hiding inside somewhere and let him in. In fact, he could be living there, what with all the amenities the place offered. But wouldn't he be discovered at some point? And why would he let Zachary in—unless he was being blackmailed.

If it wasn't Jonathan at the door, then who? Stephanie? She'd kept me waiting quite a while before finally seeing me. Had she been meeting with Zachary? Why?

Then again, maybe it was one of the several women who'd been sleeping with Jonathan, including his administrative assistant, Violet Vassar. Or maybe Zachary was also having multiple affairs like his mentor.

Finally—the big question—what had Zachary been doing while he was inside the building? Trying to find Jonathan? Going through Jonathan's desk? Stealing intellectual property—the 4-D to be specific? Or sabotaging Hella-Graphics in some way?

My mind raced with possibilities. Not a good thing for a person with ADHD. I needed to focus on the most logical points before I started off on another tangent.

I pulled up to my office, grabbed my phone from the backseat where Zachary had left it, and spent the rest of the day puzzling over unanswered questions, getting very little done on my upcoming parties. Completely baffled by Jonathan's request to find out who killed Levi, I went around in circles until my head spun like a disco ball.

By seven o'clock, Brad still hadn't come into his office, so I packed up my notes and purse and headed for my condo. The moonlit drive took me all of three minutes—I should have walked. I needed the exercise. Instead, I parked the MINI in the carport, stuck the house key into the lock, and opened the door. My three cats were waiting for me at the entryway—meowing for food, attention, or just for the hell of it.

"Hi, boys," I said, giving each one a thorough head scratching. "What's for dinner?"

Ha. I wish.

I filled their empty bowls, freshened their water, and then got myself a glass of merlot before I foraged for my own food in my nearly bare refrigerator.

Plopping onto couch with the wine and some Cheetos, I dug out my notebook and iPhone. I had three calls with no caller ID, just hang-ups, and wondered if they'd come from Jonathan. If so, he hadn't left any messages. I wondered where he was and what he was doing.

The fourth call, also without an ID, sent shivers from my head to my toes.

"Presley Parker, I'm watching you."

I held the phone out from my ear as if it had bit me and stared at it. Goose bumps broke out on my arms.

The message had been disturbing enough, but coupled with the fact that the voice was familiar, it nearly sent me diving under the proverbial covers.

It was Sarah Winchester. Or her evil twin.

A loud thud at the front door nearly gave me a heart attack. I jumped. The cats scrambled for their favorite hiding places—under the coffee table, on top of the refrigerator, and down the hall to my bedroom.

I waited, frozen to the couch, half expecting a poltergeist to start throwing forks or moving furniture around. Nothing.

After a few minutes of silence, I got off the couch and tiptoed to the front door. I opened it, leaving the chain attached, and peeked outside.

Dark. Nobody there.

I switched on the outside light but nothing happened.

Glancing up at the decorative light, I discovered what had caused the loud sound. Someone had thrown a large rock, hit the light, and broken it and the bulb. The rock lay on my porch along with broken glass.

I removed the chain and opened the door to see if anyone was lurking nearby.

Not a soul. Whoever it was had vanished.

I went around the side to see if they'd gotten the neighbor's light as well, but there were no lights on at all, and the outdoor light fixture was intact.

I swept up the glass, tossed the rock, and with a last look around, I closed the door, locked, bolted, and chained it, and returned to my tiny kitchen to make a sandwich. That would calm my jangled nerves.

"Here, kitty, kitties. You can come out now."

No sign of them, not even my attack cat.

I opened the fridge, pulled out some boysenberry jam, then got the chunky peanut butter from the cupboard and two slices of raisin bread from the countertop. I spread the jam and peanut butter on the slices, slapped the sandwich together, and sat down at my tiny table to eat.

Before I could take a bite, my iPhone rang. I looked at the caller ID: none. Jonathan or my crank caller posing as Sarah Winchester? There was only one way to find out. I took a deep breath and nervously answered the call, hoping it was Jonathan.

"Hello?"

"You were warned," came the voice of evil Sarah Winchester again.

"Not funny!" I said, hoping to provoke whoever was calling. It was all bravado—my hands shook and my heart was beating at hyperspeed.

No response. The line went dead.

I cursed, set down the phone, then decided to try Brad. No answer. I left a message asking him to call, and returned to my sandwich, but my stomach was clinched and I felt nauseated. Instead, I made a soothing latte with double caffeine, changed into my cupcake-patterned pajamas, and headed for bed to read, hoping to get my mind off things that went bump in the night—and phone calls that came from a supposed spirit.

After reading a couple of chapters that detailed the Golden Gate World's Fair of 1939, I yawned, snuggled under the covers and turned off the light. The latte did its trick of drugging me to sleep. I drifted off quickly.

The next thing I knew, I was awake, sitting upright, and covered in a cold sweat. The knocking sound at my door wasn't part of the nightmare I'd been having.

I glanced at the clock: midnight. On the dot.

Who would be knocking on my door at this time of night? Brad, I hoped.

I slipped out of bed and armed myself, just in case, with an aerosol can of spray glitter glue and an air horn, both leftovers from past events. If it was some lunatic at the door, I figured the air horn would scare him away while the glitter glue would temporarily blind him.

I switched on the hall light, and then the front porch light, forgetting it had been broken. I peered through the peephole but it was too dark to see anything.

The knocking started again, this time at the back door on the other side of my condo.

Someone was trying to scare me.

And doing a pretty good job of it.

I switched on the living room light, grabbed my iPhone from the charger, and punched in Brad's number. But before I could lift it to my ear, I heard more pounding, this time on one of the side walls. This was no gentle knock. It sounded as if someone was hitting the wall with a sledgehammer. Dropping the phone, I ran to the side window and tried get a glimpse outside, but it was pitch dark—not even moonlight could pierce the heavy layer of fog that had settled in.

Then it dawned on me. With my lights on inside, whoever was outside could see me clearly as I ran around the house like a frightened chicken.

I hurried through the living room, hallway, and bedroom, switching off lights.

Aside from a couple of incidents, I had always felt safe on the Island. I subscribe to a site called EveryBlock.com/Treasure Island, which sent me a daily e-list of police reports from the past twenty-four hours. TI mostly had petty crimes, such as auto burglaries, loud noises, intoxicated residents, trespassers, fights without weapons, and traffic stops. On occasion I read about an assault and battery or suspicious person, but they were rare.

Now, though, I felt truly terrified. I was sitting in the dark like a trapped prey waiting for a predator to come knocking on my door again.

I had to call Brad. Where was my phone?

From across the room, I heard a ghostly voice utter, "Presley! Presley!"

But this was no spirit calling from the beyond. My iPhone

was lying on the living room floor, lit up like a candle in a cave. I snatched it up.

"Brad? Is that you?"

"Presley? You okay? Or did you pocket-call me again—"

"Brad, listen," I whispered. "Someone's outside my condo. Knocking on my doors and pounding on the walls. I'm sure whoever it is, is trying to scare me"—I didn't dare say "kill me," but I thought it—"and he's doing a great job. Can you—"

"I'm on my way."

The line went dead.

There are no such things as ghosts, I told myself as I waited for the booming to begin again. My hands were trembling so hard, I didn't know if I could blow the air horn or spray the glitter. Someone was not only trying to scare me, but maybe evened wanted to hurt me. The question was, Why? Because I was asking around about Levi's murder? I hadn't even done much of that.

I huddled in the living room with my weapons, trying to figure out what was going on. My next-door neighbor was gone—his lights were still out. I could blast the air horn, but I'd probably just damage my own ears, while everyone else ignored it. I could scream, but my throat still burned from being choked.

Instead, I pondered. Did it have something to do with Jonathan? Or was there something else? Then again, it could just be random, although at this point, I hardly thought so.

Although it seemed like an hour, it was probably less than five minutes when I heard a knock at the door. This one was different. It sounded like a friendly knock.

I got up and ran to the door. "Who is it?"

"It's me," came the muffled reply from the other side.

I unlocked and unbolted the door, leaving the chain on, and peeked out, just in case it was someone who only sounded like Brad. These days, computers were capable of conjuring up all kinds of sounds, including voices.

It was him. Or a mighty convincing 4-D projection. I could feel the tension in my body melt and unchained the door.

"Boy, something's got you spooked," Brad said, stepping inside. "What's going on?"

I led him to the kitchen and offered him a beer from the fridge.

"No, thanks."

Since I'd already opened it assuming he'd take it, I decided to drink it myself and leaned on the counter and chugged a few gulps before trying to explain the noises I'd witnessed.

"I heard knocking."

"Knocking." He raised an eyebrow, like a psychiatrist trying to humor a mental patient. "You mean, like what I just did at your front door?"

I felt my face grow hot. "Yes, but much louder. And it went on and on, coming from all around the condo. Outside."

I knew I wasn't making sense, but the experience was difficult to explain, without sounding like a Looney Toon. I needed to give Brad some perspective so he wouldn't call his cop friend Luke Melvin and have me taken in as a 5150—involuntary psychiatric hold, aka crazy person. I learned that on *Law & Order*.

After a couple more swigs of beer, I filled Brad in on everything. I played back the phone calls I'd received from someone warning me to mind my own business, then told him about my threatening encounter with Zachary Samuels in the parking lot of Hella-Graphics. Brad's frown deepened as I spoke.

"Why didn't you tell me all this before?"

"I did, sort of. At least about the one phone call. I just didn't want you to get all upset and tell me to mind my own business. I'm only telling you now because I want you to help me figure out what's going on. Two people have been killed. I'm a little worried I may be next."

"I'm glad you finally recognize that," Brad said.

"Hey, I was ready for him, whoever he was." I pointed to the party weapons I'd planned to use to maim and scare off the intruder.

Brad looked over at the spray can and air horn lying on the coffee table. He shook his head, grinning. "I wouldn't want to be trapped in a back alley with you, that's for sure. I'd come out all glittery and deaf."

"Very funny." I finished the beer and stood up. Too fast, apparently. The room spun around. I remembered I hadn't had much to eat, then downed a beer.

"Whoa." Brad jumped up and held on to me.

"I'm fine," I said. "I'm just tired."

"Well, let's get you to bed. Then I'll take a look around and see if I can figure out what was making the noise."

He walked me to my room and I slipped into bed. As he turned to head out, I grabbed his hand. "You're not leaving, are you?" I said sleepily. Or drunkenly.

I pulled back the covers on the other side, inviting him to join me.

He ran his fingers through my hair. "I'm going to sit up for a while and keep an eye out, see if the knocking returns. You sleep."

I was too tired to argue.

He turned off the light. I slipped into a deep sleep and didn't hear a thing the rest of the night.

Chapter 18

PARTY PLANNING TIP #18

Séance attendees love "parlor tricks," so include a few extra thrills to give your party guests extra chills. Try "typtology"—the classic lifting of the table. To perform this trick, cover the table with a black cloth, then have someone hiding underneath lift the table on cue.

I awoke to the sound of knocking on my front door. It immediately dragged me back to what I'd experienced last night. Although my room was flooded with daylight, I broke out in a cold sweat.

"Brad?" I called, then yelled his name. Where was he? He'd promised to stay over. His side of the bed hadn't been slept in—that much was obvious.

"Presley?" I heard a muffled voice coming through the bedroom wall. Military housing was certainly cheap.

Recognizing the voice, I raced out of the room and down the hall to the front door. The pounding came again.

"Brad?"

"Yeah, it's me. Can you open up?"

The dead bolt and chain were already unlocked, but the twist lock on the knob was still engaged. I opened the door. Brad stood on the other side, two lattes in a carry-tray in one hand and a bag of what I hoped were pastries in the other.

"Lock yourself out?" I asked, taking the latte tray from him.

"You realize you don't have anything to eat or drink here, don't you?" he said, not responding to my question.

I remembered finishing off the last of the coffee, but as for pastries, they never remained longer than a few minutes in this house. "I haven't had time to go shopping."

He set the bag on the table and took off his leather jacket and hung it on the hook of a chair. His cheeks were rosy from the early-morning run to the local market. "Although you do have plenty of cat food, if we get desperate enough."

"No more knocking last night?" I asked, having slept peacefully after he'd arrived. We sat down at the table, me in my cupcake pajamas, him in his jeans and T-shirt from last night, and sipped our still-hot lattes.

"Nothing."

That figures, I thought. I felt like the girl who cried wolf.

"Did you get any sleep?"

"A little, on the couch. I didn't want to disturb you. Plus I figured I'd have quicker access to the mysterious knocker if he returned."

"You sound as if you don't quite believe me," I said, before taking a huge bite of the chocolate croissant I'd found in the pastry bag.

"If you say you heard knocking, I'm sure you did," he

said, not meeting my eyes. He quickly changed the subject. "So what are your plans today, other than hopefully grocery shopping?"

When my mouth was clear enough to speak, I said, "I'm not sure. I'd really like to find Jonathan, but I have no idea where to look. I'd also like to find out who killed Levi, but I don't want to get myself hit over the head like he did. And finally, I'd like to kill whoever it was that did all that knocking last night. But that doesn't seem likely either."

"How about this?" Brad began, after a sip of his latte. "Let the police find Jonathan. Let the police find out about Levi. And as for the knocker, stay at my place until all this is over." He gave me a long, steady look.

In the morning light, I felt a little foolish for calling Brad to come over. After all, it was no doubt some teenage vandals trying to scare me. And of course it stopped as soon as Brad arrived, which made me feel even more foolish. I decided I wouldn't call him again just because someone was trying to scare me.

"Thanks for the offer, but I'll be fine here. No one actually tried to break in. And I can always call the TI police if they do."

Brad shook his head in acquiescence. "All right, but the offer stands. You don't have to prove anything to me, Presley."

I quietly finished my croissant and wondered if I was really trying to prove something. Maybe. That I could take care of myself? I'd been doing that since my mother divorced my father when I was five. Having a mother who'd had multiple careers and multiple husbands, I'd learned to be independent early on.

Brad's cell phone rang. He answered it, mostly listened to the voice on the other end, interjecting the occasional, "Uh-huh," "Got it," and "Okay," and ending with a final "See ya." Frowning as if his pastry wasn't settling, he stood up and stuffed the phone into his pocket.

"Another cleaning job?" I asked, not especially wanting the details.

He cocked his jaw and looked at me, saying nothing.

"Brad?" Alarmed at his lack of response, I stood up to face him. "You look like you just got a call from the beyond."

He took my hand. "Listen, Presley. Pack your bags. I don't want any argument. You're staying with me tonight, understand?"

"Brad," I said, laughing nervously. "You're scaring me. What happened?"

"I don't mean to scare you, but I do want you to realize how serious this situation has become."

"What situation? What are you talking about?"

"That was Luke Melvin on the phone."

"And he wants you to clean up some kind of crime scene, right?"

Brad's dark brown eyes narrowed as he looked at me. "They found another body."

I felt the tiny hairs on my arms tingle. "Oh my God. Where?"

"At Hella-Graphics."

My knees wobbled. I held on to the chair back. "Oh God. Who was it? Stephanie? Jonathan?"

"Zachary Samuels."

*   *   *

I sat back down in my chair, completely stunned at the news. I had seen Zachary the previous day, albeit not in the best shape, but at least alive. He couldn't be dead. It didn't compute.

"Listen, I hate to leave you," Brad said, interrupting my dark thoughts, "but Melvin wants me at Hella-Graphics. You going to be all right?"

My first thought was: Lyla and Jonathan. "No," I said. "Can I come with you?" I wanted him to think I was nervous being alone—although I wouldn't be at my office. But the truth was, I was mad—mad at whoever was killing the computer nerds of Hella-Graphics.

And I wanted to have a look at the crime scene.

"Will you stay out of the way? If Melvin sees you, he'll kill me. And you'll have to do the cleanup."

"Poor choice of words, but yes, you won't even know I'm there."

"Yeah, right. This is against my better judgment. Get your stuff. Let's go."

"I'm with SFPD," Brad said into the Hella-Graphics intercom. The door magically opened. I would have to remember the secret password the next time I wanted entry.

Once inside, I trailed Brad through the lobby to the receptionist, where he picked up his visitor badge and asked for one for me, calling me his "assistant." The girl rolled her eyes, but didn't argue. Things seemed a bit chaotic there, with distraught employees standing around whispering, their arms crossed over their chests as if protecting themselves from an evil force that had invaded their work space.

Brad headed down the hall, following the directions from the receptionist, then turned back to me as I trailed behind him. "Where do you think you're going?"

"Uh . . . with you?"

"No way. I told you, if Melvin sees you here—"

"He'll kill you, I know." I pointed to the café a short distance away. "I'll be in there."

He nodded, and shot me a look that said, "And stay put."

I ordered my second latte of the day and sat down at the only empty table left in the place. The rest of the tables were filled with employees, most of them casually dressed in jeans, T-shirts, and running shoes or Birkenstocks. And most were in their late twenties or early thirties. They were all buzzing about the latest development. I got out my notebook, catching the eyes of a couple of curious employees no doubt wondering who the "new girl" was, and eavesdropped on a few of the conversations, in case someone happened to confess.

"What was he doing here?" I heard one guy with a ponytail ask.

"He was found in his old office . . ." said another with glasses and bed-head hair.

"Did you see his head? It was all bashed in . . ." said a woman with a blue streak in her shoulder-length hair and a tie-dyed T-shirt.

I took notes as I caught snatches of their comments. When their conversations turned to more personal topics— "Do you think they'll shut down the campus?" "Do they plan to talk to all of us?" "I never could stand the guy."—I tuned out and started writing down my own questions.

1. What was Zachary doing at Hella-Graphics?

Possibilities: A) Sabotaging his work (to get even?). B) Meeting with someone (who? why?). C) Returning to get something that belonged to him (entitlement?). D) Trying to find Jonathan (to protect Lyla?).

2. What was the time of death?

Possibilities: A) Soon after he'd left my car? (Last I had seen he was running down the hill being chased by a security guard.) B) Sometime in the middle of the night? (Wait for coroner's report.)

3. How had he been killed? Someone had mentioned his head was bashed in. Same MO as Levi? (Hit from behind?) Same weapon? (Candlestick?)

All I had was a bunch of questions. I needed to start looking for answers. Brad told me that answers reveal patterns, and one pattern was obvious: All three of the deceased victims had worked at Hella-Graphics—George Wells, Levi Webster, and Zachary Samuels. Two of them had had the same job—working on the 4-D project—but George was connected. He had worked as a programmer.

The signs kept pointing to Jonathan Ellington. Had he somehow lured Zachary inside the building and bludgeoned him to death? Did he suspect Zachary of hacking into the 4-D demo and changing the voice and script to embarrass him? Did he want to kill Zachary for fooling around with Lyla?

I flipped back to my original suspect list. Now that another suspect was dead, I had to rethink the whole list.

First I crossed off Zachary and wrote "Victim #3."

That put Jonathan at the top of the list again. He had a connection to all three victims. His fingerprints were on the weapon that killed Levi. He'd fired Zachary for trying to blackmail him.

Maybe George had tried to blackmail him too. And maybe those blackmail materials were what Jonathan was looking for in George's desk.

Underneath Jonathan's name were the names of the women he'd been involved with—at least the ones I knew about. But what about Stephanie? Had she been telling the truth when she said she and Jonathan had never gotten together?

Then came Lyla. Could she have murdered all these men, just to make it look like her husband was the killer? Why not? Women can do anything these days.

And last but not least was Dane Scott, CEO of Stereo-Scope, along with sidekick/fake waiter, Jerry Thompson. They were real possibilities. Hella-Graphics was losing creative staff faster than a spreading computer virus, which could only benefit Stereo-Scope. And Dane Scott, as CEO, had the most to gain if Hella-Graphics went under—especially if he had information on the 4-D Projector. Plus he had an accomplice—Jerry Thompson—who could have helped him kill the victims. Maybe Scott and Thompson somehow got the formula for the 4-D holograph and literally began killing off the competition.

I wanted to talk to Stephanie. She'd have the most inside information. She was still on my list, but she had no motive that I could see, if she was telling the truth about not sleeping with Jonathan.

Then again, maybe some other employee had a reason to kill all these people and frame Jonathan. After all, he was a jerk.

That only brought the number to several hundred . . .

The most pressing question was: Who would want these computer guys dead?

Thirty minutes later I was fidgeting in my chair at the café, tired of going in circles and not learning anything new. Some of the employees had left, others had taken their places—all were talking about the murders. I got up, threw away my paper coffee cup, and decided, in spite of Brad's warning, to take a self-guided tour of Hella-Graphics.

I felt like Nancy Drew, peering around corners before venturing deeper into the bowels of the company. Not knowing where the crime scene was, I tried to be careful not to run into Brad or Detective Melvin. If only I'd worn a cloche hat.

I had just turned down an empty hallway when Stephanie Bryson suddenly appeared from an open doorway. She looked startled to see me, but an instant later her face broke into a gentle smile. In her dark blue suit, matching scarf, and black heels, she looked almost in mourning. The only bright spot was the crystal around her neck.

"Presley! What are you doing here?"

"Hi, Stephanie. I came with the crime scene cleaner—Brad Matthews. You remember him?"

"Yes, he was at the Séance Party, helping out. I just saw him a few minutes ago." Her voice changed to a whisper. "So I guess you heard about Zachary Samuels."

"I'm so sorry," I said, not knowing how she felt about the dead guy.

"Yeah, me too. It's got everyone upset, as you can imagine. I only wish Jonathan were here to handle all this. He's so good at taking charge."

"Still no word from him?" I asked.

"Nothing. You?"

I shook my lying head. "How's Lyla?"

Stephanie made a face. "Good question. I haven't talked to her. Every time I call, she's either out or not taking calls."

I thought about what Zachary had said. He'd been worried that Jonathan might harm her. "Do you think she's all right? Has anyone heard from her or checked on her?"

"She's alive, if that's what you mean. I overheard the police say they've questioned her a couple of times. Why? You think she had something to do with this?"

"Oh no. Just concerned about her, but I'm sure she's fine. Especially if the police have been keeping tabs on her. They probably have her under surveillance."

Stephanie sighed. "I just wish I knew what was going on around here. My employees are scared. I'm scared. . . ."

I reached out and touched her arm in an effort to comfort her.

She shook her head and added quickly, "Pretend you didn't hear me say that. I've got to be strong for my staff."

"Stephanie, how did Zachary get into the building?"

"I honestly don't know. Someone must have let him in. His passkey was disabled as soon as he was let go."

"Any idea who it might have been?"

"Could have been anyone. He had friends here, but why would they let him in, knowing that's a major breach of contract and grounds for dismissal. I don't think anyone would want to risk his or her job for Zachary."

I thought for a moment, while Stephanie slid her crystal from side to side along the chain. "If no one can get in without a passkey or someone letting them in, isn't it possible that someone who works here could be the killer?"

Stephanie's hand stopped. "I suppose . . . someone who wanted these guys out of the picture, and also had access to the building . . ."

We looked at each other.

The name went unspoken.

Jonathan.

Chapter 19

PARTY PLANNING TIP #19

Think about videotaping your Séance Party so you can enjoy viewing the experience after it's over. This is also a great way to chronicle any unusual happenings that can't be explained. You might find the "reality" show called Ghosthunters interested in your findings.

"Stephanie, do you think Jonathan could be hiding in the building? It seems like there are so many places where a person could hide out."

"Not without using his pass card, and then it would show up on the security log. But I suppose it's possible, if he sneaked in somehow—like Zachary did. He knows this building better than anyone."

"I'm going to mention this to the detective," I said. "Meanwhile, you should be careful."

Stephanie rubbed the crystal as if it were a genie in a bottle. "You don't think Jonathan would . . ." She pointed to herself.

"I think everyone is in danger until the killer's caught. All the victims have a connection to Hella-Graphics—and Jonathan's on the lam. I wouldn't take any chances."

Stephanie looked away, seeming to be lost in thought. Apparently it hadn't occurred to her that she might be in jeopardy. But until we knew exactly who was doing the killing—and why—no one was safe.

Not even me, judging by the events last night.

Winding my way through a few more corridors, I found several police officers milling near a room marked PRODUCT DEVELOPMENT. A yellow police tape had been strung across the opening. There was no way I was getting past that with just a visitor's badge.

"Hi," I said to one of the officers, smiling and tilting my head.

"I'm sorry, ma'am. This area is restricted. You'll have to leave."

I don't know which pissed me off more, being called "ma'am" or being turned away without even giving me time to make up a good lie.

I was about to go pout somewhere when I heard my name.

"Parker!"

I turned around. Detective Luke Melvin stood in the doorway, dressed more like a successful CEO than a plain-clothes detective in his expensive Italian suit and shiny black loafers. Tall and lanky, he would have been handsome if he hadn't been chewing on a toothpick, a habit I find disgusting.

"Hey, Detective," I said, trying to sound like we were old friends. "How's it going?"

"What are you doing here?" he said flatly.

"I . . . I sort of knew the victim, so I thought—"

"Really? Exactly how did you happen to *sort of* know Zachary Samuels?"

"I did a party for his boss—ex-boss—Jonathan Ellington."

He bit down on the toothpick and spoke through his extra-white teeth. "Ah yes. The infamous Séance Party my brother told me about. Don't suppose you know where Ellington is now?"

"No, why would I?"

He shrugged. "You seem to have a connection to a number of homicides these days. Anything you can tell me about the vic?"

Vic? Oh, victim. Where did cops get all this jargon—perp, unsub, vic? From TV?

"He . . ." How was I going to explain this? "I . . . was in the parking lot . . . I'd just left a meeting with Stephanie and . . ."

"Why were you meeting with Ms. Bryson?"

"Uh, post-party stuff. You know. So anyway, I had just gotten into my car and . . . uh, Zachary was in the back-seat—"

"He was in the backseat?" His eyes narrowed. "How did he get in your car?"

His constant interruptions were beginning to rattle me. "I guess I left it unlocked. Anyway—"

"What was he *doing* in your car?"

"I'm trying to tell you! He said he wanted to talk to me—"

"And he couldn't just call you?"

I glared at him. "Do you want to hear this or not, Detective?"

He pulled out the toothpick and licked his lips. "Go on."

"Then stop interrupting. Zachary said he was concerned about Jonathan." I explained what I knew about Zachary being fired, which I'm sure the detective knew already. Still, I didn't want to be accused of withholding information. "So, basically, with Jonathan still on the loose, Zachary was worried about Lyla's safety."

The detective frowned. "Why would he be worried about Lyla?"

I shrugged. I didn't want to incriminate Jonathan more than I had.

"Parker," the detective said, "I'd sure like to know how you're involved in this."

"I just told you," I said. "Now can you tell me what happened to Zachary?"

"Police business," he said, and popped the toothpick back into his mouth.

"Well, what about George Wells—the supposed suicide at Hella-Graphics?"

"Supposed? Where did you get that idea? You been communicating with the dead for real?"

"No, I was talking with Teddi, George's wife, and she doesn't think he killed himself."

"Nobody ever wants to believe their loved one committed suicide. If they did, they'd have to face up to the fact that their relative wasn't happy and they didn't see it coming. They often think it's their fault—that they caused their husband or wife or whoever to do it. Denial is typical when it comes to 801s-suicides."

I wasn't going to get anywhere with him. "Well, it's been

great chatting with you, Detective, as usual. If you're done with me, I have things to do. You know the party business. It's not all clowns and balloons."

He lifted an eyebrow. "I don't know how you're mixed up in this, Presley, but if I find out you're not telling me everything, we're going to have another little chat."

"Looking forward to it, Detective. And good luck with finding Jonathan," I said, giving him a smirk.

He smirked back. "What's the matter, Presley? Your police scanner not working?"

His words wiped the smirk off my face. "What are you talking about?"

"You didn't hear?" His smirk grew bigger.

Oh God. Something had happened to Lyla. My heart skipped a beat.

"No, what?"

"Jonathan Ellington's been arrested. He was hiding at his father's care facility."

I didn't know whether to be relieved or concerned. I blurted out my first thought: "Then Jonathan couldn't have murdered Zachary. And he probably didn't kill the others, either."

The detective's smirk turned into a crooked smile. "That's faulty logic, Parker. We only caught him an hour or so ago. By the looks of things, Zachary was killed sometime during the night. And I'm guessing Ellington has no alibi."

"But . . . if he was staying at the care facility, couldn't his dad vouch for him?"

"Biased witness. Wouldn't hold up in court."

"It sounds like you've already made the judge's decision for him."

Brad appeared in the doorway. "What's going on out here? I'm trying to work, you know. How am I supposed to clean up with you two squawking in the background?"

The detective made a show of checking his watch. "Gotta run," he said to Brad, giving him a light punch on the shoulder. "Catch you later, Matthews." To me, he said, "Gotta go interrogate a suspect." Then he winked. I felt myself blush.

I turned to Brad, furious at Melvin's cocky attitude. But instead of sympathy, Brad gave me the stink eye.

"I *told* you that if you came along, to make yourself scarce! God, Presley, I can't take you anywhere."

He turned away, looking disgusted, and disappeared into the room where he'd been working. I thought about leaving, calling a cab for a ride, so as not to annoy him any further, but curiosity got the better of me. I peered into the room where Brad was working.

"Same MO?" I said, showing off my TV cop show skills.

Brad grunted.

"I'm going to take that as a yes. Grunt twice for no."

Brad sat up from his hands and knees position on the floor and sighed. He knew he wouldn't get any work done until I was finished asking questions. "All right. Basically, it looks like the same guy could have done it. Most likely he sneaked up behind Samuels and hit him over the head."

I glanced around the floor. No candlestick in sight. "With what?"

"They found a bronze statue lying on the floor nearby and took it as evidence."

"What kind of statue?"

"Looked like the Creature from the Black Lagoon."

I remembered seeing the statue on Jonathan's desk. "I loved that movie!" I said, temporarily distracted from the topic at hand. "Saw it at a retro showing of 3-D movies a few years ago. Richard Carlson and Julie Adams. Nineteen fifty-four. It was one of the earliest and best 3-D movies ever made."

Brad shot me a look that clearly said, "Your short attention span is showing."

That brought me back. "Was it heavy enough to bean someone with?"

"I didn't see it, but apparently it did the trick."

I thought for a moment. Why would Jonathan use his prized statue to kill Zachary? It would have been way too obvious if he was trying to get away with murder. I had a funny feeling the statue was covered with Jonathan's prints—and no one else's. The perfect setup for a killer who wanted to kill Zachary and frame Jonathan.

My phone rang. I backed into the hall for some privacy and answered the call I'd been dreading.

"Hi, Mother," I said wearily, figuring she'd heard the news about Jonathan's arrest.

"Presley! They've captured Jonathan and taken him to jail! You've got to do something! Stephen is so distraught. They're even talking about arresting him as an accomplice— aiding and abetting, or something like that. I think he's taken a turn for the worse."

"Calm down, Mother. First, tell me you didn't have anything to do with Jonathan hiding at the care facility."

"Of course not, darling. I knew nothing about it. In fact, I don't even think Stephen knew."

That made no sense, but it also made no sense to argue with my mother when she was fixated on something.

"Presley, what are you going to do?"

"Uh, I'm sure Jonathan has an attorney at the firm who will find him a criminal lawyer."

"That's not what I mean. What are *you* going to do to find the real killer? An innocent man's life is at stake."

Jonathan was hardly innocent.

"And this could kill Stephen."

"Mother, I don't know what I can do—"

She cut me off. "Presley, please! You've solved a couple of crimes recently. You apparently have a knack for it, as well as giving parties. There must be someone who wants to discredit or destroy Jonathan, or worse."

A name jumped instantly to mind, but before I could think it through, Mother said, "Get Brad to help you. He seems to like you. Just use your feminine wiles."

My mother had been using her wiles all her life to get what she wanted. She couldn't understand why I, at thirty, hadn't used mine—whatever they were—and hadn't been married two or three times already.

"All right, Mother. I'll do what I can. And I'll get Brad to help. But you have to stop worrying. It's not good for you. Promise me?"

I heard her sigh. "Thank you, dear. Let me know if you need my help. I love helping you with things like this."

"Sure, Mother. I'll call you soon."

As I put the phone back in my purse, I thought about the person who most wanted to ruin Jonathan. I headed for Stephanie's office and found her door ajar. She stood staring out the window, ignoring the pile of work on her desk.

I knocked.

She turned and said listlessly, "Hi, Presley." There were lines around her mouth and eyes I hadn't noticed before.

I stepped inside. "I'm sorry to bother you, Stephanie. I know it's a bad time."

"No, no, it's fine. There is no good time anymore. Is there anything new . . . ?" Her words drifted off.

"They found Jonathan."

She sucked in a breath. Her eyes widened. "Is he . . . ?"

"He's been arrested."

She shook her head and glanced out the window again. "Oh God."

"I'm sorry."

She turned back to me. "Do they know anything else?"

"That's all I've heard."

She was quiet for a moment, then said, "Do they know how Zachary died—exactly?"

"Only that he was hit from behind with a statue."

"A statue?"

"They think it's the one from Jonathan's desk."

Her pressed lips melted into a sad smile. "The Creature from the Black Lagoon. He loved that statue. It symbolized everything he'd worked for since he was a kid."

"Listen, Stephanie, I'll get out of your way, but I wondered if you had a number for Dane Scott, over at Stereo-Scope?"

An eyebrow raised. She looked as if I were about to betray her. "Why would you want to talk to him?"

"Just a hunch. He seems to be the one who gains the most from discrediting Jonathan. I thought maybe I could find out something from him or his assistant, Jerry Thompson."

She pulled out her cell phone, tapped it, and read me the number.

"You have it on your cell?" I asked, typing the number into my own cell phone.

"Oh yes. He calls here quite frequently, always trying to find out what we're working on."

I thanked her and headed for the door.

"Let me know what you learn, will you, Presley?" she asked. "If that bastard is responsible for all of this"—she paused, glancing back out the window—"I may kill him myself."

Chapter 20

It was stupid to come without my car.

Knowing the meticulous work he does, I had a feeling Brad would be cleaning up at Hella-Graphics for hours.

I pulled out my iPhone to call Delicia for a ride, when I had a thought. Instead, I switched over to Google Earth and scoped out the distance between Hella-Graphics and Stereo-Scope, figuring I could take a cab there. To my surprise, the company was located right here in the Presidio. Apparently, Lucas and Hella-Graphics didn't inhabit every building on the former military grounds. Ironically, Stereo-Scope—Hella-Graphics's prime competitor—was just across the campus.

I left Brad a note on his windshield telling him I'd gone for a walk and to call me when he was ready to leave. Then I headed for Dane Scott's place of business, trying to figure out a way to get in and snoop around. I didn't have any balloons handy for a "Surprise Balloon Bouquet," and I couldn't whip up a SUBWAY jacket without some iron-on letters. But by the time I reached the white clapboard building at the bottom of the hill, I'd come up with a plan to do just the opposite of breaking in to see him. I'd lure him out.

Unlike Hella-Graphics, the front entrance to Stereo-Scope was unlocked, allowing anyone into the small lobby. Before entering, I did a Facebook search and status check for both Dane Scott and Jerry Thompson. Scott was listed as "married." Thompson was listed as "divorced." His Facebook picture showed two young children standing with him.

At the back of the lobby stood a long desk, manned by a young woman in heavy black-rimmed glasses, with black hair and black nails to match. She looked right out of a vampire movie. She glanced up as I approached and raised a pierced eyebrow.

"May I help you?" she asked, the stud in her tongue glistening.

"Yes," I said, matter-of-factly. "I'd like to see Dane Scott."

"What's your name?"

"Presley Parker."

She looked at the computer, no doubt checking Dane Scott's schedule. Apparently not seeing what she was looking for, she asked, "Do you have an appointment?"

"No, but I have some important information he'll be interested in. It's urgent that I see him."

The girl sat back and twirled a pencil in her fingers. "I'm sorry. He only sees people by appointment."

Here we go again. Maybe I could get to his right-hand man.

"How about Jerry Thompson?"

"Do you have an appointment with him?" This time she didn't bother looking at the computer screen. She just kept twirling her pencil.

"No, but—"

"I'm sorry, but he sees only—"

"—people by appointment," I said, finishing her mantra. "Okay, then would you please tell Jerry his ex-wife is here? And if he doesn't see me, I'll be forced to leave his two children in the lobby." I glanced back toward my car as if checking on the little munchkins.

I could see the tongue stud clearly as her mouth dropped open. She blinked several times, no doubt in lieu of screaming "Oh my God!" and picked up the phone.

"Jerry? This is Katia at the front desk," she said quietly. "There's a woman here to see you . . . I know, but she says she's your ex-wife. And she's got your kids in the car . . . Yes, sir."

Katia hung up the phone.

"He'll be right out," she said. "Have a seat." She nodded toward the two brown leather couches facing each other in the middle of the room.

I felt her eyes on my back as I sat down to wait for my "ex-husband." When I stole a glance at her a few seconds later, she was clicking away on her computer, no doubt IMing everyone in the office about Jerry's ex being in the lobby. The news would be viral by the time he got out here.

I was quite proud of myself, coming up with such a great lie on the spur of the moment. But before I could gloat too much, a side door to the lobby opened and a young man stepped out. In his blue power shirt, Men's Wearhouse suit, and black loafers, he looked more like an eager company employee and less like a fake waiter.

"You're not Camille!" Jerry Thompson said, hands on his hips.

"No, sorry about that." Camille, I assumed, was his ex.

"So who the hell are you?" he continued.

I stood up, reached into my purse, and pressed the RE-CORDINGS app on my iPhone, then pulled out a business card and handed it to him. "I'm Presley Parker. We met the other day at a party."

He looked over the card, glanced up at me; then his eyes shot over to the receptionist. "Katia, call security," he demanded, his face reddening. "And have them show this woman out."

He turned on his heels, but I lunged and grabbed his arm. "I don't think you want to do that, Mr. Thompson. Or should I call you Joe the Waiter?"

He spun back around. "What do you want?" he hissed. "The party's over, Miss Parker. I have nothing to say to you."

"The police may not be so easy to escape, Mr. Thompson, even with your security people at the ready to back you up. And they'll definitely want to hear what I have to say."

He chewed his lip for a moment, his red face turning splotchy. Glancing around he spotted the nearby conference room, stepped over, and pulled open the door.

"She'll need to sign in—" Katia called out.

Thompson ignored her. He took me by the arm and

yanked me inside. Closing the door behind him, he moved over to the windows and pulled the blinds. I sat down in the chair closest to the door and tried to look relaxed and confident. Inside a beehive was raging. What was I getting myself into?

"So what do you want?" He turned around, his arms crossed defensively. "I've done nothing wrong. There's no law against moonlighting as a waiter."

"No, but there are laws against blackmail, extortion, corporate espionage, and murder," I said calmly, as if I accused someone of major crimes every day. I'd learned a lot about interrogating suspects from Detective Melvin.

Thompson exploded. He started shouting and spittle flew from his mouth. "I had *nothing* to do with any murder! Yes, I was at the party. But Levi's death shocked me as much as everyone else."

I leaned back in the conference chair. Cushy. Real leather. Made me feel like a proper CIO: chief interrogation officer. "It's obvious that you were spying at the Séance Party. But I think you were there to steal the Hella-Graphics 4-D Projector—and got caught."

"That's absurd," Thompson cried, but I noticed that he'd uncrossed his arms and was now clenching his fists, as if preparing to defend himself physically. "You have nothing on me. I'm calling security." He walked the few steps to the long conference table, his hand extended and ready to grab the multibuttoned phone that sat there.

I hastily placed my hand over the receiver to stall him. "Jonathan's been arrested," I said, playing my last card. I had run out of accusations and was throwing everything I had at him, hoping he'd—what? Confess?

Jerry blinked so many times, I thought he'd developed a tic. He pulled his hand back from the phone and tucked it into a suit pocket. A more natural color returned to his face. "Well . . . good. Then they've caught the killer. I'm not surprised. Jonathan was an egomaniacal dictator who wanted all the fame, glory, and money for himself. He deserves whatever he gets. We're done here." He started for the door, obviously planning to make a quick escape.

I stood and moved in front of him, blocking his exit. "I don't think Jonathan killed Levi—or anyone for that matter. I think you and your boss, Dane Scott, are behind all this."

His face flamed again. His hands contracted into fists.

Uh-oh. Had I really just said that?

Had I just told a probable killer that I knew what he'd done? What was to stop him from killing me? I was safe—for now—in the conference room, but once I left this building, it was open season on party planners. There was no telling when Thompson might try to silence me. Maybe he'd already tried, I thought, remembering the pounding on my walls last night.

"By the way," I continued, "your little attempt to scare me last night didn't work. And I've told the police everything, so if something happens to me, you and Dane Scott will be the first ones they'll question. After all, Jonathan is locked up. If I die, he's got an alibi."

Jerry face contorted in anger. I thought he might strike me—until a voice came over the intercom.

"Jerry?" It sounded like Katia, the multipierced receptionist.

Jerry Thompson stared at the phone as if it had suddenly come to life. Indecision about answering it was written all over his face. After another moment's hesitation, he pressed a button.

"What?" he snapped.

"There's a call for you. Do you want to take it in the conference room?" queried the disembodied voice.

He glared at me, then picked up the receiver to make the call private. Just before he turned away from me, I saw the color drain from his face. I could have sworn he said the name "Levi Webster." If it really was Levi Webster who was calling Jerry Thompson, it had to be from the grave.

Seconds later Jerry slammed down the phone. He turned to me, almost surprised to see I was still in the room, then dialed three numbers and said only, "Conference room."

Two beefy security guards arrived to escort me out the front door. I tried to maintain my dignity as they held my arms forcefully, but the stares I garnered from looky-loo employees didn't do much for my pride. Oh well. I thought things had gone fairly well for flying by the seat of my pants.

And I had the whole conversation on my iPhone recorder. I pulled out my phone and listened to part of the conversation. Then I called Brad.

"You done yet?" I asked.

"Where have you been? I've been calling you."

I glanced at my phone. I'd turned off the ringer while "in conference" with Jerry Thompson and hadn't turned it back on. Three calls from Brad.

"Sorry. Something came up. I'm on my way back to Hella-Graphics. Be there in a few minutes."

"Where are you—"

I hung up and hoofed it up the hill. Brad was standing outside, looking around—for me, I assumed. I waved. He didn't. We headed for his SUV in silence, and it wasn't until we were on the bridge that he asked again, "So are you going to tell me what you've been up to?"

"I went over to Stereo-Scope Graphics to see if I could find out more about Dane Scott."

Brad rolled his eyes. "You can't get past the front door at those places without an ID."

I smiled at him. I could almost feel my eyes twinkling.

His mouth dropped open before he hastily returned his gaze to the road. "You're kidding. How did you get in?"

"Charm. Looks. Personality. The door was unlocked. Who knows? What's important is, I talked with Jerry Thompson, Dane's right-hand man, and he's definitely hiding something. He acted very nervous and kept overreacting to my questions."

Brad stole another glance at me. "Did you find out anything?"

"Aside from the fact that he has an ex-wife? Yeah. I think he got a call from Levi Webster."

Brad frowned. "Obviously that's not possible. Levi's dead. Unless he was calling from one of those Ghost Boxes."

"No, that's just it. You should have seen his reaction when he was told who was calling. He looked like he *had* gotten a call from a Ghost Box."

"What did this Levi person say?"

We pulled off the bridge and drove down Macalla Road onto Treasure Island.

"I don't know. I was escorted out of the building at that point. But I'm dying to know how that conversation went."

We drove to Building One and parked in the lot. Gathering our things, we headed for the Art Deco front doors, flanked by giant stone statues of portly men and women, more remnants of the Golden Gate Expo of 1939.

Brad started to veer toward his office, but I called after him. "Brad, could you do me a favor?"

He groaned. "What now?"

I ignored his brief look of exasperation. "Could you find out from Detective Melvin what they discovered in Jonathan's confiscated computer, since Melvin's not likely to tell me? They should have that information by now. Maybe there's something about Levi—or Zachary—in there."

He pressed his lips together, nodded, and disappeared into his own office next door to mine. I spent the next half hour trying to focus on upcoming party events but my mind kept circling back to Jonathan—and my mother's plea to help him. In between phone calls to possible clients, I made random notes, but none of them offered any "Aha!" moments.

"Hey," Brad said, peeking in the door. "Any suspicious phone calls or strange knocking sounds lately?"

"Very funny."

He sauntered into the room and sat down at Delicia's vacated desk. Dee was off at her audition for the travel bureau that she'd been rehearsing for.

"Did you talk to Detective Melvin?" I didn't really have to ask. I could tell by Brad's expression that he had. "Well? What did he say? Did they find something?"

Brad picked up a bride and groom cake topper I had recently used at an engagement party. This one had the bride standing, dragging a reluctant groom. "It took them a while to retrieve the deleted messages, but they found e-mails to and from Zachary Samuels. Seems Jonathan found out that

Zachary was planning to sell inside information about the 4-D Projector to Dane Scott."

"Wow," I said, surprised at the revelation. After all, Zachary had denied it.

"That's not all. Jonathan threatened Zachary for betraying him."

"Threatened him? How?"

"Luke sent me a copy—I have it right here." Brad pulled a folded paper from his back pocket and handed it to me.

It read, "I'm gonna kill you, you double-crossing traitor."

Chapter 21

PARTY PLANNING TIP #21

Here's another fun trick for your Séance Party: Ask a hidden assistant to release a couple of spritzes of cologne into the room during the séance, so the participants can "smell" the presence of a female spirit. For a male, try something like Old Spice or Diesel.

Things were not looking good for Jonathan Ellington.

I dreaded telling my mother. She didn't take bad news well. She also seemed to think I was superhuman and could solve all her problems, which, of course, was impossible to live up to. The only good thing about Alzheimer's was that she often forgot my imperfections along with what she'd asked me to do. I wasn't sure, however, that this incident would be easy to forget. It seemed so personal to her.

Still, the facts were piling up against Jonathan. The motive, opportunity, means, not to mention the physical evidence—police had found his fingerprints on the weapons. That was to be expected since he touched them both, but still . . .

And now I had to add credible threats made to one of the victims, thanks to Jonathan's recovered e-mails to Zachary.

Did Jonathan really think deleting the e-mails would be enough to cover his motive? For a computer expert, it seemed pretty stupid. One thing Jonathan wasn't was stupid.

Still, SFPD had recovered the messages Jonathan had sent to Zachary when Jonathan had discovered Zachary was planning to sell the intellectual property to Stereo-Scope Graphics—for a multimillion-dollar price. Not only would Zachary be rich, but Jonathan would no doubt be ruined.

So where did this leave Dane Scott? Did Zachary manage to get him the 4-D information before he was killed—even though he swore to me that he had no such plans? Or was Zachary murdered before he could accomplish his goal?

If Dane Scott *did* receive the information before Zachary died, maybe he'd killed Zachary—with the help of Jerry Thompson—to make sure Zachary didn't talk. And that way Dane wouldn't have to pay Zachary off.

The best of both worlds.

I had to find out more about Dane Scott. But with him hiding inside that silicon fortress, he'd be nearly impossible to confront. The only way to get to him was to lure him out like I had with Jerry.

And I had just the plan.

Brad had disappeared from his office. He was probably helping Marianne with another one of her bogus requests. I'd need his help for what I had in mind, but for the time being, I'd ask Duncan Grant, skater, gamer, and computer expert, and Berkeley Wong, videographer, to lend a hand. They shared an office two doors down from mine.

"Duncan!" I said, stepping inside his office. There was no sign of Berk. Duncan, however, was sitting at Berk's desk, staring into Berk's computer screen. A bunch of gobbledygook scrolled down the screen.

He glanced over at me. "Hey, Pres. 'S'up?"

"Planning another GPS Treasure Hunt?" I asked. Duncan was the mastermind behind the GPS parties I'd hosted on several occasions. "Or are you hacking into our national security system?"

He smiled indulgently. "Not this time. Just checking to see if I fixed Berk's computer. It had a meltdown this morning."

"Oh no. Did he lose all his work?" Berk stored most of his videos on his computer, although he could probably get most everything back from his posts on YouTube.

"Nope. It's working now. Just doing a diagnostic."

"You're amazing," I said, in awe of anyone who knew more about computers than I did . . . which was probably everyone. Brad was also computer savvy, but there was no one quite like Duncan. It's a wonder he didn't work for the National Security Agency or some other supersecret high-tech place. Barely twenty-one, he didn't seem eager to enter the real world, and preferred doing his own thing. All while carrying a torch for Delicia.

"Listen, I need your help," I said.

He looked up. "Of course you do." Relaxing back in his chair, he folded his freckled hands over his ragged Space Aliens T-shirt. His tangled, curly red hair looked as if it hadn't been combed in days—if ever—which was normal for him.

"I want to send an e-mail to the CEO of a company and I can't find his address. Is there any way you could get it?"

"Depends," he said swiveling in his chair. "What have you got?"

I gave him Dane Scott's name, company name, and Web site address—it was all I had, aside from some articles I'd found on the Internet. "Not much, is it?"

Instead of answering me, he started typing furiously on the keyboard. I swear it was less than two minutes before he came up with DWScott2000@StereoScope.com.

"How did you do that?" I marveled at him.

"E-mail search engine. There's a bunch of them. This one—e-mailaddress.com—is one of the best. I could prob-ably find Amelia Earhart, Jimmy Hoffa, and the Bermuda Triangle's e-mail addresses if they existed."

"I'm impressed. Thanks so much."

"Later," he said, already refocused on Berk's computer screen.

Delicia was back when I returned to our shared office.

"Hey. How'd the audition go?" I asked as I sat down at my desk.

She gave me a long, dramatically downcast look, then broke out into a grin and clapped. "I got the part! I got the part! I'm Miss Baghdad by the Bay for the San Francisco Tourist Bureau!"

I jumped up and hugged her. "That's wonderful! I'm so happy for you. You'll be great."

"At least I'll be able to afford the rent this month. And it's going to be fun, playing all these different characters."

That gave me an idea.

"Dee, I've got the part of a lifetime for you. Doesn't pay much, only a handful of people will see you, but it could be very satisfying. What do you think?"

"What—you need me to play another fortune-teller and tell you who your killer is? I'm a good actress, but not that good."

"Actually, you'll be perfect!" I told her my plan.

Brad appeared in the doorway, his eyebrow raised. "What are you two plotting? You look very suspicious."

I grinned. Dee giggled.

"Just the man I was looking for," I said. "Got a question for you. And since you seem to have all the answers, I'm betting you can answer this one."

He touched his forehead and closed his eyes, pretending to read my mind. After a few seconds, he opened his eyes and said, "You want to know what I'm making for dinner tonight?"

"That too," I said, "but first, is corporate espionage illegal? I mean, can you get arrested for trying to steal secrets from another business? It seems so common these days."

Brad sat on the corner of my desk. "Yes, it's illegal. I've never had to clean up after it, but Luke has all kinds of stories about corporate spying. The most famous one was an employee at Bristol-Myers Squibb who had downloaded a bunch of the company's secret processes so he could start his own business in India. He got something like ten years. Why? Are you about to commit a felony?"

I ignored his witty repartee. "How did they catch him?"

"Bristol had computer security specialists who caught on. They tracked his e-mails, texts. Those guys aren't stupid. That's why companies hire them."

"I had no idea it was so prevalent."

"These days corporate spying is pretty extensive and sophisticated. They hire professional sleuths, tap telephones, intercept text messages, get cell phone records, hack into computers, go Dumpster diving—all the stuff the CIA does."

"Amazing. How do companies protect themselves?"

"Most businesses hire private security, mainly because the legal system is way behind on what constitutes espionage—and what's just healthy competition."

"The same goes for corporate sabotage?" I asked.

"Yep. That trusted insider may be a mole—anyone from an engineer to maintenance man to a salesman to an inspector."

"Or a cleaner?" I said, tongue in cheek.

He grinned. "Yeah, I've stolen enough intel from Killer Parties to start my own party business."

I laughed. "Are most of these guys caught and arrested?"

"Some are caught, but only a few go to jail. Mostly they end up as lawsuits. It's a dangerous risk, but the payoff can be high."

Aha. Just what I needed as leverage against Dane Scott and his talking puppet, Jerry Thompson.

I spent the afternoon getting ready to party once again—at the Winchester Mystery House. It was short notice, but Mia agreed to let me use the actual séance room this time, since the guest list would be smaller. She sounded surprised to hear that Jonathan had been arrested for murder and said she thought he was innocent. For such a brief relationship, he must have been quite the lover. I cringed at the thought.

Next, I prepared the guest list. Besides my team—Dee, Brad, Duncan, Berk, and myself—I jotted down the guests of honor and then Dane Scott and his yes-man, Jerry Thompson. Then I added Mia from the mansion; Lyla, Jonathan's soon-to-be ex-wife; Violet Vassar, his administrative assistant; and finally Stephanie, who would serve as a resource for information. I threw in my mother and Stephen Ellington to prove to them I was trying to find out the truth.

I drafted a copy of the e-vite, with Sarah Winchester herself doing the honors. I had Duncan create an animated spirit, with audio personalized to each guest, then ended with the Five W's of Party Invitations:

What: Another Séance Party
Where: The Winchester Mystery House
When: Tomorrow night
Why: To ask Sarah Winchester to reveal the killer . . .
Who: ?

I sent the first invitation to Dane Scott's previously private e-mail address. Sarah Winchester gave him a very "good reason" to attend, telling him she "knew all about his corporate espionage and would share it with the police, the district attorney, and worse—the local television station"—if he didn't respond positively in his RSVP. For Jerry Thompson, I had Duncan add audio from my iPhone recording of our meeting.

I wondered how much time I'd get for extortion.

I finished the rest of the invites, personalizing them based on what I knew about each guest. The ones to Lyla and Violet were a little less threatening, but still compelling (Lyla's affair with Zachary and Violet's unmentioned internship at Stereo-Scope Graphics). Stephanie and Mia got simple invitations asking them to be there for "an important update" in the case. Finally, I called my mother—she doesn't do e-mail—and asked her if she and Stephen Ellington would like to attend. "Of course we would," she said. I told her I'd arrange transportation for them both.

After I hung up, I had a frightening thought. If this plan backfired on me, I might be putting my mother in danger. Maybe I hadn't thought this through enough. Desperation will do that to a person.

While I waited for the RSVPs to pour in, I started prepping for tomorrow night's party—a séance to end all séances. The whole thing felt a bit like the denouement of an Agatha Christie novel, with all the suspects gathered in the parlor.

Only this time, the prime suspect, Jonathan, would be missing.

Chapter 22

PARTY PLANNING TIP #22

Increase the spook factor by including automatic writing at your Séance Party. Tell a guest to ask a question, then have your "medium" go into a "trance" and write an answer on a sheet of paper, using his or her nondominant hand.

I checked my e-mail and found four responses to my e-vite. None of them was from Dane Scott or Jerry Thompson. If those guys didn't show up, my plan would fall apart. I scanned the RSVPs I'd received:

Mia wrote, "This should be interesting. I'll be there."

Lyla answered simply, "Yes."

Stephanie said, "I hope to be there, if nothing else gets in the way! Fingers crossed."

Her answer reminded me of something, but before I could remember what it was, a new e-mail popped up.

From: Stereo-Scope.com
To: Killer Parties

Subject: Séance
We'll be there, along with our attorneys.
    —D.S. and J.T.

Whoa. It looked like there would be a couple of hefty party crashers at my last-minute Séance Party. I only hoped I knew what I was doing.

I burst into Brad's office and found him at his computer. "Brad! I need to see Jonathan." He looked up from the screen and sat back in his chair, lacing his hands over his chest.

"Last I heard, he was in jail, Presley," Brad said. "Visiting days are Saturday and Sunday."

I pulled up a chair, sat down, and leaned toward him. "Seriously. I need you to call Detective Melvin and get him to let me see Jonathan. I have a plan that I hope will prove Jonathan's guilt or innocence."

"They usually do the proving in a court of law, Pres," he said. "Besides, I thought this whole Séance Party you're putting on tomorrow night was your plan. Aren't you going to scare the bad guys from Stereo-Scope into confessing?"

I sat upright. "Stop mocking me!"

"Sorry." He frowned, turning serious. "Why do you need to see Jonathan?"

"He's going to be the one who accuses the killer of the murders."

Brad chuckled. "And how is he going to do that? I'll say it again—Jonathan's in jail."

"I *know* that. That's why I have to see him. To videotape him for the séance."

Brad shook his head. "First of all, I don't know if I can

convince Luke to let you in. I don't have that kind of influence."

"Yes, you do."

Brad sighed, then continued. "Second, Jonathan's probably not going to cooperate with any of this."

"I think he will, especially if he's innocent. Would you just talk to Melvin and try to get me in? Please? I'll deal with the rest of it."

Brad cocked his jaw. I could read his face easily, and it clearly said, "Resistance is futile; I give up." He pulled out his phone and called the SFPD.

"Thank you," I mouthed, then ducked out of his office and into the one next door. I had to get Berkeley Wong and Duncan Grant on board or, misquoting a Borg, my efforts would be futile. I found them punching keys on their computers, looking as if they were about to shoot, maim, or blow up each other—virtually.

"Berk!" I said manically.

"Ha!" Duncan said, his fist shooting up in the air. I took it that he had won the skirmish. Not to worry. These dead players came back to life quickly, ready for another round of warfare.

"Thanks a lot, Pres," Berk said. "You made me lose. Now I'm dead." In fact, he looked quite lively in his *Twilight* T-shirt, tight jeans, and bright green Chuck Taylors. He'd gelled his spiky black hair just enough to make it stand up like he'd been shocked in an electrical outlet.

"'S'up?" Duncan asked, still grinning from his win. It was midafternoon and he was still in his SpongeBob pajama bottoms, his Space Aliens T-shirt covering his thin chest.

Going shoeless also appeared to be part of his fashion statement today.

"Guys. Listen, I need your help," I said, breathless from excitement.

"Sweet," Duncan said. "I love helping you with your parties."

"I'm in," Berk added. "As long as I can upload what I tape onto YouTube."

I filled them in on my plan. Then Berk showed me how to use one of his Flip Video camcorders to tape Jonathan—if I got the chance to see him in jail. Next, I got Duncan to agree to do a little computer work for me. In return, I offered to pay their rent for a month. They, like me, were also underemployed. I figured I could always take it out of Jonathan's pocket if I proved him innocent.

I left the guys trying to rekill each other and stopped by Brad's office on the way back to mine. He was on the phone so I returned to my office to fill Dee in on my plan.

"So, this time you want me to play the Great Mesmer?" she asked, clarifying. "A man?"

"Yes," I said. "Can you do it?"

"Of course I can!" Dee said. "I played Peter Pan in my college production. With a wig, a mustache, and a magician's outfit, I should be pretty convincing. This is going to be awesome!"

After we worked out some details, I checked on Brad to see if he'd talked to his buddy, Luke.

"Did you talk to him?" I asked.

"Yep."

"So . . . what did he say?"

"You can have five minutes with Jonathan, under the supervision of a guard. That's it. Be there at three o'clock p.m."

"Oh my God, you're amazing!" I wanted to kiss him but this wasn't the time or the place. "How did you do it?"

"Let's just say, he owes me from a poker game."

"I owe you big-time! How about I make dinner tonight at your place?"

"I thought you couldn't cook."

"I can cook," I said, not meeting his eyes. "I usually don't have time."

He eyed me suspiciously before answering. "Okay, you got a deal. But if I have to have my stomach pumped, you're paying for my hospital stay."

"Very funny," I said before I dashed back to my office.

I sat down in my chair, took a deep breath to calm myself, then realized no amount of deep breathing would help with the upcoming tasks. Not only could something go wrong with every step of my plan, but I could get myself into some serious jeopardy if the killer decided to kill the messenger.

And worse, I felt bad about lying to Brad.

I didn't really know how to cook.

Brad accompanied me to 850 Bryant: the location of the Hall of Justice, the main San Francisco Police Department, and the county jail. I'd been to the jail before, to see Delicia when she'd been mistakenly arrested for murder. I didn't like the place any more now than I had back then. The SoMa— South of Market—location felt seamy and unsafe, the concrete building imposing, and the relentless sadness I imagined behind those walls was depressing.

After passing through the metal detector, where I'd had

to temporarily relinquish my iPhone, keys, and purse, I collected the Flip camera that Berk had lent me, and waited in the empty meeting room for Jonathan to appear. Memories came flooding back as I sat staring at the pale pink walls. When I'd visited Dee, it had been during regular visiting hours and the room had been filled with families and friends of the inmates. The noise—laughter, tears, excited conversations—had been loud and distracting. Now, with me as the only visitor, the room was deathly quiet—and lonely.

While I waited, I practiced videotaping the picnic-style tables and benches, the ticking clock on the wall, the official signs that warned visitors of potential misconduct. Berk had taught me how to use the simple gadget and had sworn it was foolproof, but I still worried I'd forget to remove a lens cap or turn on a wrong button and erase everything. I guess we'd see about that.

A heavy metal door on the far side of the room clanked, then creaked open. Jonathan Ellington entered, his usually erect shoulders slumped, feet and hands in shackles, his eyes darting around. He was accompanied by a uniformed officer, instantly reminding me that Jonathan was here for a capital offense, not tagging buildings with spray paint or driving while texting. His skin appeared drawn and pale, his mouth drooped, almost as if he'd had a stroke like his father, but his eyes lit up when he saw me.

"Presley!" he said, maneuvering around the shackles to sit down on the end of the bench opposite me. "They said I had a visitor, but I had no idea it would be you. What are you doing here?"

He reached out a hand to touch mine, but the guard called

out, "No touching." His hand contracted, like a startled turtle pulling its head into its shell. I had a feeling he would have liked to do the same with his whole being.

"I only have five minutes," I said, "so I'll be quick. I want to videotape you."

His eyebrows rose. "What for?"

"I'm having another Séance Party tomorrow night and I want you to appear—at least, in spirit."

He squinted at me, as if I might belong in the criminally insane section of the jail. "I don't understand."

"Listen, Jonathan. I'm trying to prove whether or not you killed those guys. That's why I want you to make a surprise appearance at the séance and say these words. If you're really innocent, then I'm hoping the real killer will be exposed."

I pulled out a single sheet of paper from my jeans pocket and pushed it over to him.

He picked it up, his steel bracelets jangling, and scanned it.

"You're kidding."

"I'm not."

"You really think this will work?"

"I . . . don't know. I hope so. It's certainly worth a try."

I glanced at the clock on the wall. If Melvin had been serious about having only five minutes, I had just three left to get this done. Holding up the video camera, I said, "Are you ready for your close-up?"

He frowned, but said, "I guess so."

I put his face in most of the frame, trying to block out the details of the jail meeting room, then nodded, indicating for him to start. He took a last glance at the script, faced the camera, and said the first line I'd written for him:

"Yes, it's me. I'm out of jail . . ." He paused.

". . . And I know who killed Levi and Zachary . . ." Another pause.

"Furthermore, I have the evidence to prove it . . ."

Finally, Jonathan pointed his finger outward and said, "It was you—"

I stopped taping and smiled at him. "Perfect."

He raised an eyebrow. "That's it?"

"That's it." I checked the tape before I turned the camera off, to make sure I hadn't messed up. "Now, if you're superstitious, keep your fingers crossed."

He looked down at his hands. "That's about all I'm able to do right now."

"Time's up!" the officer said.

I gave Jonathan a last smile of encouragement and said, "Hang in there." It was all I had at the moment.

We rose, and I watched Jonathan shuffle back to the door that led to the jail. I couldn't help feeling sorry for him, in spite of his usually cocky attitude and scandalous disregard for women. I had a feeling that my mother was right—this man hadn't killed anyone. He was a lover, not a killer.

But if that was true, someone hated him enough to make it look like he had.

And I was going to prove it.

Tomorrow night at my encore Séance Party.

Chapter 23

After a quick side trip to the care home on Van Ness Avenue to reassure my mother and Stephen Ellington about Jonathan's well-being and my plans to help get him released, I returned to the office and spent the rest of the day preparing for the party. By six I was ready for a break and when Brad stopped by I was packing up my things.

"Looking forward to dinner," he said.

Oh my God. I'd forgotten all about my promise to make dinner. I quickly recovered and said, "Yeah . . . hope you like it. One of my specialties."

"You want to ride with me or follow me over?"

"Uh, I need to feed my cats, get my mail, pick up a couple

of things. I'll meet you at your place, if that's okay." We headed to the parking lot.

"Sure. Want me to come with you to your condo?"

"No, no. I'm sure I'll be fine for the few minutes I'm there."

"Okay, but keep your phone handy. If you see anything suspicious, call me. I can be there in two minutes."

I felt guilty lying to him. He was such a great guy. I gave him a quick kiss as a promise of more and got in my MINI, while Brad headed for his Crime Scene Cleaners SUV. Minutes later I was at my condo, still wondering what I was going to serve Brad for dinner.

Me and my big mouth.

Night was falling quickly and blanket fog had begun to seep in. I grabbed the mail, unlocked the front door, and opened it slowly, half expecting the boogeyman to jump out at me. When I'd come home this morning to feed the cats, everything was fine, but that didn't stop me from feeling jumpy now that it was getting dark.

Maybe I should have had Brad accompany me, I thought. But after nothing more had happened the other night, I'd felt silly calling him. I was sure the sounds had been caused by teenage vandals or a couple of drunks who were out having what they considered a good time.

Inching the front door open, I listened for any unusual noise. The creaking of the door alerted my cats that I was home, and they ran to me as if I were their long-lost mother.

"Hey, guys," I said, giving each a head massage, tummy rub, or back scratch, depending on their preference. The cat bowls still had traces of the morning meal, but I filled them up, freshened the water, and sat down in a kitchen chair with a glass of merlot to go through the mail.

Bills, ads, flyers, coupon books, and a single envelope with my name computer-typed on the outside. No return address. I hoped it was a check from one of the several parties I'd recently hosted—I needed the money. I tore it open.

Inside was a folded sheet of paper. I unfolded it—and nearly peed my pants. I was looking at a Photoshopped collage of six pictures.

Each one of me.

Me coming out of my office building yesterday—I could tell by the clothes I'd worn.

Me leaving Brad's house this morning.

Me in the parking lot of Stereo-Scope Graphics.

Me entering the Hall of Justice to see Jonathan.

Me dropping by my mother's place.

Me returning to my office building wearing the same thing I was wearing now—black jeans, a T-shirt with a replica of a Ouija board on it, and my black Mary Janes.

I held up the envelope with trembling hands to study it. No stamp. I hadn't even noticed that when I'd torn it open. That meant someone had been following me, had come to the Island—to my *home*—and put the letter in my mailbox. I picked up the sheet of photos again and stared at them.

The last one had been taken only a short while ago.

How could someone have followed me throughout my day taking pictures without my knowledge?

And they had even beaten me home.

With sweat prickling my forehead, I picked up my purse, stuffed the envelope and letter inside and grabbed the closest cat—Cairo. "Hey, kitty. That's a good boy," I said reassuringly as I carried him quickly to my car. I placed Cairo inside, along with my purse, closed the door so he couldn't escape, then ran back, and picked up Thursby from the couch and Fatman from under the coffee table. I returned to the car, and with all three cats safely inside, I ran back and locked the front door to my condo, got in my MINI, and headed up Macalla, toward the Bay Bridge.

Instead of driving directly to Brad's place, I drove to the city. I couldn't go to Brad's empty-handed, not when I'd lied about being able to cook. One of my favorite places to pick up to-go food is practically right off the bridge exit, a little place in trendy SoMa called The Butler and the Chef. I phoned in my order on the way, hoping I didn't get caught using my cell phone while driving and end up in jail, and asked for two Croque Monsieurs, two ham-and-cheese quiche slices, and some pâté. I also told them I'd call when I got there so they could bring the food out to me, explaining that I couldn't leave the car. The reason: My bewildered cats were climbing all over me.

I drove into the parking space reserved for takeout customers and let them know I was there. When the waiter arrived with my order, I had him put it the trunk to keep it away from my hungry cats. Unfortunately, they could smell it with their supersensitive cat nostrils and I had to listen to a trio of meowing all the way back to Yerba Buena Island.

I parked in the narrow slot behind Brad's house and dialed his number.

"Presley?" he answered breathlessly. "Are you okay? I've been worried."

"I'm fine, Brad, but I need help carrying a few things in from the car. Do you have a couple of large cardboard boxes with tops that close?"

Silence, then, "You've got that much food?"

"Just bring them," I insisted, and hung up.

Moments later Brad arrived with two boxes the size of small microwave ovens. He reached for my car door but it was locked. I eased the window down an inch. "I'm going to open the window in a minute and I want you to shove one of the boxes inside as fast as you can."

He peered in, frowned at what he saw, and shook his head. "You're kidding me. What are your cats doing here?"

"Playdate," I said, "with Bruiser."

"Very funny. They'll eat him alive. Seriously, why are your cats in your car?"

"It was an emergency. I'll explain once I get them inside. Now shove one of the boxes in, please."

He did what I asked. I put the two smaller cats in the boxes and closed it up, then passed it out to Brad. He gave me the other box, I put the last cat inside, then folded the top closed. The cats complained, but I reassured them as I opened the car door, eased out the second box, and started for his house.

"Careful," I said to him as he followed me, carrying the first box.

Brad opened the door, balancing his box on his leg, and waited for me to go inside. I set my box inside the front door; then Brad entered and set his down.

I glanced around. "Where's Bruiser?"

"Probably sleeping on my bed."

"Will you shut him in there, then let my cats out? I have to get a few more things from the car."

I ran out, grabbed my overnight stuff and the bag of food from The Butler and the Chef. When I returned, I located

Brad in the kitchen, holding a glass of wine. He popped a handful of something into his mouth and gulped it down with a big swallow of the wine.

"What are you doing?"

"Taking drugs," he replied. "Claritin."

I'd forgotten about his allergies. "Sorry about this. Hope it's not too inconvenient." I briefly explained that I didn't want my cats home alone with a maniac loose. I held off showing him the pictures I'd received until I'd had another glass of wine.

I sipped the glass of Treasure Island Merlot he offered me while I set the table and the cats cased the place. Fatman made himself at home under the kitchen table, Thursby sniffed and scratched at the bedroom door, and Cairo complained about the food in the dog's dish. In the distance, I could hear yapping. Bruiser, vanquished to Brad's bedroom.

"Go watch TV," I told Brad so I could prepare the food. He turned on the news in his man cave and sat down on the black couch.

Meanwhile, I found three mismatched bowls, divided the pâté into thirds, and added bits of quiche to each bowl. As soon as the makeshift cat food was ready, I called the kitties and they came running. Finally, I opened the last containers, set the French sandwiches on plates, and microwaved them to heat them up. When I turned around to place them on the table, I found Brad standing in the doorway, looking puzzled.

"You're not making dinner," he said. "You bought it!"

I sighed. "Sorry. I had no choice. Something came up. I'll tell you about it after I've finished this wine."

Brad filled up our glasses and we sat down to the reheated

food. Raising my glass, I said, "Cheers." We both took long sips. Before taking a bite, Brad asked, "So, what happened?"

I reached over to my purse, pulled out the envelope, withdrew the paper with the photographs of me, and handed the sheet to Brad.

He studied them for a few seconds, his face growing cloudy, the furrow at his eyebrows deepening.

"This is serious, Presley. This guy—or whoever—has obviously been stalking you and knows where you live. You did the right thing, getting out of there and coming here, but we've got to tell Luke about this. You're in real danger."

I'd been looking forward to sleeping with Brad, more for the safety and comfort of his arms than the attention of his other body parts—but it was not to be. Instead of being reassured after talking with Detective Melvin, I was even more frightened. He'd warned me in no uncertain terms that although Jonathan was locked up, someone—a cohort?—was threatening me. And Detective Melvin had been a police officer long enough to know not to take threats lightly. He knew I was temporarily safe with Brad, but he told me not to go alone anywhere until I stopped "stirring things up," as he put it.

So I was restless most of the night. Three displaced cats on the bed and a whining dog in the next room didn't help either. Nor did my recurring nightmare of Sarah Winchester, who kept trying to tell me something that I couldn't understand.

The next morning I awoke to minor aches and pains, not used to Brad's firm bed. I showered, whipped up my specialty—burned toast and overcooked eggs—then served the eggs to my hungry cats, who had polished off the gourmet people food and refused to touch Bruiser's dog food.

Brad and I were about to head out when he got a call for a cleaning job—a cat lady in the Fillmore district had died, her body undiscovered for days. "Apparently her cats had started nibbling—"

I plugged my ears. "Stop! Don't tell me!" Yuck. Note to self: Remember to pick up cat food before my own cats started nibbling on me in the middle of the night.

Brad pulled my fingers out of my ears. "Remember what Melvin said. You need someone with you at all times, at least until this party is over tonight."

"I know. As soon as I get to TI, I'll have my crew with me all day."

"You're still planning to go through with this?"

"Of course!"

"You really think Jonathan is innocent?"

I hesitated a moment, then said, "Yes," as convincingly as I could. I still wasn't absolutely sure, but I'd promised my mother I'd do what I could to find out the truth. I thought of another promise I'd made to Teddi Wells. Maybe this would lead to the truth about her husband's supposed suicide.

"Okay, well, I've got to run," Brad said, grabbing his black jacket. "I'll walk you out."

He escorted me to my car, gave me a duplicate key for his house, headed for his SUV, and drove off.

Dew sparkled on my MINI in the early sunlight that was trying to break through the fog. After glancing around to make sure I wasn't still being followed, I gave a sigh of relief and I unlocked the car. Being stalked made me feel vulnerable and paranoid. Luckily, I only had a few short miles to my office at Treasure Island until I'd have an entourage.

I opened the car door and started to get in—then froze.

The passenger's seat was covered with torn photographs, like giant pieces of confetti. I reached down to study a piece, then another, and another. More pictures of me—from the moment I'd left my house with my cats last night, to my trip to the restaurant, to Brad's house afterward. All torn into pieces.

Someone was still following me. They'd broken into my car.

And Brad was gone.

A chill ran down my back as I swiveled my head side to side, searching for my stalker. Seeing nothing, I peeked into the backseat to make sure no one was there, then slid inside the car and punched down the locks. I needed to get myself over to TI and my crew ASAP, but my hands shook as I tried to start the engine. Third time was the charm. I revved the engine and gripped the steering wheel, then glanced at the window on the passenger side.

There was a small slit at the top.

No one had actually gotten in my car. I'd left the window open a crack. They'd slipped the photos inside.

Jamming the gearshift into reverse, I stepped on the gas and backed out of the space with a jerk. Moments later I'd left Yerba Buena behind, and was headed for my office building on Treasure Island.

Pulling up to the parking lot at Building One, I checked my rearview mirror again.

No one was there.

Chapter 24

I parked the car, still glancing over my shoulder, and headed for my office.

"You look like you've seen a ghost. You okay?" Dee asked.

"There's a lot of that going around," I said. I didn't want to tell her the latest news, afraid she and the others might back out of helping with the séance. Then again, I thought, I might be putting their lives at risk by not disclosing the details. I finally decided that whoever was stalking me wouldn't try anything as long as I had company. Safety in numbers, they always say.

"I'm fine. Just nervous about the party," I added when I felt her eyes still on me. She knew me too well, but apparently she ignored her intuition and started asking what she could do to help. Within a couple of hours we'd gathered everything I needed for the improv séance and were ready to head over to the Winchester Mystery House. The rest of my crew—Duncan, Berk, and Raj—caravanned, following Delicia and me in my MINI. I prepped Dee on her role as I drove, and by the time we arrived at the mansion, we were both excited about the upcoming possibilities and anxious to get it over with.

Mia greeted me and my crew in the gift shop, ready to lead us to our destination. "Follow me," she said, and we did, taking a new route to avoid tour groups. By showtime— eight p.m.—the house would be closed to everyone but us.

"Sweet," Duncan said, his eyes as wide as crystal balls. He hadn't been with us for the original séance and seemed in awe of the place.

We wound through the life-sized puzzle box that Sarah Winchester had called home. Once we reached the small séance room, I delegated tasks to my crew. Brad said he'd come later, after his cleanup job, and bring Mother and Stephen Ellington. He'd also arranged to have Detective Luke Melvin there as well.

Duncan and Berk brought in a small round table and chairs, while Dee and I arranged the tablecloth and accessories we'd be using for the event. I kept the decorations minimal, placing only votive candles at each seat rather than the lethal candlesticks, and added a trick crystal ball in the middle of the table that would fill with smoke on cue. Raj helped Berk set up the cameras and microphones we'd be using, and Duncan prepped the computer in the adjoining room so it would be ready to conjure up the new "spirit" of Jonathan Ellington. It might not be as impressive as the state-of-the-art 4-D Projection, but it would get the job done.

I hoped.

At six, Brad arrived from his latest cleaning job.

"Glad you're here," I said, wanting to give him a hug but not in front of the others.

"You all right?" he asked softly, looking me over.

"I'm fine. Everything's going according to plan. We'll be ready for the guests when they come in"—I checked my watch—"less than two hours. What about Mother and Stephen?"

"Luke's having them picked up in a van by a plainclothes officer. They should be here around seven thirty."

"I'm hungry," Berk suddenly whined.

"I'm starved!" Duncan seconded.

I looked at Brad, who said, "I could eat—but not that overpriced cafeteria food they serve here."

I offered to buy a quick dinner at Santana Row, and everyone jumped on it. The evening was pleasant so we walked the few blocks to the Italian place, ordered spaghetti, salad, and a bottle of Chianti. Brad and I argued over the check—he won—and we walked back to the Mystery House eager to welcome our guests. What a great crew I had.

The place was closed to the public by the time we returned. The house, as usual, looked ominous in the moonlight, and I shuddered as we entered, not just from the air that had turned cool. After Mia led us back to the séance room, I did a last check to make sure everything was ready, then sent Dee to change into her Mesmer costume. As ready as we could be, I left the crew behind to take their places, and headed for Sarah Winchester's formal waiting room, where visitors began their tour, and waited for the rest of the guests to arrive.

Mother and Stephen Ellington entered soon after, thanks to Detective Melvin, who'd chauffeured them himself in a van outfitted for wheelchair access.

"Oh, Presley, darling. This is so exciting," Mother said. "Isn't it, Stephen?"

He gave a half smile and blinked with one eye several times. I knew he'd put a lot of hope into my plan to prove Jonathan innocent, and I felt the burden of his trust wash over me.

"We'll do our best, Mother." I gave what I hoped was a reassuring smile to Stephen. I turned to Detective Melvin and asked if he would carry Stephen to the séance room.

"It would be my pleasure," he said, and swept the thin, frail man up into his strong arms. Mia led the way, and Mother followed, leaving me alone in the waiting room. I reviewed the guest list, praying they would all show up. Stephanie had offered to bring Lyla, and I assumed Dane and Jerry would come together, apparently with their lawyers.

Otherwise, it would be an event planner's worst nightmare—hosting a party where nobody came.

Waiting was agonizing.

I had prepared for the séance to the point where it would almost host itself. There was nothing more to do. Hopefully, tonight I would find out that Jonathan really was innocent—and uncover the killer.

I flipped over a couple of pages in my notebook and found copies of the deleted e-mails that Jonathan had written to Zachary, thanks to Brad. Something bothered me about them.

Would Jonathan really threaten Zachary via e-mail, knowing how easily his deleted e-mails could be retrieved? He was, after all, a computer expert.

And why would he use a statue from his own desk to kill Zachary?

Like a magic trick, everything changed right before my eyes.

Quickly, I phoned Duncan and told him I wanted to make a change. He said it was "No prob," and hung up just as Stephanie and Lyla arrived. Distracted by my new plan, I robotically offered them wine that had been placed in the waiting area. Both accepted; Lyla took a seat on a nearby bench and sipped her wine while reading her phone messages. Stephanie paced the room, playing with her necklace, her sharp heels echoing on the hardwood floor.

I checked my watch for the umpteenth time. It was eight thirty—half an hour past the party start time. The last two guests—Dane Scott and Jerry Thompson—still hadn't arrived. If they didn't show up soon, my plan wouldn't work.

The door to the waiting area open and in walked Dane Scott, Jerry Thompson, and a woman I didn't recognize, all escorted by Mia Thiele.

"Sorry we're late," Dane Scott said, without a hint of apology on his stern face. He and Jerry both wore suits—perhaps they never took them off. As an abnormal psychology instructor, I knew that dressing formally all the time was a sign of insecurity, much like getting numerous degrees or joining brainiac organizations. They needed such things to make up for their lack of self-confidence and self-worth. I wondered if these two fell into that category.

As for the woman, she wore a gray pantsuit, a large ruby brooch, and power red Manolos. Classic overachiever.

Dane Scott caught me staring at her and said, "This is Holly Simone. She's our company attorney."

I nodded at her, she ignored me and glanced around the room as if assessing its worth.

"Well, glad you all made it," I said, mentally wiping away a virtual sweaty brow. "Since we're all here, we'll begin. Please follow Mia. She'll lead us to the actual séance room that Sarah Winchester used to contact the spirits."

While the guests formed a single-file line behind Mia, I held back a few seconds to alert the crew that it was showtime. I quickly caught up with the group by following their voices after taking one wrong turn and winding up in one of Sarah's many bedrooms.

"Please take your assigned seats," I said, after I entered the crowded room where Stephen and Mother were already seated at the table. They appeared anxious: Mother whispering to Stephen and patting his hand, while Stephen's eyes darted from person to person.

I studied the guests as they searched for their place cards and sat down, their candles already lit. Mia looked wide-eyed and excited, and had come dressed in period costume. Her long black dress looked much like the one Sarah Winchester had worn in the photograph in her office. She grinned as she scooted in her chair.

Stephanie wore her usual business attire: a severe maroon suit, matching maroon heels, and a colorful scarf that hung down on either side from her neck. As usual, she held the crystal in her hand, no doubt thinking about Jonathan and what had happened last time, and hoping for protection.

Dane Scott's perpetual frown and heavy eyebrows made him look even more irritated as he stared at his folded hands, his knuckles white, his thumbs twiddling. Sitting next to him, his sidekick, Jerry Thompson, kept glancing at his boss, perhaps for cues on how to act. He mimicked everything Dane did, right down to the folded hands and twiddling thumbs. Their attorney sat on the left of Dane, her lips pressed together, waiting patiently for something to happen so she could no doubt spring into action.

Lyla had finally put her cell phone away. She looked bored, as if the last time she'd been to a séance, no one had been murdered. Had the woman even cared for Jonathan? Or had she just married him for his status, wealth, and good looks?

Detective Melvin had slipped in while the guests were busy finding their places. He'd tried hard not to dress like an off-duty cop, wearing khaki slacks, a Hawaiian shirt, and loafers. I'd almost laughed when I saw him walk in earlier. Now I was getting used to the casual look.

Standing behind an empty chair opposite one other empty chair, I greeted the small crowd. "Thanks for coming, everyone. I know you all want to find out if Jonathan is really the one behind these murders. That's why I've arranged this séance—only this time we have a real medium."

Before anyone could react, the lights dimmed and a puff of smoke arose from across the room. A short, big-bellied man appeared, wearing a black suit, black shoes, even a black shirt. Only the black silk cape attached to his shoulders seemed out of place. His cheeks were rosy, his black hair was slicked back, and he sported a bushy black mustache that covered his small mouth.

Pretty, petite Delicia was truly a chameleon when it came to costumes and makeup!

"Please welcome Mesmer the Great, our medium for tonight's party," I said, then took my place at the table between Stephanie and Lyla.

The Great Mesmer took a bow, using his/her cape for dramatic flourish. All eyes—some wide, some narrow—watched the odd-looking man as he took his seat at the head of the table. He said nothing, just took in a deep breath, exhaled slowly, and closed his eyes.

Suddenly the crystal ball in the center of the table turned from clear to smoky. Mother gasped.

"Please, join hands," Mesmer's deep voice boomed.

"Are you—" my mother started to say.

"Silence!" Mesmer commanded. Mother blinked. Mia jumped. Stephen didn't react; I wondered if he was hard of hearing or if his reflexes had slowed. Dane Scott raised an eyebrow, apparently not used to being spoken to in such a tone, while Jerry's eyes grew wide as he looked at his boss for cues. Stephanie had let go of her crystal, while Lyla just stared at the odd man giving orders. I caught a glimpse of Detective Melvin shaking his head, reminding me he wasn't into this sort of thing, even to catch a murderer.

The lights dimmed further, thanks to a well-hidden Brad, leaving only the candles to illuminate the room. In the fluttering darkness, I started to feel a little nervous myself.

"Join hands," Mesmer commanded, he gripped the hands of guests on either side—Mother's on the left and Mia's on the right. I hoped Mia wouldn't be able to tell she was holding on to a female hand. After a few seconds, Mesmer took in another deep breath, let it hiss out, then began rolling his head around. I prayed he didn't lose the wig or the mustache.

Finally Mesmer's head slumped forward; guttural mumbling tumbled out of his mouth, his lips barely moving as he conjured up a spell. A wind blew through the room—Duncan was right on cue with his preset fan—and the candles flamed out, leaving us in utter darkness. Without windows in the room, not even moonlight could pierce the blackness.

Someone squealed; I couldn't tell if it was from delight or fear.

The crystal ball began to glow a bloodred color.

An image materialized inside the ball—the image of a tiny Jonathan Ellington. Duncan's computer wizardry was working perfectly.

I heard Dane Scott's distinct laugh, followed by Jerry's high-pitched laugh. No wonder. The display looked hokey, nothing like the Hella-Graphics 4-D Projection of Sarah Winchester. More like the Haunted Mansion spirits at Disneyland.

But the laughter died as Jonathan began to speak.

"Yes, it's me. I'm out of jail . . ."

Heads turned from side to side, as the guests tried to get a glimpse of one another reflected in the red glow. Jerry whispered, "Dane, that's Jonathan's voice!"

"Shut up," Dane hissed.

Jonathan continued. ". . . And I know who killed Levi and Zachary . . ."

Next to me, I heard Stephanie gasp. She jerked her hand from my grip and reached for her crystal.

"Furthermore," Jonathan's image said, "I have the evidence to prove it . . ."

The image paused.

The room grew silent.

Jonathan extended his finger and stopped just before it reached me. "It was you—"

I heard a chair fall backward. A door burst opened, light streamed in from the next room, and I saw a figure bolt from the room.

Mia got up and switched on the lights. Everyone looked around, a little dazed.

One person was missing from the table.

The one Jonathan Ellington had pointed to: Stephanie Bryson.

Chapter 25

PARTY PLANNING TIP #25

After your Séance Party, reveal all your tricks to your guests so they won't fall victim to fraudulent mediums. Plus, they'll get a kick out of seeing "how it was done." Note: The great magician, Harry Houdini, who made it his mission to expose phony spiritualists, once visited the Winchester Mystery House.

I dashed after Stephanie, leaving the stunned guests behind.

As I bolted through the door where she'd made her getaway, I called out for Detective Melvin and Brad.

No sign of them.

Right now it didn't matter. I had to follow Stephanie before I lost her for good. The problem was, she had a few seconds' lead on me, and had disappeared into one of the most baffling and confusing mazes ever built. And like Hansel and Gretel, if I didn't have bread crumbs or a GPS to follow, I would be hopelessly lost.

Not to mention, it was dark in here. If only I'd grabbed my cell phone, I could have used it as a sort of flashlight.

The narrow hallways deep inside the mansion allowed no moonlight in, so I had to feel my way, stopping every few steps to listen for Stephanie's footfalls. The clicking of her stilettos on the hardwood floors would have been relatively easy to follow if the echoes hadn't been misleading and the house hadn't been so twisted. I found myself repeatedly running into dead ends or bumping into walls. Sarah Winchester had meant to fool the spirits and keep them from finding her. That worked for human beings as well.

At one point, just when I thought I was getting close, I tripped over a doorjamb and fell, slamming my knee against the floor. It ached when I rose—I'd injured it once before when someone at another party tried to kill me—but I could walk/limp. But I'd lost time, and paused, listening intently for those killer heels. After a few seconds I picked up the sound again, and wound my way through more passageways, up a staircase, and deeper into the bowels of the house. All in utter blackness.

I sensed she was getting farther away.

"Stephanie!" I called when I'd caught my breath. Running mazes wasn't one of my best athletic activities and I was winded. I hoped either she'd answer, or that someone would hear me and help give chase. "Stephanie, I'm not going to hurt you. I just want to talk."

"Leave me alone!" a hysterical-sounding Stephanie hollered back from some distance away. How far, I had no idea. "I warned you, Presley. I left those messages on your phone and those pictures in your mailbox and car. I even tried to scare you off by banging on your door like an angry spirit. But you didn't listen. Now leave me alone or you'll end up like the others."

Good: The more she talked, the more I'd get a bead on where she was.

Bad: She wanted to kill me, like she had the others.

"Stephanie, I know what Jonathan did was despicable, using you and all those other women. But don't make things worse than they are!"

Dead silence.

I tiptoed forward in the darkness, hoping to hear her breathing, if nothing else. Unfortunately, the old wood floors creaked beneath me, giving away my location.

I turned a corner in the darkness and listened.

A scream.

Only a few feet away.

"Stephanie! Are you all right?" I called.

Nothing.

I continued forward, still feeling my way through the halls and passageways like a blind woman, and praying I didn't trip again and lose her. I had a feeling that once she was out of this house, she was gone.

I had a sudden thought and a chill passed through me. Maybe that scream I'd just heard wasn't what I thought it was. Maybe Stephanie wasn't really in trouble.

Maybe she was trying to lure me somewhere and . . .

Oh God. Was I walking into a trap?

Stephanie was not a stupid woman. Superstitious, yes, with her horoscopes and charts and lucky crystals and knocking on wood. But she'd cleverly planned and executed—so to speak—her plot to seek revenge on Jonathan.

And she'd fooled us all.

I slowed down again and listened.

A moan.

Coming from a short distance away.

Maybe she really was hurt. After all, I'd almost broken my kneecap.

I entered the next room on tiptoe and immediately recognized where I was—the infamous Daisy Room. Unlike the inner rooms of the mansion, this one allowed moonlight to stream through the muted yellow stained-glass windows, giving the room a shadowy glow. Suddenly I remembered— Sarah Winchester had been trapped in here for hours during the 1906 earthquake.

I glanced around, certain I'd heard a moan coming from here. I spotted one of the daisy-themed windows—it was broken, shattered to pieces. Most of the shards and bits of colored glass lay on the other side of the window but a few had fallen inside.

Had Stephanie crashed into the window trying to escape?

I scanned the dimly lit room, searching for her. I expected to find her huddled in a corner, nursing some kind of wound, maybe bleeding. Or unconscious.

Instead, I caught movement in the corner of my eye.

Before I could react, Stephanie lunged at me from behind the door to the room. Something in her hand glinted in the moonlight. She raised her fist, giving me only a split second to see that it was wrapped with her scarf.

In it, she held a knife-long razor-sharp piece of broken glass.

I threw up my hands defensively just as Stephanie brought down the jagged shard.

I screamed as the shard plunged deep into my hand. Blood spurted from my palm. The pain made me woozy and the room began to spin. I pressed my fingers to the gash, hoping to staunch the flow of blood and keep myself from passing out.

But the room continued to spin. My legs crumpled, and I fell to the floor, hitting my hip and elbow hard as I landed.

I looked up as Stephanie loomed over me in the semi-darkness, her eyes wild, the dagger of glass held high again. Leaning on my sore elbow, I kicked at her stilettos with all the adrenaline-fused strength I had—not to mention a good strong pair of Mary Janes.

Her legs buckled as she lost her balance and she fell to the floor like an inexperienced ice skater. She landed on her butt, and I thought I heard a crack—either the floor, the glass shard, or her tailbone. She let out a string of curses that I doubt sailors or Kathy Griffin would even know.

As soon as she'd caught her breath, she rolled over and pushed herself up, shaking with anger. "I'm gonna kill you!" she screamed, then lunged again, the dagger still intact and in her scarf-wrapped hand.

The scarf was soaked in blood.

"You've cut your hand," I yelled at her, hoping to distract her. I also hoped to attract the attention of anyone nearby, but I knew that in a twisted mansion like this, it might take hours to find us. And that would no doubt be too late—for me.

She glanced at her hand, her eyes wild with both fear and rage. Then she turned that rage toward me, lunging again with the shard. I rolled to the side and found myself trapped in a corner of the room. Glancing around for any kind of weapon to defend myself, I saw nothing—nothing but a pipe that started halfway up the corner to the ceiling, and out of the room.

One of Sarah Winchester's listening tubes.

"Stephanie! Listen! Do you hear him?" I shouted the words up into the tube, praying someone would hear me. At the same time, I wanted to distract Stephanie, who seemed to believe in all this spiritualism stuff.

She stopped in midair. Listening.

"I don't hear anything," she said tentatively.

"A voice. I can't make it out . . ."

Stephanie continued to listen. Now that she was temporarily distracted, I wanted to get her talking.

"Stephanie, what did Jonathan do to you?" I continued to speak loudly, hoping my words reached the tube. Mia had said that the servants could hear Sarah calling from this room after she became trapped, but they couldn't get to her because of the damage the earthquake had caused.

"*Jonathan* didn't do anything," she said, nearly spitting out his name. Her face contorted as she spoke.

Good. She was talking. And loudly too.

"But he must have done something to you. He used women as if they were his personal toys. Did he seduce you? Promise to leave his wife? What?"

"He didn't do anything!" She screamed the words, then turn the right side of her face toward me. "Look. At. Me!"

I could barely see her in the moonlight coming from the broken window.

"What? I don't understand. . . ."

And then I did.

I saw it.

The large red splotch on her face no longer covered with makeup. Wiped away with sweat and tears. The birthmark that disfigured an otherwise attractive woman.

"Do you really think Jonathan would have anything to do

with someone like me?" She was screeching now. Hopefully loud enough to be heard through the listening tube.

"But you know how superficial he is. And you're vice president at a company that's about to go viral. Isn't that enough?"

"Not after what he did to me."

"What did he do, Stephanie?"

"He laughed at me," she said, giving a little laugh herself. "He didn't just turn me down when I suggested we . . . get together. He laughed. Of course I knew all about his affairs and what he was like. But to him I wasn't a woman. He only wanted them young, blond, and sexy."

"But why kill Levi? Why not Jonathan?"

"Killing Jonathan would have been too easy. He wouldn't have suffered enough. I had to destroy everything that meant anything to him."

"So you killed Levi—and Zachary—and then framed Jonathan. Why?"

"I've been planning this for two years, ever since Zachary created the 4-D Projection. I found out Zach wanted more money from Jon, and Jon refused to pay him. Not only that, he fired Zach. When Jon came up with this séance idea— which personally gave me the creeps—I went to Zach and told him I had a plan."

"Your plan was to get Zachary to help you disrupt the séance and expose Jonathan for what he was. But then you killed Levi. Why?"

"I had to find out if he knew what Zach and I had done."

"And?"

"And, yes, he'd figured it all out, after putting all the pieces together."

"So you . . ."

"Killed him? Isn't it obvious? I had to or he'd have told Jonathan and ruined everything."

"And then you made it look like Jonathan had done it," I said, as it all fell into place.

Her eyes narrowed in the dim light, but she said nothing. What was she thinking? Or planning next?

"Did Zachary know you killed Levi?"

"No, Zach thought Jon did it, too. He knew about Jon's affairs and believed me when I told him Jon had killed Levi thinking he was the one who'd exposed him."

"So you convinced Zachary to make that new message for the séance, and promised him—what? More money? The job of VP when you took over Jonathan's CEO position after Jonathan was arrested for murder? You stood to gain a lot if your boss was out of the picture."

A thin smile appeared on her lips. I'd figured it out.

The hand with the glass knife inched upward again.

I was running out of questions to keep her talking.

"So . . . you sent those e-mails, didn't you? And deleted them, knowing experts would be able to retrieve them. That was clever, because you knew Jonathan wouldn't see them." I thought giving her a few compliments would help me stall for time.

The smile remained. So did the shard in her bloody hand.

"You . . . must have arranged for Zachary to enter the building. Then you killed him with Jonathan's statue. Only, I can't figure out why you got rid of Zach. He was your ally, so why did you kill him?"

She shrugged. "Zach finally figured out I killed Levi. He came to see me, told me he didn't want to be involved in murder. He was going to turn me in. I had no choice."

I had no choice. There it was.

Stephanie raised the shard higher over her head, now grasping it with both hands. She was moving in for the kill.

I huddled in the corner, trapped, and covered my face with my arm.

Seemingly from the walls, a disembodied voice echoed the name, "Stephaaanniieeee. . . ."

The voice of a dead man: Zachary Samuels.

Chapter 26

✿ *PARTY PLANNING TIP #26*

Add a little personality to your Séance Party by bringing a few famous souls back from the dead. Hire a celebrity impersonator to channel the voices of stars like Elvis Presley ("Thank you very much"), Marilyn Monroe ("Happy Birthday, Mr. President"), and Mel Blanc ("That's all ffffolks!").

Even in the semidarkness, I could see Stephanie turn a whiter shade of pale.

"Zach . . ." she whispered, eyes searching the moonlit room.

"Stephanie . . . I'm here . . ." the voice said.

If I hadn't known about the listening tubes, it would have scared the shit out of me, too. But Stephanie didn't know—she hadn't taken the tour—and she literally dropped to the floor, both hands covering her mouth, the unmistakable look of horror on her face.

I didn't hesitate. While she cowered in fear, repeating the name "Zachary," I shoved her down flat so she landed on her stomach. She screamed when pieces of broken glass cut her hand.

And then I sat on her.

She stretched back, making short jabs with the dagger she still held, but I raised my foot and brought it down forcefully on her wrist.

She screamed again in pain and the shard tumbled from her bloody grasp.

I unwrapped the soaked scarf from around her hand and tied one end to her damaged hand. I grabbed at the other hand, yanked it behind her back, and roped her hands together. I continued to sit on her as she writhed under me, drooling and shouting profanities, her face twisted in agony. The splotch on her face was clearly evident.

Feeling like Horton the Elephant, I yelled toward the listening tube, "We're in the Daisy Room! Get Mia to show you. Hurry!"

"On our way," Brad's steady voice came through the tube.

His was the first face I saw entering the Daisy Room door fewer than three minutes later. Good timing, as Stephanie was still kicking and screaming and trying to break free. Behind him were Mia, who I was sure led him here, plus Detective Melvin. Mia punched on the lights.

Brad lifted me off Stephanie, who seemed to have finally lost steam. Now that I had backup, she lay there silent, eyes closed, deflated as a morning-after party balloon.

Detective Luke Melvin knelt down and admired my homemade handcuffs, then removed the scarf and cuffed her with the real thing. Backup, in the form of two uniformed officers and two EMTs, arrived moments later. One EMT bandaged Stephanie's wounds, while the officers read her her rights and placed her under arrest.

The other EMT wrapped my hand in gauze and tape, and checked my knee to see if I'd broken anything. My clothes were a bloody mess.

"You okay?" Brad asked gently.

"Yeah." I glanced down at my bandaged hand and tried to wiggle my fingers. "I just hope I can play the kazoo again, or at least blow up a balloon again. If not, I may be out of business." I grinned at my own version of the old joke to show him I was really all right.

Brad glanced around at all the broken glass. "Very funny. By the looks of things, she nearly killed you. How did she break the window?"

I hadn't thought about it. "I don't know . . ."

Detective Melvin interrupted. "With her heel," he said. "See how the crack webbed out from that small hole?" He held up a portion of a pane that he'd retrieved from the other side of the window. "Then she found a big piece to . . ." He left off the rest of the sentence but the meaning was clear.

Brad looked at me in disbelief. "How did you manage to stay alive until we found you?"

"I kept her talking until I spotted the listening tube. You know how some women love to talk. Plus, I knew she was very superstitious, so I tried to scare her a little. Then you guys caught on and really played that up. Which reminds me, how did you bring Zachary back to life like that?"

"Duncan—that kid's not only a skater and gamer, he's an electronics wizard too," Brad said. "He's got voice-changer software on his computer and he used something called a voice comparator to create Zachary's voice."

I'm sure I looked completely baffled. He explained, "Basically, he called Zach's cell phone and imported his recorded answering message. He used that as a reference for its pitch and timbre. Then he recorded his own voice, saying the word "Stephanie." Finally he used the comparator to match the pitch and timbre with Zach's. I thought it sounded pretty close to the answering machine message, especially for doing it on the spot like that."

"Apparently, Stephanie did too—thank goodness. It scared her nearly to death."

The EMT looked up at me. "You're going to need stitches, ma'am," the cute young EMT said, finishing his ministrations.

I nodded.

"You want us to take you to the hospital or do you have someone who can drive you?"

Brad raised his hand as if volunteering in class. "I'll take her."

Mia led us back to the gift shop, where my staff was anxiously waiting. They'd already packed up most of their gear and were just standing around for word from me. There were hugs all around, a few tears from Delicia; then Brad whisked me off in his SUV to San Francisco General. My hand still throbbed and I felt a little dizzy, but not so bad that I couldn't keep talking the whole ride over.

"Will Melvin release Jonathan now?"

"I'm sure he will," Brad answered.

"Mother and Stephen will be so happy. What's going to happen to Stephanie?"

"Good question. She'll need a smart lawyer. And maybe a straitjacket."

"I just don't understand why she went over the edge," I said, mostly to myself. "She had a great job. She was smart. She was attractive, in spite of her birthmark. And women have survived being dumped before."

"She wasn't dumped. She was laughed at."

I thought for a moment, then said, "One thing still puzzles me. George Wells. How does he fit into all this?"

"Luke has a lead he's following on that."

"Really? What? Did Stephanie kill him too? It wouldn't have been easy hanging him! But she said Zachary refused to help her when it came to murder so he couldn't have done it for her."

"She didn't kill him. He really did commit suicide."

"You're kidding. It can't be a coincidence."

"It's not. He was a mole for Dane Scott, just like Jerry Thompson, who posed as a waiter at the party. George was paid a lot of money to pass Hella-Graphics intel over to Stereo-Scope. He was living large—the house in Pacific Heights, the boat, the exotic vacations, not to mention all the stuff he bought his wife and three daughters. But when George couldn't give Dane the kind of information he wanted, Dane threatened to expose him as a corporate spy if he didn't pay all the money back. George was caught between a rock and a hard place. He knew he was looking at twenty years easy. He couldn't face jail, or the shame he'd be bringing to his family. So he hung himself, right there in his office."

"Poor Teddi. I'm sure she had no idea he was mixed up in all this. I hope they get Dane Scott, too. What a cutthroat business."

"Yeah, not much different from the event-planning business," Brad said. "Meanwhile, Stephanie was planning to destroy Jonathan and take over. She was just waiting for Zachary to complete the 4-D technology, while learning all she could about it."

"Like I said, smart lady. Too bad she used it for evil," I said.

"I guess there will always be women who feel they need a man to fulfill their lives, even those with successful careers, like Stephanie and my mother."

Brad looked at me. "What about you? Don't you need a man in your life?"

I grinned. "Sure. Someone to bring me lattes and clean up after my parties and have hot sex with now and then."

Brad smiled widely. "You think we have hot sex?"

I said nothing as he pulled into the parking lot of San Francisco General. I felt that familiar tingle rising and wondered if we could find a quiet linen closet or unused operating room for a few minutes.

My hand didn't hurt at all now.

Chapter 27

PARTY PLANNING TIP #27

If your Séance Party is a great success and you want to host an encore, give it a twist by adding a special theme within a theme. Then invite guests to your Alien Contact Séance Party, Dead Movie Stars Séance Party, or Departed Pets Séance Party.

I woke up in my own bed to the smell of coffee and the sound of howling cats and kitchen noises. Bless that man, I thought, stretching out the sleeping kinks. I immediately regretted it, when my sore muscles, bruised hip, and fresh stitches in my hand protested.

I glanced at the time. Past nine! How had I slept so late? The drugs. Thank God for the drugs. Now that they had worn off, I was ready for more. Then I remembered I'd promised to meet Mother, Stephen, and Jonathan for breakfast at Mel's Diner so Mother could make sure I didn't look as bad as I sounded when I talked with her last night.

Rolling gently out of bed, I headed for the shower before Brad saw me in such disarray. I looked bad enough with all the cuts and bruises and didn't need to subject him to hair fright. Finally clean, dressed in fresh jeans and a long-sleeved purple shirt that covered most of my wounds, I padded out to the kitchen. Brad was sitting at the table, sipping his latte and reading the paper. I wondered if we'd all made the news.

"Morning," I said, then pointed to his coffee. "Got one of those for me?"

He set the paper down and looked me over. "It's in the microwave, ready to be reheated. How you feeling?"

"I could use some more heroin, or whatever it was they gave me. But a good, strong intravenous latte might do the trick."

He grinned and pulled out a chair. "Sit down. I'll get it for you. Help yourself to a cranberry muffin there. Can you eat one-handed?"

"Nothing keeps me from a cranberry muffin," I said, stuffing a bite into my mouth with my good hand.

Brad brought over the reheated latte and set it on the table, then leaned over and kissed me softly on the lips. That was about the only drug I'd need to get me through the day. Of course, I'd need a booster shot when it was bedtime.

The group had already assembled at the table when we arrived at Mel's. Mother was dressed to maim, if not kill, in a silky purple suit that matched my blouse, and a pink blouse with a big fluffy ribbon tied under her chin. Her eyelids were dusted in a shimmery lavender, her champagne hair glinted under the lights, and her pink lipstick matched her blouse.

Stephen sat in his wheelchair, which was pushed close to the table. One side of his face seemed alert, the other lacked personality. But he brightened and gave a half smile when he saw me, and it felt good to add a little cheer to his day.

Jonathan, on the other hand, looked pale and distracted, as if his body was present but his mind was elsewhere. Instead of his usually enthusiastic, overbearing greeting, he simply smiled as he moved over in the booth to accommodate us. Was that remorse on his face? Embarrassment? Defeat? I couldn't tell.

"Presley, darling! How are you?" Mother studied me, looking for signs of my encounter with Stephanie the night before. "Your face . . ."

I touched my cheek where I'd hit the floor when Stephanie attacked me. I thought I'd covered the bruise well with makeup, but my mother saw through my disguise.

"I'm fine, really, Mother," I said, as I slid in next to Jonathan in the large semicircular booth. Brad squeezed in next to me. I deliberately sat by Jonathan in an effort to keep the two men apart. Jonathan shot a sideways glance at me as I settled in, nodded to Brad, then returned to studying the napkin he was folding and refolding like an accordion in front of him.

"Are you sure, dear?" Mother insisted. "Have you seen a doctor?"

She'd apparently forgotten where I'd ended up last night—at San Francisco General. Another sign of her short-term memory loss.

"Yes, Mom. Three doctors, in fact. They all said I'm going to be fine." I tucked my bandaged hand in my lap so she couldn't see it and ask more questions. "How are you, Stephen?" I asked, redirecting the conversation to Jonathan's father.

"Much better," he said, "now that Jonathan is out of jail."

Although his speech was somewhat slurred, I heard what I wanted to hear.

Jonathan lifted his head and smiled. "Yeah, he's doing great. Rehab begins tomorrow and that should do wonders for his mobility, right Dad?"

Throughout this whole ordeal, the love between father and son remained strong and was still evident. If nothing else, Jonathan and I had one thing in common: a close bond with an elderly parent.

Once we'd ordered, Mother peppered me with questions about Stephanie. I wasn't hungry after my latte and muffin and just had orange juice, but Brad ate a he-man plate of bacon and eggs, while Jonathan just poked at his omelet.

I filled Mother and the others in on the details of Stephanie's twisted reasons for killing Levi and Zach—they got in the way and knew too much. And why she'd tried to kill me—likewise.

"That poor thing," Mother said, forgetting for a moment that the poor thing tried to silence me with a glass shard. But that was Mother—always rooting for the underdog, even if the person was a killer.

"She'll get the help she needs in the psychiatric ward," Brad said, wiping bits of breakfast off his mouth. "And then she'll get her own private cell."

Jonathan cleared his throat, set down his coffee cup, and wiped his own mouth with his napkin. "Presley . . . ahem . . . I don't know what to say, other than thank you. You're not only a great party hostess, but you essentially saved my life, and probably the lives of others as well. I owe you."

I felt my face flush. "Oh . . . you really should thank my mother. If it wasn't for her . . ."

Mother looked at me, a little bewildered, then said, "I told you she was San Francisco's premiere party queen. I'm so proud of her."

"Well, you were right, Ms. Parker," Jonathan said to Mother, then turned back to me. "Presley, I have a check for you." He pulled a folded prewritten check from his shirt pocket.

I opened it and read the amount. He'd doubled my fee.

"Oh, Jonathan, this isn't necessary—" I started to say.

"Yes, it is. And by the way, I'm doubling the donation amount for the American Stroke Association as well." He glanced at his dad. Was that a tear I saw in Stephen Ellington's rheumy eyes?

I folded the check and thanked Jonathan.

"What are you working on now, dear?" my mother said, breaking the silence that had settled over the table.

I sighed, and shot a glance at Brad. "Well, Brad got me hired for a big event in exchange for discounted rent in my new office building. It's not for another few months, but it looks like I'll be planning a mini-Expo, a tribute to the one that was held on Treasure Island seventy years ago, only on a much smaller scale."

"What fun!" Mother said. "Your grandmother Granny Constance was there, you know. She was a Pan Am Clipper Ship Hostess on the Magic City. Are you planning a Gayway?"

The fair's "Gayway"—which had nothing to do with San Francisco's Castro district—had been the most popular part of the Expo, especially Sally Rand's Nude Ranch, a peekaboo adult playland featuring scantily clad women frolicking in little more than colorful ostrich feathers.

She didn't wait for my answer. Instead, she said, "Did you

know that the Expo was considered a financial flop, and closed early, over four million dollars in debt?"

Brad whistled.

Stephen raised an eyebrow.

Jonathan squirmed in his seat and grimaced. "Speaking of which," he said, glancing at each of us in turn. "I'm selling what's left of Hella-Graphics. ILM is interested in the 4-D projector and a couple of other companies are too. I think it's time." He glanced at his dad, who gave him a crooked smile.

I'd been wondering what Jonathan had planned to do after all this, but the news still came as a surprise. I knew he'd worked hard to create his innovative products and build his business.

"What will you do next?" I asked.

He shrugged. "Not sure. Maybe work on some kind of product that helps stroke victims like my dad. I'm pretty good at gathering talent and inspiring them to create something visionary."

I hesitated, then asked the other question that had been on my mind. "What about Lyla?"

He shook his head. "That's over. We were both cheating on each other. Hers was more from revenge, but still, that's no way to be married. In fact, I'm off women for the time being. I just want to focus on my dad."

"Now we're both going to rehab," Stephen said proudly. "Just not the same kind."

I took a sip of orange juice and decided to bring up one last loose end. "So George Wells really committed suicide?" I said more than asked, confirming what the police had ruled.

Jonathan nodded solemnly. "You know, I sensed something was up, but I had no idea he was under such pressure. The whole idea of Hella-Graphics was to make it an enjoyable place to work."

Apparently, having a personal trainer, a slide between floors, and a coffee barista wasn't enough to keep the employees happy. Maybe a psychologist would be a better hire.

I thought about Teddi Wells and how hard it was for her to accept her husband's death as a suicide. The guilt she must have been feeling for not knowing—or not seeing—how depressed he had been, how trapped he had felt. It would take time—and her own therapist—to cope with those unresolved emotions. I made a mental note to have coffee with her this week just to talk and let her know I cared.

"Well, I've got to run," Mother said, winding up the conversation. "I have bocce ball this morning, and Curves this afternoon. Then a bunch of us are watching a *Golden Girls* marathon. We're going to dress up as our favorite character from the show. Guess which one I'm going to be."

"Blanche, of course," I said. The men looked bewildered.

"How did you know?" Mother asked.

I knew my mother all too well. And I hoped to go on knowing her for a long time to come.

Brad and I escorted my mother to Jonathan's car while Jonathan wheeled his father along. He had picked up both his father and my mother from the care center, and promised to return them safely.

"Presley!" my mother said, suddenly looking alarmed. "I've lost my purse again!"

I glanced down at her side and pointed to her Coach bag. "It's right there, Mother."

She followed my pointing finger, recognized her bag, and clutched it tightly to her side. "Thank goodness!" she said as she stepped into the car, visibly relieved.

Just before he got into the driver's seat, he paused and looked at me. "Thanks again, Presley—for everything." I nodded. He slipped inside and drove away.

Brad took my good hand and we walked slowly to his SUV. Still feeling the pain of my bruised hip, I favored my good leg, and used Brad's strong arm for support. When we reached the car, he held the door for me, then went around the car and got in. I had my iPhone in my hand and was scanning messages when he asked in an English accent, "Where to, madam?"

I grinned, shut off the phone, and dropped it into my purse. "To the Bat Cave, Alfred."

"Ah, don't tell me we have another case, Batgirl."

"Not a case, a party. Where do you think I could rent some bats this time of year?"

Brad eyed me as if I now needed my own psychiatrist. "Bats? I hate bats." He shivered.

"Well, you better get over that, because Lucas Cruz wants a 'wrap party' to celebrate finishing his latest film." Cruz, the resident movie producer on the Island, rented one of the Pam Am Clipper hangars for filming. It wasn't unusual to spot Robin Williams, Danny Glover, or Margaret Cho coming or going.

"A bat party?"

"Nope. A Vampire Party."

"That should be interesting," Brad said, raising a lascivious eyebrow. "Maybe we should go back to your place and get in the mood. I'll wear one of your vampire costumes—actually just the cape—and you can . . ."

"Down, boy," I said, giggling. "First we need to make a little side trip."

"Where to?" he asked.

"Colma."

"Colma . . . aka 'The City of Souls'? What for? That place gives me the creeps. It's nothing but cemeteries."

I smiled. "I know. That's exactly why Cruz wants to host the Vampire Party there. If we hurry," I said, channeling Béla Lugosi's Transylvanian accent, "we can look over the graveyards and be safely home before darkness falls . . ."

Brad grinned at me and started up the engine.

How to Host a
Killer Séance Party

So you want to chat with Elvis? No problem—even though he's been dead for decades. Just host a séance, hold hands around a crystal ball, and wait for the spirits to appear. . . . Ideally, at the circle you'll want a few true believers, a couple of skeptics, and one or two who are open to the possibility of the supernatural. And don't forget the medium—real or not. It's time for a ghost-whispering Séance Party.

Invitations

Invite the skeptics and believers with a "message from the beyond . . ." Cut out a white circle, glue the top edge to a black card, and write, "The Spirits Are About to Speak . . ." on the outside. Underneath, glue another white circle and include the party details. Or draw a ghost on a white card with a speech bubble providing the information. Or outline your palm, draw lifelines, and write the details along each line, indicating their "future" at the party. Include a tarot card or a lucky rabbit's foot.

What to Wear

As the hostess, you might dress up as a gypsy, or wear all black with a lacy scarf. Tell the guests to come in costume, dressed as a character from the twenties, when the séance was in its heyday. Or suggest they come as a witch, sorcerer, or fortune-teller.

Decorations

You'll need a dark room to host the séance, one with draperies that will keep out the light from outside. Set a round table in the middle of the room and drape it with a black lace tablecloth. Set a crystal ball (or an upside-down fishbowl) in the center of the table. Light candles around the room and play spooky Halloween music in the background. Set hanging pictures at an angle, and string fake cobwebs along the lights and furniture, or in the corners of the room. Download creepy pictures from the Internet, frame them, and set them on tables or hang them on the walls. Get an accomplice to help you with some simple séance gimmicks while you summon the spirit world. (See Games and Activities for examples.)

Games and Activities

Scare the goose bumps out of your guests with a few ghoulish games and spooky surprises!

Summon the Spirits

Have a real séance with a hired medium. Or put on your own séance and set the scene with lots of spooky gimmicks. Have the attendees sit at the table and hold hands. While you close your eyes and mumble to the spirit world, have your accomplice do some of the following tricks. Tie fishing line to a picture on the wall and move it slightly. Do the same to the draperies. Knock softly, then louder, on the wall. Turn on a fan and blow out a candle or two. Start up a fog machine. Spray the guests with a sudden blast from a squirt gun. Have sheeted ghosts pass through the room. Use a speaker or karaoke machine to create the voices.

Channel the Spirits

After the guests are thoroughly spooked by the unseemly spirits, it's time to channel the dead. First, tell a little background to continue the spooky mood and put on a theatrical performance as you call the spirits. Then bring back someone famous from the past that everyone knows, such as Elvis, Queen Victoria, or Marilyn Monroe. Have the accomplice imitate the voice, and answer questions from the attendees, such as "Elvis, how did you die?" "Ah ate too many pork rinds—thank you verah much."

Ouija Board

Get out the Ouija board, choose a couple of guests to sit opposite each other, and ask questions. Take turns so everyone gets a chance to hear answers "from the Other Side." You might even include some preformed questions the players must ask, such as "Who will meet the man of her dreams next?" or "Who in the room is keeping a deep dark secret?"

It's in the Cards

Read up on fortune-telling with tarot cards. Then predict each guest's future using the cards.

Predictions

Have the guests make up predictions for each guest. When everyone is finished, choose one guest to read her predictions—then guess who created it.

Movie Madness

Rent creepy movies that feature ghosts and other strange creatures, such as *The Others*, *The Ring*, *Thirteen Ghosts*, *Ghost Ship*, *Ghostbusters*, *The Haunting*, *The Legend of Hell House*, *Poltergeist*, *The Shining*, *What Lies Beneath*, or *Ghost*. Share them with the group.

Refreshments

Make your own fortune cookies. Buy prepackaged sugar cookie dough. Roll out the dough as thinly as possible, cut into circles, fold the circle, curve it into a "C," and pinch the ends, leaving a small opening. On small strips of paper, write down funny fortunes, such as "You will learn to play the violin," "You will marry a clown," or "You will come back as a mule." When the cookies are lightly browned, let them cool, then insert the paper predictions. Make a devil's food cake for a centerpiece, topped with tarot cards or the crystal ball.

Favors, Prizes, and Gifts

Tarot decks make great prizes and favors, along with lucky charms, scary movies, a book of ghost stories, creepy sound tracks, and astrology books.

Party Plus

Invite a "real" medium, psychic, or tarot-card reader to your party to lead the séance or predict the future.

For more party ideas, check out *Ladies' Night: 75 Excuses to Party with Your Girlfriends* by Penny Warner (Adams-Media).

Read on for a sneak preview of
Penny Warner's next Party-Planning Mystery,

HOW TO PARTY WITH A KILLER VAMPIRE

Coming from Obsidian in Fall 2012.

PARTY PLANNING TIP

With the popularity of vampires today, why not host a Vampire Party! Take your pick from the Twilight *saga,* True Blood, The Vampire Diaries, Buffy the Vampire Slayer, *Bram Stoker's* Dracula, *or Anne Rice's* The Vampire Lestat. *Or give your party some bite and invite all of them!*

It should have been a dark and stormy night, à la Hollywood, but the October moon was full and the sky cloudless. I stood quietly in the cemetery, feeling as if I were viewing a film. But there were no cameras, and this was no movie.

I watched as the tall, pale twentysomething man dressed in tight black jeans and a black chest-hugging T-shirt suddenly appeared from out of nowhere. He seemed to glide toward the wide-eyed, raven-haired young woman who waited for him. She wore a flowing white dress, sheer and low-cut, that displayed her obviously enhanced breasts. Leaning seductively against a towering headstone, her long hair swirling in the night breeze, she smiled at the man in black approaching her. He held a glass of bloodred wine in his hand.

I felt like a voyeur, but I couldn't take my eyes off this mesmerizing couple.

He offered her the glass, not taking his eyes from hers. "This is very old wine. I hope you'll like it."

She wrapped a porcelain hand around the stem, her lacquered red fingernails tinkling against the glass. "Aren't you drinking?" she asked, her eyes reflecting the bright spotlights. She took a sip.

Staring at her with intense dark eyes, the young man parted his full mouth, revealing white teeth that glinted in the light. "I never drink *wine*."

I almost laughed out loud at the familiar line. Count Dracula had said the same thing to Renfield in the 1939 film. But when the man in black suddenly jerked, as if having a spasm, I gasped. Seconds later he shot up into the air like a rocket, and disappeared into the branches of a eucalyptus tree.

"Awesome!" I said, clapping. I could feel my heart racing.

I looked around, certain I'd be joined in a round of cheery applause. But when I saw frowns on the faces of those nearby, I stopped.

"No! No! No!" Lucas Cruz yelled from behind me.

Cruz, as everyone called him, was the eccentric producer/director at CeeGee Studios, located on Treasure Island. Five years earlier he had set up his computer graphics/film company in one of the long-empty Pan-Am clipper ship hangars on the island. Since then he'd produced a number of sci-fi and horror films, which featured his cutting-edge special effects. One of his films had starred local San Francisco resident Robin Williams as Cosmo Topper in a remake of the popular 1937 ghost film *Topper*. In spite of Robin's talents, the movie had quickly gone to video.

Cruz had hired me to plan a wrap party to celebrate—and publicize—the end of production on his latest horror film, *Revenge of the Killer Vampires*. I'd seen a few clips of the jump-the-shark spoof of vampire flicks that had ravaged theaters around the country. The two "hot" young stars—Jonas Jones, who played the vampire, and Angelica Brayden, the love interest—would no doubt become *ET*, TMI, and Gossip Guy regulars once the film debuted. And I was lucky enough to have just witnessed a preview of the mini-performance from the movie that would be performed at tomorrow night's party.

The wrap party would have been simple enough to host if it hadn't been for the fact that Cruz wanted the event held in a cemetery—"for the ambience." After overcoming my initial resistance, I researched the possibilities online, and I found a *Wall Street Journal* article that mentioned the growing popularity of murder mystery events, scavenger hunts, and other events held in cemeteries. Hollywood Forever cemetery in Los Angeles projected movies onto mausoleum walls. Davis Cemetery in California offered bird walks and poetry workshops. Others presented Shakespeare festivals, family picnics, and even weddings.

The idea behind this: "To nurture warm feelings about the cemetery."

Weird, I thought, but why not?

I made some calls and found San Francisco's few cemeteries unreceptive to the idea. The City had been forced to move many of its cemeteries, due to rising costs of land and lack of space, and those that remained didn't readily open their doors for entertainment purposes. But when I contacted the powers-that-be in neighboring Colma, I got lucky.

While the historic town of Colma is quaint, with brick-paved roads, ornamental streetlamps, a railroad depot, a retro city hall, and ethnically diverse restaurants, Colma is better known as the final resting place for the who's who of San Francisco's dearly departed. Among its permanent residents—newspaper tycoon William Randolph Hearst, business magnate William Henry Crocker, *San Francisco Chronicle* founder Charles de Young, the infamous self-proclaimed Emperor Norton, and baseball legend Joe DiMaggio. Even Sheriff Wyatt Earp had come to rest in Colma. It's now known as "the City of Souls," and it's also where many former deceased San Franciscans have been "relocated." In fact, now the dead outnumber the living one and a half million to sixteen hundred.

After Cruz paid a hefty rental fee, the city administrator agreed to let us host our party at Lawndale, one of the older, neglected cemeteries that had gone bankrupt, thanks to the plethora of the more prestigious cemeteries—sixteen, to be exact—that had opened in the area.

Cruz had quickly found the spot in the cemetery he wanted—a large open-air mausoleum with a patio surrounded by acres of untended headstones. At the moment, production crew members from CeeGee Studios were working out the logistics of "vampire flight" gone wrong. Two men were trying to retrieve Jonas from the treetop, while others attempted to fix a glitch in the rigging that was supposed to lift the young star up and away in a dramatic disappearing act—but not up and into a tree. It looked as if Jonas, aka Count "Alucard"

("Dracula" spelled backward), was going to need more flying lessons and a better pulley system.

Still, I was impressed, and I thought the party guests—the primary stars, select film crew, important media, and a few local dignitaries—would be at tomorrow night's party. That was, if they weren't too superstitious to enter a graveyard.

I didn't relish the idea of hosting a party in a graveyard— it seemed somewhat disrespectful—but Cruz had promised to make a large donation to the charity organization of my choice. That was something I insisted on when I hosted large parties for clients. This time I'd chosen the American Red Cross. Given the type of party, it seemed appropriate to help out an organization known for their blood drives.

"Watch the trees, for God's sake!" Cruz yelled, as crew members adjusted the young actor's hidden flying gear. "I want him lifted up and over that whatchacallit—that monument there—not flung around like Peter Pan on crack. This is supposed to be thrilling, not embarrassing! Reporters and photographers from TMI, Gossip Guy, and Buzz Online will be here tomorrow night!"

Cruz ran both hands through his thinning hair, a habit he had when he was anxious or upset. It was probably why he had thinning hair. He wasn't the easiest person to work with, and I sensed I'd regret taking on this job, but in the past he'd helped me out with some of my parties that required unique lighting, background decor, or special effects. So, even though I'd been buried under a pile of party requests since I'd hosted the séance party at the Winchester Mystery House, I felt I owed him and couldn't turn him down.

Besides, helping one another is what we Treasure Islanders do.

While Cruz and his crew continued to work on the "disappearing Dracula" glitch, I went over final plans for the party decorations with my own crew. Tonight we were setting up the lighting, unloading the larger props, and doing logistics; tomorrow we'd turn the old mausoleum into a mini-Transylvania.

Delicia Jackson, part-time actress and my office mate on T.I., was in charge of the "vampire black" and "bloodred" helium-inflated balloons, and she was currently tying them to headstones and monuments in the designated party area. Tomorrow she'd dress for the theme, in a sexy "Vampira" costume. No wig needed: Her long black hair was perfect for the part.

Berkeley Wong, my events videographer, had already helped Cruz's crew with the atmospheric lighting—headstones with eerie backlights, indirect spotlights, and dozens of candles. He'd be back again tomorrow night to videotape the event.

Duncan Grant—gamer, computer whiz, fan of extreme sports, and Berk's office roommate on Treasure Island—was busy connecting wires behind some gravestones. He'd been thrilled when Cruz had hired him and a few of his friends as movie extras. At the moment he was hooking up the creepy voice recordings he'd made earlier on his computer, and placing tiny speakers around the party area. Each time someone walked past a headstone, a disembodied voice said, "I vant to suck your blood," "What a long neck you have," or "Bite me."

Everything was going to be perfect, I promised myself.

"Those are awesome!" I called to Brad, my . . . whatever. I refuse to call him "boyfriend." The hunky crime scene cleaner, who also rented office space on the Island, had volunteered to help out. At the moment he was setting up Styrofoam tombstones made by graphic artists at CeeGee Studios. Each marker had been hand-painted to look cracked and crumbling, then lettered with funny epitaphs, such as, *"To follow you, I'm not content, How do I know, Which way you went?"* and *"Here lies a man named Zeke, Second-fastest draw in Cripple Creek."*

"As long as I don't find my name on one of these . . ." Brad said, securing a fake headstone to the front of a real one with duct tape.

I opened a box and began sorting through the "necklaces" that I'd be placing on the portable party tables, soon to be covered with black tablecloths. I'd ordered dozens of little wooden crosses and small rubber bats, which I planned to set at each place, along with plastic vampire fangs that doubled as napkin rings. But it was the centerpieces that would catch the eyes of most guests tomorrow night. I'd had mini-coffins made out of Plexiglas that would be filled with red-tinted water and topped with a floating black rose candle.

I hummed as I worked, probably because I found most cemeteries serene and relaxing, with their expansive lawns, color spots of flowers, and statues of weeping angels. While the lawns had turned brown and the flowers had long ago died here at Lawndale, the headstones were still intriguing, documenting lives often taken prematurely by complications of childbirth, disease epidemics, or wars. Lawndale also had a pet section called "Pet's Place," reserved for burying animals. Not to be confused with Stephen King's *Pet Sematary*, where the pets actually came back to life after they were buried, this one was filled with tiny headstones featuring names of well-loved cats and dogs, interspersed with the occasional parakeet, gecko, or monkey.

I suddenly sensed someone standing behind me. Half-expecting Brad again, I turned around and came face-to-face with a grizzled old man in a frayed Forty-Niners baseball cap, dirty overalls, and a plaid flannel shirt. His tattered brown boots were caked in mud, his beard caked in bits of dropped food. Backlit by the work lights the crew had constructed, the man seemed to loom larger than life.

"What the hell is going on here!" The man spat, then grimaced, revealing a row of crooked yellowed teeth. He swung the beam of a heavy flashlight around the crew. Everyone stopped working and stared at the man—and at the large shovel he held in his other hand.

I was about to explain when Cruz bounded over, nearly tripping over a cord. "I should ask you the same question, buddy," he said to the man, who was nearly twice his size. While Cruz might have had a big bark, I had a feeling this guy had a bigger bite. Those creases in his aging face weren't made by lots of smiling.

"I'm the owner and manager of Peaceful Kingdom, and you're on private property." He spat again, and I realized his lower lip was filled with chewing tobacco.

Reluctantly, I stepped up to take over from Cruz, who had a short fuse. While the big old guy held a menacing flashlight and shovel, I still had some garlic bulbs in my hands, and I knew how to use them if it came to that.

"Hi." I reached out a garlic-free hand. "I'm Presley Parker, from Killer Parties. We're hosting a wrap party for a recently completed film, and we have permission to be here."

"A what party?" he asked, ignoring my hand—thank God—and aiming the flashlight right in my eyes. He reeked of alcohol, tobacco, and dirt.

I shaded the glare. "A wrap party," I said, enunciating. "To celebrate the end of—"

"I don't care if it's a crap party—you cain't have it here!" He gave his shovel a menacing shake.

"I'm afraid we can," Cruz said. The flashlight shifted to his face. "I don't know anything about your Peaceful Kingdom or whatever, but you don't own this place. We have documentation from the City of Colma allowing us to rent Lawndale Cemetery for our event."

"Listen, you maggot, and listen good. My name's Otto Gunther. Me and my wife, Carrie—God rest her soul—we own this here cemetery, and you're trespassing. So git."

"We're not going to 'git,' Otto," Cruz continued, "but we are going to call the police and have them settle this." He turned to me and pulled out his cell. "Right, Presley?"

I glanced at the others, who had gathered to watch the real-life drama. No one looked particularly frightened, but they did seem eager to find out what would happen next. Except for Brad, who was nowhere in sight. I looked back at Otto. His angry expression was easily visible in the party lighting.

Or was that an expression of fear I saw behind those bloodshot eyes and rigid grimace?

Otto's hand shook as he held the flashlight on Cruz. "You're trespassing on hallowed ground, people, and you're disturbing the dead. The owl portends that if you're not gone by midnight, Death will follow. . . . Death will follow. . . ."

He turned and vanished back into the darkness.

Cruz looked stunned at the man's own special effect of appearing and disappearing, then shook his head. "'The owl portends?' That's all I need. A nutcase in a cemetery . . . and a flying monkey in the trees. What else can go wrong . . . ?" He was still muttering as he returned to the problem at hand—fixing the vampire's own disappearing act.

I looked into the dark recesses of the cemetery where Otto had disappeared, and wondered about the unkempt giant of a man. Where had he gone? And why had he claimed to be the owner of Peaceful Kingdom, whatever that was? At the moment, his kingdom didn't look so peaceful.

Great. I was just starting to relax and now this. Cruz was right: What else could go wrong at our upcoming vampire party? If it was anything like some of my other events—everything.

By midnight, the decorations were in place, the vampire was able to disappear without a glitch, and rough cuts of the film were ready to be viewed on the side of the large mausoleum. In spite of the fact that I kept looking over my shoulder, I'd seen no more signs of Otto Gunther. At this point I should have been eager for tomorrow night's party. But the threats the old man had made—or implied—had unnerved me. These days it seemed as if every crazy person was ready to shoot a gun for any reason. I'd read in the online news yesterday that some guy had killed another guy over a parking place in the City.

Of course, in a city like San Francisco, that might have been justified. But still.

"I'm pooped. You ready?" came a voice from behind.

I jumped. "Brad! Don't sneak up behind me like that! Especially in a cemetery." I checked the new Mickey Mouse watch that Brad had given me after I'd hosted a surprise party for his brother, Andrew. "Where have you been?"

"Loading stuff into the SUV."

"So you didn't see that ginormous old guy who stopped by to threaten us?"

"What guy?" He scanned the area.

"Never mind. Just don't sneak up on me again. Don't you watch horror movies?"

"Nope. Just crime dramas and police shows. Horror movies give me nightmares."

I felt my tension melt away with him standing next to me. "You're kidding, right? I didn't think anything scared you. Except the maggots you sometimes clean up at your crime scenes."

He crossed his muscular arms over his muscular chest, almost causing me to have a muscle spasm. "I'm not afraid of maggots. I just hate them."

"Horror movies are only make-believe, you know," I said, teasing him. I happened to love them.

"That doesn't stop Freddy from invading my dreams, the way he does in those *Nightmare on Elm Street* movies." He shivered.

It could have been that the cold was seeping into the cemetery. Or not. I was sure Brad could take down Freddy, Jason, and Michael Myers quicker than a kiss from a vampire, but it was fun to see this vulnerable side of him.

"Well, let's get out of here before that old guy comes back with a killer backhoe," I said, referring to the mysterious Otto. "We've done all we can here tonight, and it looks like everyone else has packed up and left. We'll finish the rest tomorrow."

"You got somebody watching over all the stuff we're leaving behind?" Brad asked.

"Oh yes. Cruz brought a couple of his security guards, and I hired Raj for extra security. He's around here somewhere. . . ." Scanning the darkness, I spotted my favorite T.I. security guard shining his trusty flashlight into the dark recesses of the cemetery, no doubt searching for illegal gravediggers from Dr. Frankenstein's lab.

"Who's there?" Raj suddenly called out from several yards away.

I followed the beam of his flashlight as he swung it back and forth through the rustling eucalyptus trees, trying to penetrate the darkness.

Uh-oh. Was Otto back?

I spotted a small circle of light in the darkness, about eight or ten feet up in the air. The tiny, intense beam seemed to hover over a headstone, as if suspended in midair, then seemingly bounce to the next, defying gravity.

This was not Raj's flashlight beam. Not unless he'd learned to levitate.

For a moment, I thought it might have been one of Lucas Cruz's special effects. But Cruz and his gang had already left.

And this wasn't in my party plan.

Neither was the scream that followed.